HAPPY HOLLOW

BY
GARY BARGATZE

Warfield

Upcoming titles in the
Your Winding Daybreak Ways series

Hurricane Creek

Hollow Rock

McGill

Cabedelo

Thunderwood

Babylon, A Human Requiem

For more information about the series, visit the author's

website www.garybargatze.com

HAPPY HOLLOW

GARY BARGATZE

—————————————————

RIGOR HILL PRESS

For Fred and Jean, who pointed the way

HAPPY HOLLOW

1

As THE GUNS fell silent at Appomattox, the gods were
already shaping the next battlefield. None of us realized
the target would be narrowed this time to just eight square
miles overlooking the Mississippi. We each believed we had
our own reasons for leaving our homes and settling on the
bluffs—organizing a parish, opening a school, fleeing a master, practicing law, or healing the sick. And then again later
on we had our own reasons for staying once the ungodly
attacks began in earnest—blind faith, a sense of duty, and an
unfathomable willingness to race toward death as the masses
fled in panic.

I believe my reasons for coming to Memphis were
straightforward. I needed a job and wanted to return to western Tennessee where I had grown up. After recurring bouts
of winter fever, I'd finally completed my training and landed
a teaching position at the prestigious Westminster Academy.
The preparatory school's only English lecturer had died of
the cholera in December, and they quickly hired me to replace him for the spring semester. In his most recent correspondence, Mr. Taylor, the headmaster and cofounder of the
academy, insisted I arrive the afternoon of the thirty-first and
promised to be waiting at the old Memphis terminal to escort

me to my lodging, which he stressed would be within easy walking distance of the school.

So after crossing the Hatchie River Bridge at Brownsville on the thirty-first, the Nashville & Northwestern engineer opened the throttle and raced the last forty miles southwest to Memphis. We were desperately behind schedule. Earlier in the day we had been diverted to a siding just up the road from my old family farm near Warfield. The conductor had apologetically explained a maintenance crew was finishing repairs to the rail bed, which had washed out during the last evening's flooding.

When we finally reached Memphis, I shifted to the opposite side of the car and gazed out the partially frosted windowpane trying to spot Master Taylor. In his last letter he had lightheartedly counseled me to be on the lookout for a tall, handsome fifty-year-old fellow sporting a substantial moustache, thick sideburns, and a fashionable charcoal bowler. And as I stepped out onto the platform, I immediately discovered the most likely of candidates, a dapper middle-aged gentleman leaning against the station wall with one leg up, smoking a stubby cigar and towering over the swirling crowd of passengers and greeters.

I confidently approached the fellow and half asked and half declared, "Master Taylor?"

"Good work, Thomas! Welcome to Bluff City! Here, let me help you with your bags. We'll go out through the waiting room there. I parked the carriage near the front entrance."

After stowing all my belongings, we climbed up onto the carriage bench and headed south on Second Street. Master Taylor turned and embarked on my orientation. "Well, Thomas, we're now coming into Memphis proper. Our academy's down the street there between Court Square and the new Peabody Hotel. Every now and then you'll see Bedford Forrest, President Davis, or even General Bobby Lee leaving the Peabody to take a stroll around the square.

"It's my favorite spot, Thomas. The soul of Memphis, a refuge for everyone. You'll see. There'll be the nurse with the baby carriage, the lovers walking arm in arm, and even a tramp or two just off the overnight freight sleeping on the wrought-iron benches. . . . You'll love the landscape there: mature cypress, magnolia, and cedar trees, a classical fountain, marble statues, and promenades lined with roses and lilies. It's a natural wonder surrounded by the hubbub of the warehouses, jewelry shops, and dry goods stores; a sanctuary from the rumblings of the ice wagons and drays; a shelter from the din of fruit men touting, 'Strawberries, fresh strawberries,' and the newsboys shouting, 'Get your *Avalanche*, just five cents! Read all about it in the *Appeal*, robbery and murder in the Pinch! A scandal brewing at Fort Pickering!' I just know you'll love the square. It's a place to reflect and get your bearings."

Master Taylor steered the mare to the right and then to an immediate left into an alleyway behind a row of impressive two-story brick homes. He then pulled hard on the reins, stopping behind a red carriage house trimmed in white with large timbered doors. Master Taylor jumped down, swung the doors open, and announced, "Well, we're home!"

"We're home?"

"Yes. You and I. We're home."

"You're putting me up in your own house? I really couldn't, sir . . ."

"Everything's gonna be just fine, Thomas. My family and I discussed it right after you accepted the position. We've plenty of space here—ten rooms for six people—and honestly, it'll save the school some money." He continued jokingly, "Now how on earth could you refuse such a deal with free room and board? And besides, you'll have extra money to court the handsomest belles Memphis has to offer."

I smiled, embarrassed, and responded, "I don't know what to say, Master Taylor."

"'Thank you' will be quite enough, Thomas."

I extended my hand and said, "Well, then, thank you, sir. I really mean it. Thank you."

After parking the carriage and unharnessing the mare, Master Taylor grabbed my heaviest suitcase and led me up a slate walkway toward the back entrance to the house. As we entered the hallway, he motioned for me to drop my things off on a ladder-back chair and follow him up the stairway. "I'll send Aaron down to fetch your things in a little while. Let's get on up to the dining room. It sure smells like the ladies have cooked up a rib-sticking meal."

As we climbed the narrow steps, the headmaster shouted our arrival. "Emma! Emma! We're home!"

A lady's voice responded urgently, "Preston, you fellas get on up here quick like lightnin' before everything gets cold. We started puttin' the victuals on the table when we saw you pullin' up behind the carriage house."

Quickly turning the corner and entering the dining room, we found three ladies busily arranging platters and covered dishes on a double pedestal table. Master Taylor approached the two ladies on his left, gave each a brushing kiss on the cheek, and launched the introductions: "This beautiful young lady here's my wife, Emma. Been married now going on twenty-nine years. Can you believe it? And this is our daughter, Amanda. Folks say she's the spitting image of her mama . . . and I say just as beautiful too. Amanda's completing her course of studies at the Market Street School here and will be enrolling at Mary Sharp College in Winchester next fall."

Master Taylor pivoted, stretched his arm out to his right, and said proudly, "And this is our adopted daughter, Hannah, who's lived here with us the last few years along with her brother, Aaron." The beautiful dark-haired young woman nodded, smiled shyly, and immediately returned to setting the table.

Mrs. Taylor ushered me around to my assigned seat and said, "We're all so happy you'll be stayin' with us. We're gonna sit you right here. It's a special place." And then raising her voice for all to hear, she announced, "This'll be Thomas's chair from now on, right here next to Aaron and across from Hannah." She then paused to survey the room and continued, "When you're finished there, Hannah, go fetch your brother. I think he's in his room workin' on his studies."

Several minutes later Hannah returned with Aaron. He was carrying a book with his index finger marking the spot where he'd left off reading. I squinted to see the cover: a translation of Manzoni's novel, *The Betrothed.* Master Taylor again did the introduction. "Thomas, this is Aaron, our adopted son, who's finishing the academy and will be enrolling at the University of the South this fall. It looks like you'll be having Aaron in your literature class for his last semester at Westminster. From the moment he stepped through the door here he's always said he wanted to be a writer or a journalist."

The ruggedly handsome young man extended his hand confidently. "It's nice to meet you, sir. I'm looking forward to your class."

"Likewise, Aaron." And pointing to the book in his left hand, I added, "I hope we get a chance to discuss Manzoni. It's a compelling description of the Italian plague."

Master Taylor signaled for us to take our seats and then mistakenly assuming I was an inveterate churchgoer, immediately put me on the spot by asking me to offer up the dinner prayer. There was no time now to explain I hadn't yet made my peace with the gods. I just lowered my head and relied on memory and cadence to recite the words I'd heard my mother pray hundreds of times before. "We thank Thee, O Lord, for this food, for this family, for this day, and the many blessings you've bestowed upon us. In Jesus' name we pray. Amen." Everyone echoed heartily, "Amen."

After everyone piled his or her plate with ham, sweet potatoes, and mustard greens, Mrs. Taylor opened the conversation. "Well, it's just two more days now until the reception at the Overton. So, Preston, dear, ya lookin' forward to meetin' your first royalty?"

Master Taylor responded brusquely. "As long as I can avoid that scoundrel, Custer. I know people describe him as charismatic and daring, but he's a little too flamboyant for my taste. I've heard he's been at the duke's side ever since the big hunt with Buffalo Bill Cody in the Nebraska Territory earlier this month."

Seeing the confusion on my face, Mrs. Taylor interrupted her husband. "Apologies, Thomas. Czar Alexander's third son, the Grand Duke Alexis, will be arrivin' right here in Memphis day after tomorrow, and the city's holdin' a reception ball in his honor at the Overton Hotel that evening. Ya see, the Grand Duke's been tourin' the country since last November. All the newspapers have been followin' his progress from New York to Washington, from Omaha to Louisville, and now he and his entourage are on their way here. Ya see, that's why we wanted you arrivin' on the thirty-first—so you could go with us to the reception Friday night." Mrs. Taylor beamed. "We're really lucky they've chosen Preston to be on the reception committee. Only eight hundred tickets total, and Preston got some of 'em for us! I tell you, we'll make a fine foursome, you and Amanda, Preston and me. Now tell me, isn't this excitin'?"

"I'd . . . I'd love going along, Mrs. Taylor, but it's impossible."

"How so, Thomas?"

"I . . . I don't have the clothes for such an affair."

Mrs. Taylor responded enigmatically, "Don't you worry now, Thomas. I know we'll find somethin' here suitable that fits. We'll look into it right after dinner."

Following a long-standing family tradition, everyone helped clear the table; and since it was Amanda and Hannah's week washing the dishes, the rest of us were free to do as we pleased until the formal family hour at half past eight. Explaining he had to review the academy ledger, Master Taylor excused himself, and Aaron returned to his room to finish reading the last few chapters of Manzoni's narrative.

Mrs. Taylor slipped her arm beneath mine, guided me toward the spiral staircase at the front of the house, and said, "Let's go upstairs, honey, and see what we can find for you to wear Friday night." When we got to the landing, we turned and headed down a long, gaslit hallway lined with Neo-Grecian wall sconces depicting Hermes, Hera, Zeus, and a host of other unknown deities comprising the Greek pantheon. As we approached the end of the hallway, Mrs. Taylor pointed toward the last door on the right and said, "Thomas, this'll be your room from now on. I'm sure we'll find somethin' in there for you to wear. Let's light the lamps and see what we can find."

Mrs. Taylor swung open the doors of a massive oak wardrobe filled with an extensive collection of men's formal clothing. She began sorting through the suits draped on some newfangled hangers Master Taylor had purchased on his last trip back East. "Not this. . . . No, not this one. . . . No, no. . . . Aha! Here, honey, try this one on."

She handed me a dark gray jacket and draped the matching trousers over a chair. I slipped the jacket on over my crumpled traveling shirt.

"Now how does that fit?"

"Maybe the sleeves are a tad long, Mrs. Taylor, but other than that it feels pretty good. Look okay?"

"Debonair, darling. Now go over there on the other side of the bed and take a look in the mirror."

"Not bad, if I must say so myself. I mean other than the sleeves."

"Sleeves are an easy fix. I'll pin 'em, and Hannah can make the adjustments tomorrow mornin'. I'll step out now, Thomas, so you can try on the trousers. Call me when you're decent."

I quickly pulled on the pants and shouted, "Okay, Mrs. Taylor! All set!"

She stepped back into the room. "How they feel, dear?"

"Well, they come down just about right on my boots, but they're a tad tight in the waist. Probably the second helpings tonight. But all in all, a pretty good fit."

Mrs. Taylor began walking toward the door and said, "Get changed back into your street clothes now, and bring the suit with you down to the parlor. We'll be meetin' in there for the family hour in a little while."

After Mrs. Taylor left, I collapsed back onto the bed and began surveying my new room through the flicker of soft lamplight. It appeared to be more a museum than a chamber. There were pictures, certificates, flags, and weaponry carefully placed throughout the room, perhaps chronicling a young man's progression from childhood to the military. Curiosity got the better of me. I got up, walked over to a chest of drawers in the corner, and inspected the extensive collection of memorabilia surrounding the bureau. On the wall above the chest was a framed certificate of enlistment declaring:

STATE OF <u>TENNESSEE</u>

CITY OF <u>MEMPHIS</u>

I, <u>Michael W. Taylor</u>, born in <u>Shelby County</u> in the State of <u>Tennessee</u> aged <u>eighteen</u>, and by occupation a _____ DO HEREBY ACKNOWLEDGE to have voluntarily enlisted this <u>twenty-fifth</u> day of <u>April 1862</u>, as a SOLDIER in the ARMY OF THE CONFEDERATE STATES OF AMERICA for the period of <u>twelve months</u>, unless sooner discharged by proper authority: Do also agree to accept such bounty, pay, rations, and clothing as, or may be established by law. And I, <u>Michael W. Taylor</u>, do solemnly swear, that I will bear true faith and allegiance to the CONFEDERATE STATES OF AMERICA. Sworn and subscribed to, at <u>Memphis, Tennessee</u>, this <u>twenty-fifth</u> day of <u>April 1862</u>, SIGNED: <u>Michael W. Taylor</u>. BEFORE: <u>First Lieut. Benjamin Wilkinson, CSA.</u>

To the left of the certificate hung a Sharps carbine and to the right a cavalry officer's saber with intricate ornamental etching running the length of the curved blade. Resting on top of the chest of drawers were a rare LeMat revolver and a red cavalry battle flag with wide blue crossbars and twelve white stars. As I reached down to pick up the pistol, Aaron entered through the open door carrying everything I owned. "Excuse me, sir. Father asked me to bring your bags up. He said he'd like you to join him downstairs in his study once you've settled in."

I thanked him and then pointed to the enrollment certificate above the bureau. "Aaron, forgive me, but since this is going to be my room, can you tell me a little about this fellow, Michael Taylor?"

"Only the little bit I know. Never met him but consider him my brother—left for the war in '62, and I didn't come here to live until late '67, long after the war was over. My parents have never had much to say about him, and I've been reluctant to ask."

"Well, perhaps I can find a polite way to pose a question or two to the Taylors without it looking like prying. I grew up around here during the war and met a lot of soldiers on both sides. I'd love to know more about him. His possessions here are trying to tell a story I don't quite understand." I slowly turned away and began walking toward the door. "Please tell Master Taylor I'll be down in a few minutes."

"Yes, sir," he replied and hurried off down the hallway.

After changing out of the formal attire, I dropped the suit off with Mrs. Taylor and headed over to the study. I knocked tentatively and half whispered, "Master Taylor?"

"Come on in, Thomas, the door's open."

As I stepped in, Master Taylor looked up from behind several large piles of paper and said, "I only need to make a couple more entries. Please make yourself at home. Forgive the mess. I hate this part of my job the most. I've tried mending my ways, but I always backslide, putting off the postings until the end of the month. My deceased partner, Thaddeus Westminster, used to love balancing the books. But now sadly, it's fallen on me to make everything right. And in an odd way I find the bookkeeping both boring and terrifying."

When he lowered his head again behind the stacks of assets and liabilities, I moved over to the bookshelves lining the walls and explored the headmaster's vast collection. The only word to describe it is *eclectic*. Most collectors focus on a single topic, a time period, an author or related authors, or works of a specific geographic region. But Master Taylor's library spanned the ages and the full range of political, philosophical, literary, and scientific thought.

The first book I picked up was an eighteenth-century printing of the Egyptian *Book of the Dead*, a millennia-old compilation of magic spells designed to guide the deceased on the long, dangerous journey through the underworld to paradise. Next was a seventeenth-century edition of Lucretius's Epicurean poem, *De Rerum Natura*, which suggested the moral responsibility of man is far superior to organized religion. Then I examined a copy of Ovid's *Metamorphosis*, a collection of poetic tales ranging from the creation of the universe to the relationship between the gods and man.

One after another the shelves produced surprises—Dame Juliana Berner's fifteenth-century *Treatyse of Fysshynge with an Angle*, the most complete early reference on fly fishing; Hobbes's political and religious discourse, *Leviathan*, emphasizing the subordination of the individual to the state; Adam Smith's eighteenth-century *Wealth of Nations*, arguing diametrically that individual freedom and free markets produce prosperity; and George Catlin's incomparable recent record, *Illustrations of the Manners, Customs, and Condition of the North American Indian.*

As I reached for Harrington's *Oceana*, the reluctant accountant stood up and exclaimed, "Thank God, that's finished! Now a respite for another month. . . . So, Thomas, did you find anything interesting there?"

"You have an unbelievable library, Master Taylor. Titles I've heard about but never seen. How long have you been collecting?"

"I guess you could say almost all my life. My father was a collector and passed the love of books on to me. Many of the works here belonged to him; but as my personal finances have allowed, I've continued adding to the collection. My latest acquisitions were Darwin's *Descent of Man* and Jubal Early's *Memoir of the Last Year of the War for Independence*."

When the headmaster mentioned the Confederate general's memoir, I sensed an opportunity to redirect the conversation. "Master Taylor, speaking of the war, I hope you won't mind my asking, sir, but . . . the things in my room—the weapons, Michael Taylor's certificate of enrollment . . . Forgive me, sir. A close relative?"

The headmaster eased back into his chair and said reflectively, "I wish more people would ask. . . . Michael's our son. We were heartbroken when he announced he was joining the army. Emma and I had to put a brave face on it, you know. After all, he was eighteen and determined to join the fight. He left in April '62. We had occasional letters from him over the years describing various battles and his rise through the ranks of General Forrest's cavalry. Battles at Murfreesboro, Chickamauga, Tupelo, and Nashville."

"My brother, Robert, also reported to General Forrest,"

I interjected. "He was a captain. Headed up Robert's Raiders. Died late in the war. I'll bet your son knew Robert. As Mama always said, 'It's a small world.'" I looked down, embarrassed by my exuberance, and said, "Sorry, Master Taylor, please go on."

The headmaster nodded and continued. "Well, a wounded neighbor returning home delivered Michael's last correspondence in February of '65, more than a month after he'd finished it. That's the way he'd write, describing the events of a few weeks or even months in a single note.

"I'll never forget the last pages of that final letter. They were dated New Year's Day, 1865. The somber opening paragraphs had described the rebel defeat at Nashville mid-December '64. Michael then explained he and his men had been ordered to protect General Hood's retreat across the Tennessee River into Alabama. But you could tell his spirits were rising again in the last pages as he recounted the Battle of Devil's Gap on Christmas Day '64. Michael said they'd laid a trap for the bluecoat cavalry, which was in hot pursuit of Hood's army. He described how he and his boys had stopped the charging Feds cold atop Anthony's Hill—swooped down the rise on them and fired round after round into their fleeing ranks.

"As I said, that was the last we heard until a Confederate officer in full regalia appeared at our door toward the end of May '65. He was a distinguished-looking fellow about six feet tall; dark brown eyes; long, black beard; and wavy, iron-gray hair. He was holding a large leather valise in his left hand. 'Preston Taylor?' he asked. 'Yes, sir,' I replied. He extended his hand and introduced himself. 'Nathan Forrest, sir.' The uniform, the name, and the familiar suitcase immediately sent a wave of dread coursing through me. I spontaneously asked, 'General, you have news about Michael?' He deflected the question with a question of his own, 'May I come in, sir?'

"While walking down the hallway, I instinctively called out, 'Emma, hurry to the parlor!' When the general and I reached the room, I motioned for him to take a seat in one of the gold-damasked chairs. I sat down on the settee across from him and said nervously, 'Let's wait a moment. My wife should be here soon.' When Emma arrived, I introduced her to the general and then asked her to join me on the settee. Her eyes immediately focused on the valise sitting at the general's feet. She whispered hesitantly, 'You've . . . you've come to speak of Michael, haven't ya?'

"The general answered solemnly, 'I'm sorry, ma'am, but I've come to discuss unpleasant things. Your son, Michael, died in action last month. Died a hero on the first of April, just a few days before the surrender at Appomattox.'

"Emma slowly lowered her head onto my shoulder and began sobbing, 'How? Where? Did he suffer?' General Forrest leaned forward and responded sympathetically, 'Our orders were to stop the Feds from takin' Selma, Alabama, which throughout the war had produced weapons and distributed critical supplies to our men. We first engaged the enemy at Six Mile Creek some fifty miles north of Selma, and we carried on a runnin' battle with Wilson's troops for the next forty-eight hours. We were sorely outnumbered, but our boys fought proudly and bravely.'

"His voice deepened as if he had returned to commanding his forces in the field. 'I ordered our thirteen hundred boys to take up positions six miles north of Plantsville straddlin' the crossroads leadin' to Randolph and Maplesville. We had to take a stand here and keep the Yankees out of Selma. After the last of Crossland's brigade moved into position, Boone's scoutin' party arrived with a bluecoat cavalry in hot pursuit. As the Feds neared our position, I ordered point-blank rifle fire, which quickly emptied a number of the Federal saddles. But the Yankees dismounted and continued drivin' forward, pressurin' our inexperienced militia on the right. When the flank finally gave way, I ordered our men to fall back toward the ford at Dixie Creek. Sensin' our retreat, the bluecoats quickly remounted and raced down the slope toward our infantry. We had to stop 'em now or our soldiers would be annihilated.

"'I turned to Major Taylor and said, "Let's go get 'em!" He relayed the order to his escort company of elite cavalry, which immediately moved up into mounted spear formation. Michael and I formed the point and led the counter charge toward the oncomin' Yankee cavalry. After the thunderous collision of our forces, their superior numbers quickly swallowed us up. But Michael was still at my side. We began firing our revolvers and hacking away with our sabers. It was fierce, close-in, hand-to-hand combat. We were all so tightly packed together, none of us could move. The screaming, bleeding mass of horses and men was being swept toward a nearby forest line. When we reached the woods, I again gave the order to fall back.

"'As we spurred and wheeled our horses toward the woods, a Yankee shot my horse right out from under me. Seeing my predicament, Michael raced over, reached down, and pulled me up into the saddle behind him. Wilson's men quickly closed the gap and began slashing again with their sabers. When Michael swung his horse to the right to give me a better shot, a young Fed lunged toward us, missed me, and caught Major Taylor in the chest. I grabbed the reins from him, continued firing, and managed to keep the dogs at bay.

"'We rode long and hard and finally shook the bluecoats somewhere near Plantersville. When I realized they'd given up the chase for now, I signaled my troops to halt and shouted for several of Michael's men to quickly dismount and help me ease the Major down from his horse. One of the fellows who raced over was my trusted physician, Dr. Cowan, who immediately evaluated your son's condition. And after less than a minute he looked up, shook his head, and announced what I had suspected all along: the wound had been fatal. I then ordered the men to carry the Major down among the pines and dig a respectful grave worthy of a hero.

"'I want both of you to know your boy was like a son to me. He joined my staff in July '62 not long after I became brigadier general, and Michael remained at my side until the very end of the war. You should be proud of his service and sacrifice. There was no one who served more bravely or gave more for the cause and for his men than your son.' The general paused, reached down for the valise, handed it to me, and said, 'Here, I've preserved a few of Michael's effects. And . . . and his men insisted you have our prized twelve-star battle flag.'

"Then General Forrest stood up, removed the saber from his belt, and handed it to me. 'This was Michael's' he said. 'He carried it into every battle. I'm sure he'd want you to have it.' The general then moved toward the settee, placed his left hand on Emma's shoulder, extended his right hand to me, and said, 'I'm so sorry; I . . . I feel I've let you down. My duty to the Confederacy, of course, was always to be aggressive and win, but my personal mission from the beginnin' was to protect my boys from harm. I'm truly sorry.' With that, he slowly turned away, and I followed him to the door. And that was the last time we spoke with the general face to face. But every year on the first of April he still sends a note around inquiring of our situation and letting us know he remembers and cares."

2

As Master Taylor rose from his chair and moved to the front of his desk, I said, "I'm sorry for your and Mrs. Taylor's loss, sir. I hope time has helped heal your sorrows."

He shook his head and replied, "Sad to say, Thomas, that was only the beginning of our troubles." He paused reflectively. I remained silent. I sensed he needed to continue telling his story. "At first Emma became agitated, but she gradually fell into a deep depression. She spent a lot of time alone in Michael's room. That's when she conjured up the idea of making a memorial of his effects. And it was also hard on our little girl, Amanda. How could a ten-year-old understand she wasn't the cause of her mother's sadness and strange behaviors—walking the halls late at night, calling out Michael's name and saying she was past bearing another son?

"We tried the best doctors and the latest remedies, but nothing seemed to work. Emma wasn't eating well and was rapidly losing weight. So based on the doctors' recommendations we committed her to a private sanitarium for rest and observation. After six months of treatment, the doctors released her into my custody. Time, rest, and the medical care seemed to have done her some good. She had gained back some of the weight she'd lost, and the color had returned to her cheeks. Even the warm smile was back occasionally. But I wrestled with the fear her progress would fade once she spent time again in the house and the room where Michael grew up.

"And I lived with that fear until Aaron and Hannah came into our lives. It was no more than a month after Emma returned home when our Episcopal priest, Father Webber, paid a visit and fulfilled a mission. After inquiring of Emma's health, the priest revealed a second reason for stopping by. You see, to save the parish some money he and some volunteers had emptied the church's communal privy pits and transported the contents in open carts to Happy Hollow 'for burial.' Happy Hollow's the marshland beneath the bluffs where the Wolf River meets the Mississippi. The combination of refuse, brush, and river mud forms something of a foundation where poor folk raise houses on stilts using sheet metal, scrap wood, and the like.

"Father Webber said while they were emptying the carts, he noticed a couple of youngsters picking through the trash near the riverbank. He approached them and asked if he could help. They replied their older brother was really sick and they hadn't eaten in well over a day. The priest asked where they lived, and they pointed toward a makeshift heap of shacks sitting back about thirty yards from the water's edge. Father Webber said he convinced the children to guide him through the muck to their hut where he found their much older brother in a soiled bed. He was unconscious, feverish, and breathing shallowly. After summoning a doctor and nurse, Father Webber drove the youngsters back to the parish house for food, fresh clothing, and temporary shelter.

"The good father then lowered his head and reported that unfortunately not even the best medical care could save the young man. The priest said that after learning the poor fellow had died during the night, he immediately returned to Happy Hollow to scour his effects for information about the family and for any next of kin who could care for the children. Father Webber said he was about to give up when he discovered a large bound notebook sandwiched between a pair of shabby mattresses. It was the young man's journal covering the years from before the war through late 1866."

Master Taylor walked over to his bookcase, retrieved a tattered notebook, and handed it to me. As I carefully turned the pages, he said, "Father Webber gave me the journal to share with Hannah and Aaron when they got a little older. It was invaluable in learning the family's history. The young man's name was Isaac. A Charleston dealer had sold Isaac's mother, Mourning, to a plantation owner, a Master Clary, of Jackson, Tennessee. Clary was a widower whose wife had died in a steamboat explosion at Vicksburg the year before Mourning's arrival in Jackson. Isaac's mother told her son he was born in the summer of '43. In the margins near that entry, he had later noted his brother, Aaron, was born in September '53 and his sister, Hannah, a year and a half after that. Isaac described how he and his siblings were raised 'with privileges' much to the annoyance of the rest of Master Clary's slaves. The squire and his wife had had no children; so he treated Isaac, Hannah, and Aaron as if they were his own.

"The tone of the diary changed from innocence to sadness after the war began. Times were tough economically for the region, and the bluecoats continuously harassed Master Clary, requisitioning his horses, cattle, forage, and corn to supply Grant's occupying army. And the nature of the diary changed again in December 1862, but dramatically this time from sorrow to outright anger and hatred for the Union forces. It was after General Forrest had torn up Grant's rail lines east and west of Jackson that the Feds exacted revenge on purported sympathizers throughout Madison County.

"Isaac recounted how Lincoln's men had ridden up to the house, dragged Master Clary out into the rain, charged him with aiding 'villainous Forrest,' and summarily put a bullet through his head. After stripping the property of valuables, foodstuffs, and the remaining livestock, the Feds allowed Clary's slaves to remain on the property and fend for themselves. Some weeks later Mourning took her eldest son aside and divulged just what you might have guessed: Master Clary had treated Isaac and his siblings differently because they were indeed Clary's children. From that point on, Isaac seethed inwardly every time he saw a Union soldier marching or riding through town."

Reacting to the brutal injustice, I couldn't resist jumping in. "Did Isaac do anything about it? I mean, did he get involved in the war?"

Master Taylor shook his head and said, "He sure did. After Mourning assured him that the family would survive on the plantation, Isaac made his way to east Texas and became a scout for Terrell's Confederate Cavalry Regiment. He and his comrades patrolled the Gulf Coast; helped blunt a Union foray into Texas during the winter of 1863–64; and then the following spring defeated General Bank's forces at Mansfield and Pleasant Hill, Louisiana, thus ending the Fed's one-hundred-and-fifty-mile advance up the Red River. He and his men remained in southern Louisiana until near the end of the war and then returned to Texas as heroes.

"When his regiment was mustered out in '65, Isaac returned to Jackson only to discover his father's mansion had been torched and the plantation abandoned. He later learned from a sympathetic clergyman that all of Master Clary's former slaves had fled to Memphis after experiencing harassment from the locals as the Confederate cause became more desperate by the day. Isaac then traveled to Memphis to continue his search for his missing family.

"After several days of dead-end leads, he finally located Hannah, Aaron, and Mourning in Happy Hollow. They were sharing a dilapidated hut with a family that had fled Mississippi after Lincoln's proclamation. Isaac moved into their crowded space, worked odd jobs, and began collecting wood and rusted metal from up and down the riverbanks to raise his own 'mansion on a hill.' He made an ironic observation that much of his building material came from the greatest disaster on the Mississippi, the sinking of the steamboat *Sultana*, which exploded only weeks after the war ended, killing seventeen hundred Union troops just released from Confederate prisons."

I looked up from the journal resting on my lap. "I remember that sinking, sir. It was all the news at the time."

Master Taylor nodded. "Well, Isaac reported he and his family moved into their new hut just in time for Christmas of '65. While there were no presents or tree, everyone felt they had been given the greatest gift of all, their own place to live. After the first of the year, the war hero resumed searching for a permanent job but without success. By God's grace Mourning and Isaac managed to find just enough work to get by. They often proudly observed they were poor but enjoyed their freedom. The next passage in Isaac's journal announces bitterly that the 'good fortune' has ended. In May '66, Mourning died of the smallpox and Isaac became the sole source of support for the family. And as Father Webber learned only a month later, the diary ended because Isaac had come down with a deadly fever that left the orphans to scavenge the filthy bog for food.

"Well, as I said earlier, Father Webber paid a visit and fulfilled a mission. I now believe he wanted to assess Emma's health before offering up his daunting proposition. He cleared his throat, leaned in toward us, and said, 'Some of the congregants, the elders, and I have concluded we can't let the children return to Happy Hollow. Admittedly our motives are mixed. While some quote the scriptures, others talk about taking care of the families of our Confederate heroes. We discussed potential adoptive parents and settled on you. We believe you and your family would offer the children a loving, comfortable place to live. Amanda could become an older sister for Hannah; and you, Preston, could enroll Aaron in your Westminster Academy. I know you must be thinking of the added expenses; but the congregation has already agreed to pay a monthly stipend to help defray the costs. Do you think it's possible?'

"So it appeared the church, the priest, and the orphans had adopted us rather than the other way around. I first looked over at Emma, who nodded her approval, and then turned back toward the supplicant priest and replied, 'As Jesus said, "With God all things are possible."' Father Webber leapt from his chair, enthusiastically hugged both of us, and said, 'God bless you; you'll never regret this act of kindness.' Yes, and I remember Father Webber uncharacteristically staying for lunch that day. But what I remember most about the visit is the final broad smile he shot back over his shoulder as he bounded down the front stairs toward his carriage. He realized that with the help of God and Confederate prayers, he had indeed fulfilled his mission."

Master Taylor eased down off the front of his desk and said, "Well, looking back over the last six years, I guess I'd have to say Father Webber's suggestion was good for all of us. The church members have treated Hannah and Aaron as respectfully as they would a child of their own color. Amanda has learned the responsibilities of an older sister, the children have filled the void in Emma's broken heart, I've watched a young scholar grow, and Emma has lovingly nurtured them into respectful, caring adults."

"Something to be proud of, sir," I replied.

The headmaster smiled, pulled his watch out of his vest pocket and said, "We'd better get to the parlor in a hurry. I'm sure Emma and the children have been waiting to begin our family hour."

As we entered the parlor, Master Taylor apologized profusely. "I'm so sorry we're late. We got to talking, giving

Thomas the lay of the land and, well, you know how it is."

Mrs. Taylor laughed out loud and said affectionately, "After all these years, Preston, yes, we all know how it is. You've never been sparin' either with the words or the stories." She patted the cushion on the settee, motioning to me to join her, and explained, "Wednesday night's special for us, Thomas. We've been holding these family get-togethers for years. There's no format; we talk about anything from Shakespeare to the latest goin's on. But to remember the Lord's blessings we always include a scripture and sing a hymn or two. So, Aaron, I believe it's your night to read the passage. What have you chosen, dear?"

"Well, it's been almost six years since Isaac died—since Father Webber saved us from Happy Hollow and you and Father brought Hannah and me here to live. So in honor of the three of you I've chosen a passage from Psalm 107:

> O give thanks unto the Lord, for he is good: for
> his mercy endureth for ever. Let the redeemed
> of the Lord say so, whom he hath gathered out
> of the lands, from the east, and from the west,
> from the north, and from the south. They wan-
> dered in the wilderness in a solitary way; they
> found no city to dwell in. Hungry and thirsty,
> their soul fainted in them. Then they cried
> unto the Lord in their trouble, and he delivered
> them out of their distresses. And he led them
> forth by the right way that they might go to a
> city of habitation. Oh, that men would praise

the Lord for his goodness, and for his wonder-
ful works to the children of men!

Master Taylor looked over toward his wife and said proudly,
"The Lord works in mysterious ways, doesn't he, Emma? We
lost Michael and gained a daughter and son in return. Praise
God you're both here with us now." He then turned to his
younger daughter and asked, "So, Hannah, it's your turn and
then Amanda's to lead us in song…tell us the hymn you've
selected for tonight?"

As she rose from her chair and walked toward the old upright, Hannah responded, "Aaron and I thought 'Come, Thou
Fount of Every Blessing' married up well with Aaron's psalm."
She slid onto the bench, struck the opening chords, and sang
in a sweet soprano. We all joined in on the popular hymn:

> Come, Thou Fount of every blessing,
> Tune my heart to sing Thy grace;
> Streams of mercy, never ceasing,
> Call for songs of loudest praise.
> Teach me some melodious sonnet,
> Sung by flaming tongues above.
> Praise the mount! I'm fixed upon it,
> Mount of Thy redeeming love.

"Oh, I love that old song praising God's blessings," Mrs. Taylor said. She then softly repeated, "Streams of mercy, never
ceasing / Call for songs of loudest praise." She paused, turned
toward the large crucifix hanging on the far wall, and became

lost in an otherworldly reverie, which we honored until the hall clock finally and divinely intervened.

Master Taylor looked over toward Amanda and said, "It's your turn, dear; what will you play tonight?"

"'Light Shining Out of Darkness,' Father," she answered. "We don't hear it as often in church, but the hymn has a message similar to Hannah's and perhaps has even more to say." Amanda eased into Hannah's spot on the bench and began playing and singing in a dramatic soprano voice. We followed along, but nowhere near as proficiently as we had with Hannah's more familiar song:

> God moves in a mysterious way,
> His wonders to perform;
> He plants his footsteps in the sea,
> And rides upon the storm.
>
> Ye fearful saints, fresh courage take,
> The clouds ye so much dread
> Are big with mercy, and shall break
> In blessings on your head.
>
> Judge not the Lord by feeble sense,
> But trust him for his grace;
> Behind a frowning providence,
> He hides a smiling face.

After finishing the reading and the two hymns, the conversation quickly shifted to more worldly matters—Alexis's grand tour of America and his scheduled arrival in Memphis on Friday. Our parlor drama played out in two acts. The first centered on Alexis's visit to the hunting grounds, where Master Taylor, Aaron, and I took the lead while the ladies crocheted silently in the background.

"Can you imagine that?" Master Taylor asked. "General Sheridan, Buffalo Bill, and Custer working a deal with Chief Spotted Tail to have six hundred Sioux warriors greet the duke and put on a show of war dances, bow-shooting, and horsemanship. I read they gave the Sioux twenty-five wagonloads of flour, sugar, coffee, and tobacco."

"Probably the only way they got the Sioux to show up for the ceremony and gain permission to hunt their lands," I suggested.

"But to tell the truth they got even more than that," Master Taylor replied. "Ironically, the Russian guest had to bail out his American hosts. I understand things got pretty riled when good old Custer got tanked up and made a pass at Chief Spotted Tail's sixteen-year-old daughter. The duke had to step in and smooth things over, offering the chief hunting knives, blankets, and bags of silver dollars. I hear order was finally restored when everyone passed around a peace pipe in Sheridan's tent."

Mrs. Taylor looked up from her half-completed shawl and objected, "Even if Custer's one of the handsomest men alive, his behavior's inexcusable. And to top it all off, I believe he's been married for some years now."

With Mrs. Taylor's comment, the ladies took center stage and the men faded into the dimly lit backdrop for the second act.

"Is the Grand Duke as handsome as Custer, Mother?" Amanda asked.

"By all accounts he is. Wavy hair, full beard, tall, sturdy physique. He's in his early twenties and unmarried to boot," Mrs. Taylor replied.

"The reception ball at the Overton will be so exciting," Amanda exclaimed. "I suspect a dance would be unlikely; but I hope I at least get a chance to speak with him. How should I address him? Grand Duke? His Imperial Highness?"

Master Taylor interjected, "Why not a dance? You're one of the most beautiful belles in Memphis." And then just as quickly he withdrew again from their conversation.

"Be careful what you wish for," Mrs. Taylor said. "By all accounts he's a ladies' man. I read he's already fathered a child with a poet's daughter eight years his senior. When the tsar got wind of it, he put an end to the affair like Johnny on the spot."

"Perhaps it was just a mistake, and he learned his lesson," Amanda replied.

"On no, my dear. The newspapers are full of the young duke's excesses with the ladies. He went to see a touring opera company in Buffalo and sent the lead soprano a bracelet studded with diamonds and turquoise. Do ya think it was just a gesture of his appreciation of her operatic skills? I don't think so. Next in Chicago, Sheridan introduced Alexis to the Dutch custom of making New Year's Day calls upon the ladies. You can only imagine what happened at the end of that day. Then in Saint Louis the duke attended the burlesque show, *Bluebeard*, where the actress, Lydia Thomson, sang "If Ever I Cease to Love." There are rumors flitting about she performed the song for him privately during a rendezvous after the performance—and mind you, how can I say this oh so delicately, she was almost twice his age. Scandalous, I tell you. While one newspaper reports Alexis's infatuation with the sister of his Indian guide, another describes a young acquaintance's unsuccessful journey from Saint Louis to Omaha hoping to become the duke's wife. And finally, there's a dispatch out of Saint Louis that Alexis became enamored of a young dance partner from Kansas, who was already betrothed to marry a respectable gentleman from Saint Louis in the fall."

At this point we rejoined the ladies' conversation for the denouement. "I agree, Emma, y'all must be on your toes with the young Romanov," Master Taylor said. "But as long as you ladies are aware of his . . . ah . . . tendencies, you can enjoy his visit and still hold him at bay. It's a win for both sides. He gets the flirtatious adulation he requires, and Memphis makes a lot of money and gains the respect of the Yankees up North. This is what Pinson, Davis, Hill, and I emphasized at our reception committee meetings. And look what's happened so far. The newspapers are saying the shelves of the finest milliners and clothiers have emptied in advance of the reception dinners and balls. Business hasn't been this good since before the war—and that's not all. The visiting journalists will file enthusiastic reports about the rise of the New South and how we've regenerated ourselves culturally, politically, and economically. This will bring prestige and power to Memphis. It will make us all proud again!"

As Master Taylor spoke about "regeneration" and the "New South," he became more animated, and his rich baritone grew increasingly loud. About halfway through the soliloquy, he rose from his chair and began pacing rhythmically to the forceful pattern of his speech. And just as he completed a revolution of the parlor, he shouted his rallying cry, "It will make us all proud again!" There was a brief pause, and then the room erupted spontaneously into sustained applause.

"An inspirin' way to end the evenin', my dear," Mrs. Taylor said. "But honestly, all this talk just sharpens the anticipation and makes the waitin' that much more unbearable. Let's hurry to bed now; and when we awake tomorrow, the festivities will only be a day away. . . . Here's a lamp, Thomas. Amanda and I will see you up to your room."

We climbed the staircase, walked the length of the ghostly hallway, and stopped outside Michael's door. "There's a pitcher full of fresh water in the basin and a clean towel on the dry sink," Mrs. Taylor said. "Sleep well, Thomas. We're all so happy you're here."

I undressed and quickly crawled in beneath the thick goose-down comforter. As I lay in the starlit darkness, I first reflected on my generous host and his wife. I concluded Master Taylor was a flawed but decent man reflecting the sentiments of many folk living in western Tennessee. You didn't have to be around him long to pick up on how he felt during the war. He had passionately supported Forrest and the rebels, silently despised the Federal occupiers, and believed emancipation could destroy the economic underpinnings of the South.

But when the war ended, he was able to change. Perhaps a deep-seated trait unearthed by one of Father Webber's homilies. Perhaps the death of a son in a dying cause. I don't know for sure how or why it happened, but I can testify Master Taylor had made the long journey from Southern sympathizer to the guardian of mulattoes whom he mentored and loved as his own.

While Master Taylor lived in the present, I sensed his wife had never really escaped the past. She was a living anachronism, a faded Southern belle longing for the gentility, customs, and comforts of the Old South. She just couldn't come to grips with her diminished status in a new society, which had leveled the very social distinctions she had learned to value as a young lady of privilege.

So she now lived in a shadowy region somewhere between fantasy and reality, between yesterday and today, which helps explain her obsession with every detail of the young Romanov's visit. While standing before the mirror donning the evening silks, rich laces, and long kid gloves she planned to wear to the reception ball, she would be transported back to the vanishing decorum of her antebellum past.

It was apparent to me that over the years she had learned to layer on a cosmetic verve and charm to hide a yearning for the old ways and her profound mourning for a fallen son. Because of a deep love for his dear Emma I believe Master Taylor had misread his wife's feelings. More than anything he wanted her to heal, and he thought mistakenly Aaron and Hannah would help fill the unspeakable void. Sad to say, after my interaction with Mrs. Taylor that first day, I suspected I would be her next attempt at mending a broken heart. But I didn't hold out much hope for her success.

During the darkest days of the war, my old schoolmaster and I debated the meaning of the very psalm young Aaron excerpted for family hour that evening. While Aaron's experiences had led him to the opening lines offering praise and thanksgiving for God's deliverance, my life had compelled me to focus on the reality of the latter verses:

> They that go down to the sea in ships that do business in great waters; these see the works of the Lord, and his wonders in the deep. For he commandeth, and raiseth the stormy wind, which lifteth up the waves thereof. They mount up to the heavens; they go down again to the depths. Their soul is melted because of trouble. They reel to and fro and stagger like a drunken man, and are at their wits' end. He turneth rivers into a wilderness and the watersprings into dry ground; a fruitful land into barrenness, for the wickedness of them that dwell therein.

As I drifted off, I gave thanks for my position at the academy, for a place to call home, and for a family to replace the one I lost during the war. I wasn't praying, mind you. Despite my mama's admonition to pray often, I had learned early on that prayers are rarely answered. And I have the war and a crowded family cemetery to prove it. But in deference to my mama's memory and her beliefs, I offered up these words of thanksgiving not to the gods but to the anonymous starry night.

3

MASTER TAYLOR HAD surprises in store for us that
we would remember for the rest of our lives. Despite Friday breaking dull, drizzly, and cold, the headmaster was much
more cheerful than usual. Perhaps he realized his work on the
reception committee was over and it was now time to enjoy
the elaborate festivities. He had advised everyone the night
before to rise early, dress in their Sunday best, and be ready to
leave the house precisely at noon.

After we all piled into the carriage, Master Taylor drove
us over to the Memphis depot. Crowds of excited onlookers
had already begun lining both sides of the main thoroughfare
running between the station and the Peabody Hotel, where
the duke would be staying for the next six days. When we
pulled up in front of the terminal, Master Taylor jumped
down, helped the ladies exit the carriage, and then instructed
us to wait for him on the platform while he hitched the mares.

When Master Taylor arrived, he immediately asked the
police sergeant to collect the six officers milling about the
crowd and to meet him at the west end of the station. After
no more than five minutes, the meeting broke up, and the officers set about roping off a wide lane running from the edge
of the platform to the station entrance. Master Taylor then

curiously asked us to join him within the restricted area away from the other spectators.

As the minutes passed, the crowd grew and became increasingly excited and boisterous. I overheard the waggish stationmaster describe the din as loud enough to "deafen the ears of an ass." Every few minutes a prankster would scream out, "There's the train!" which would be followed first by gasps and then by loud groans and laughter once everyone realized they had been tricked by another false alarm.

The bedlam continued until the crowd felt the first rumblings of the real locomotive rounding the last bend and approaching the terminal. The engineer sounded the whistle twice and slowed the train to a stop, perfectly aligning the Grand Duke's car with the post and rope stanchions on the platform. The station doors swung open, and the official welcoming committee walked past our group and boarded the train to greet the Grand Duke face to face. While Messrs. Pinson, Haynes, and Hill were visiting with Alexis on the train, Master Taylor instructed us to line up side by side against the ropes next to the wives and children of the other reception committee members. And for the next ten minutes we stood there like soldiers at attention all in a row—Master Taylor, Mrs. Taylor, Amanda, Aaron, Hannah, and me.

The hubbub of laughter and shouting continued until the coach car opened and the welcoming committee exited followed by Alexis, General Custer, and a substantial ducal entourage. Mr. Pinson, a former officer in the Confederate army, moved along the row of family members with the Grand Duke making the introductions. To his credit, even after touring Mammoth Cave the day before and traveling much of the night, Alexis spoke through a translator with each person standing in the receiving line, including the youngest children.

Hannah and Amanda took their cue from Mrs. Taylor, who smiled warmly and curtsied impeccably, no doubt just as she had been schooled beginning at the age of five. Perhaps because his reputation preceded him, I quickly concluded the more beautiful the young lady being introduced, the more time Alexis spent in conversation with her. And my suspicions were proudly borne out the following morning when, mind you, two reporters lightheartedly made the same observation in their lengthy columns describing the Grand Duke's arrival.

Once the royal procession had passed by, we filed in behind the group and followed them out through the terminal into the street. We could barely hear Master Taylor's instructions over the roar of the crowd standing ten deep on both sides of the boulevard. He was actually trying to reveal another secret—trying to tell us to quickly get into the carriage because we were going to be a part of the welcoming parade riding up the cheering avenue to the Peabody Hotel.

When we reached the Peabody decked out with large Russian and American insignia, Master Taylor led us up the stairs to the fifth floor where he revealed his next surprise: we would participate in the official welcoming ceremony in the Grand Duke's suite hosted by Memphis's popular mayor, the Honorable John Johnson. The hotel staff had assembled the finest accommodations for the luxurious rooms: rosewood furniture, large gilded mirrors, carved marble tables,

Belgian carpets, and three paintings by the Swiss-born and former Memphis resident Carl Gutherz, "The Assumption of the Blessed Virgin," "Descent from the Cross," and "The Household Saint."

The hotel had also spared no expense in preparing a lavish banquet for the Grand Duke and our welcoming party: oysters on the half shell, chicken gumbo, turkey, beef, boiled lake trout, mashed potatoes, hominy, stewed tomatoes, spinach, and coconut cream pie with vanilla ice cream for dessert. But the most remarkable aspect of the afternoon was the enormous crowd that had assembled outside the hotel entrance and continued cheering until Alexis made an appearance on the balcony and tipped his hat several times. Only then did the throng of well-wishers disperse and allow the duke and his entourage to rest a little before the evening festivities began at nine o'clock.

After returning home to freshen up and change into our formal evening wear, we drove to the Overton Hotel and joined four hundred other couples who had gathered in the elegant dining room, which had been converted into a grand ballroom for the gala reception ball. The hotel staff had added elaborate decorations to the hall, including new chandeliers; Russian and American flags; red, white, and blue bunting; elaborate floral arrangements; and wreaths of evergreen.

Alexis and his retinue relaxed in reserved suites on the upper floors of the hotel until it was time for their grand entrance at precisely half past nine. As the Grand Duke walked out onto the dais at the far end of the ballroom, Professor Handwerker's fifteen-piece orchestra struck up Sousa's latest march, "The Review," and a gas device spelled out "Welcome, Alexis" in flaming letters above the proscenium of the temporary stage.

After patiently greeting the attendees for the better part of the next hour, the Grand Duke honored Colonel Pinson's wife with the first dance. Then it was time for Master Taylor's final two surprises of that memorable day—he had miraculously arranged for Mrs. Taylor and Amanda to dance the next two waltzes with the Grand Duke. And as his daughter took her turn gliding across the floor with the crowd looking on, Master Taylor turned and said proudly, "It's been a fine day today, hasn't it, Thomas?"

"One I'll certainly never forget, sir, that's for sure." And then under my breath I murmured, "Perhaps the gods just overlooked us today."

We barely had time to recover before the second great social event of the season was upon us—the first Mardi Gras in Memphis only six days after Alexis and his entourage boarded a steamer for their journey to New Orleans. While trying on the elaborate costumes the ladies had crafted for us, I said to Master Taylor, "I've heard about the Mardi Gras in Mobile and New Orleans, but why start a celebration here in Memphis?"

Master Taylor shook his head slowly and replied, "The city was in a bad way physically and spiritually after the war ended. Honestly, it was a quagmire of poverty, filth, misery, stench, the carpetbaggers and the Freedman's Bureau, political graft and corruption, uncollected taxes. . . . The city was teetering on the brink. And worst of all, no one at town hall was trying to straighten things out. It was a divided city. You had the Union military, the merchants and traders, the old aristocracy, and the Irish, German, and Italian immigrant laborers. Everyone was fighting everyone else, and no one was strong enough to exert any control. It was just a mess.

"But thank God for General Greene. He fought the Yankees all through the war, mostly in Missouri and Arkansas. Returned to Saint Louis to find his former partner had bankrupted his business. He then moved here in '68. Became an agent for Knickerbocker Life and then started his own insurance company last year. I bought a small policy from him to help Emma, you know, with the final expenses. I believe he was the right man at the right time. I think it took someone from the outside with some leadership skills, business acumen, and attention-grabbing showmanship to get all the factions working together."

Master Taylor stopped the narrative to put on his costume wig, and I considered what he had told me. Although I followed the war closely, I hadn't heard about General Greene and was fascinated by the role he played in rebuilding Memphis.

Having secured his wig, Master Taylor picked up where he had left off. "Greene's most daunting task was to build a team to fund, publicize, and manage the 'big shindig,' as he called it. He first went to the wealthy businessman, Joe Specht, and made his pitch. He needed Joe to sell the merchants on financing a Mardi Gras celebration to help save their shops. Next he called on Colonel Galloway, editor of the *Daily Avalanche*, whom he persuaded to provide much-needed publicity to get the project up and running. And finally, he asked Lou

Leubrie, owner of the New Memphis Theater, to manage the production, choose an overall theme, and design the supporting theatrical effects for the celebration.

"General Green and his team set right to work; and by last December, Leubrie had led an exploratory delegation to New Orleans to see how 'the big boys did it.' After Leubrie reported back to the committee, Galloway published a series of articles in the *Avalanche* touting the benefits New Orleans derived annually from their celebration. And with Galloway now stoking the fire, it was Specht's turn to visit the merchants and collect the 'donations' for the decorations and the floats."

Master Taylor paused, walked over to the full-length mirror, adjusted his jacket, and asked, "How do I look?"

"You strike a commanding pose, General Washington," I replied. "And how about me, sir?"

"Outstanding, my Lord. More imposing than Cornwallis himself."

So only days after Alexis left, we once again squeezed into Master Taylor's carriage and headed downtown, this time for the inaugural Memphis Mardi Gras. Our destination was Leubrie's New Memphis Theater, which would be our base for that day's activities, filled with parades, floats, brass bands, tableaux vivant, and masquerade balls.

We left the house in costume at the early masking hour of ten o'clock in the morning. Dressed as Washington and Cornwallis, Master Taylor and I were the odd men out both in theme and historical epoch. Since the rest of our family had agreed to participate in the grand tableau, "The Legends of

Greece," our ladies chose flowing gowns and floral wreathes and Aaron was fitted out handsomely in realistic leather armor. While heading up Jefferson toward Third, a smile came across my face as I supposed this would be the closest I'd ever get to the heavens, sitting here in the carriage next to the striking Hannah and surrounded by gods and goddesses—Athena, Hera, Aphrodite, and Zeus.

It didn't take us long to realize General Greene and his lieutenants had a huge success on their hands. Half the city's population of forty thousand had filed out into the streets and filled the midway, the taverns, and the hotels. The *Daily Avalanche* reported excitedly the following day that "kings were arm in arm with peasants; princes hobnobbed with Biddies; Saracens and Crusaders were inseparable as Siamese Twins; Bismarck drank liquor with Louis Napoleon; and Lord Cornwallis and Washington danced a Highland Fling to the music of 'Sugar in the Gourd.'" General Greene's vision had successfully begun to tear down the walls dividing the city. Aristocrats raised a cup with merchants; Yankees danced with rebels; and Irish and German immigrants shared their favorite drinking songs.

Just after sunset the grand torchlight parade got under way at the old Charleston Depot and moved down Adams Street toward the reviewing stand at the Overton Hotel. Our family got to ride the whole way. Master Taylor and I were on the "American History" float highlighting de Soto's discovery of the Mississippi River at the bluffs. And after appearing in their tableau vivant, Emma, Amanda, Aaron, and Hannah starred on the "Fall of Troy" float, which won the grand prize for beauty, thematic relevance, and creativity.

When the parade disbanded at Court Square a little past nine o'clock, many of the revelers headed off to one of the makeshift ballrooms created just for the festivities. As we walked over to the New Memphis Theater to dance the night away, we saw a lot of folks letting their hair down with impunity. Everyone had obviously read the police chief's public dispensation posted on the telegraph poles proclaiming there would be no fines for "too much spirits."

But the bawdy atmosphere of the streets disappeared as we entered the aristocratic decorum of Leubrie's theater. Emma slipped her hand up under Master Taylor's arm, smiled broadly, and said, "Preston, I've died and gone to heaven." All the old families were there: the Brinkleys, the Hills, the Mallorys, the Overtons, and the Randolphs. And Mr. Leubrie had even hired a special orchestra out of New Orleans to capture the authentic spirit of a Shrove Tuesday carnival and help recapture some of the beloved memories of an antebellum past.

It didn't take me long to learn our participation in the Grand Duke's reception and the Mardi Gras celebration wasn't an anomaly. The Taylors took their jobs as parents and cultural mentors seriously. So during my first full year in Memphis, the family and I attended concerts featuring the former slave turned pianist, Blind Tom Wiggins, and the celebrated conductor, Theodore Thomas, offering up the US premier of Wagner's *Ride of the Valkyries*. We saw plays starring Edwin Booth and Fanny Janauschek as Macbeth and Lady Macbeth, and then Frank Mayo as the titular character in a new play, *Davy Crockett*. And before the presidential election, we heard a well-received lecture (some say a campaign speech) by Horace Greeley, who argued President Grant should stop the Reconstruction, pull all his Federal troops out of the South, and let the states return to conducting their own affairs again.

4

THE MONDAY FOLLOWING carnival marked the beginning of the second semester of the school year. Since it was my first teaching position, I felt a bit anxious, but the nerves were much more about anticipation than fear of failure. I actually felt prepared because Master Taylor had shared the deceased lecturer's syllabus for the course I'd be picking up midstream. In fact I was impressed with Mr. Karrigan's approach and literary selections and felt comfortable carrying on the second semester with only a few significant changes to his challenging outline.

Before taking ill in December, Mr. Karrigan had covered the Pentateuch; Plato's "Euthyphro" (I'm sure he also introduced the Socratic dilemma); Dante's *Inferno* (the classic I discussed with Master Hudson during planting season on the family farm); Montaigne's "Of Cannibals" (perhaps Mr. Karrigan's subtle attempt to inject his own beliefs about the recent war. What did Montaigne say? "I conceive there is more barbarity in eating a man alive, than when he is dead; in tearing a body limb from limb by racks and torments . . . than to roast and eat him after he has died"); excerpts from Galileo ("I've loved the stars too fondly to be fearful of the night"); Shakespeare's *Merchant of Venice* ("If you prick us, do we not bleed?"); and Descartes' *Discourse on Method* ("I supposed all the objects ever entered my mind when awake had in them no more truth than the illusions of my dreams").

According to the syllabus, Mr. Karrigan was scheduled to teach *Robinson Crusoe* at the end of the first semester. But then he died unexpectedly and the search for his replacement spilled over into January, so Master Taylor pushed Defoe out into the second semester. Since every schoolboy had read *Crusoe* more often than they'd read the Bible, I decided to challenge the class with Defoe's less familiar novel, *A Journal of the Plague Year*. I believed the raw nature of the account would draw the students in ("'Throw out your dead!' . . . 'Where am I?' . . . 'Where are you?' says Hayward. 'Why, you are in the dead-cart, and we are going to bury you.'"). And once the students had engaged, we could then discuss the spiritual meaning of historical events in Defoe's works.

In deference to my old teacher, Master Hudson, I added Wordsworth to Mr. Karrigan's pre-Romantic "Graveyard Poets"—Parnell, Young, Blair, and Gray. There was method to my madness. Master Hudson had lent me Wordsworth's *Lyrical Ballads* to supplement my studies. I remembered the preface; Wordsworth said he was experimenting with a new form of poetry—rejecting the difficult classical style of earlier writers and crafting poetry based on the "real language of men."

Focusing on this concept of a "real language" would provide the rationale for the most significant changes I would make to Mr. Karrigan's syllabus. Instead of emphasizing the later Romantic English poets, Byron, Shelley, and Keats, and the Romantic and Victorian novelists, Austen, Scott, Thackeray, and Dickens, I would cross the Atlantic and introduce the "real language" and immediacy of recent and current American writers including Irving, Hawthorne, Whitman, and Poe.

So Master Taylor and I left the house together early that Monday morning following carnival. He said he wanted to introduce me to the faculty before the boys showed up for classes. We walked up Main Street past the Peabody Hotel to Madison, where Master Taylor stopped in front of a three-story brick building with four large chimneys, a wide porch, and columns extending the length of the structure. There was a singular stained-glass oval centered above the main entrance.

Master Taylor pointed toward the building and said, "Welcome to Westminster Academy, Thomas. Let's go in, do the introductions, and get you settled."

"Looking forward to it, sir," I replied enthusiastically.

We climbed the stairs to the top floor and found everyone congregating in a large open space most likely used for gymnastics, since there was a piano at one end of the room and stacks of wands, rings, and dumbbells at the other. The staff appeared to be discussing what they had been doing over the holiday hiatus. Master Taylor motioned for me to follow him. We walked up to the group nearest the landing, politely interrupted, and began the introductions. The names came fast and furious. I couldn't remember whether it was Mr. Crosby or Mr. Shelby who was from New Jersey and taught arithmetic or whether it was Mr. Meacham or Mr. Gage who was from Mississippi and lectured in history or whether it was Mr. Martin or Mr. McKinley who was from Memphis and instructed the upper and lower classes in music and art.

When the blur of introductions ended, Master Taylor put his arm around my shoulder and guided me out into a long hallway of individual faculty offices. We walked down to the northwest end of the building and entered the corner space, which was as large as Master Hudson's one-room school I'd attended before leaving home for college.

"This was Mr. Karrigan's old office," Master Taylor said. "He'd been here a long time. Before your arrival, I spoke with Mr. Martin, who'd have inherited the room because of his seniority; but he graciously relinquished it, suggesting you take the office because he was going to retire at the end of the school year. Come on over here, and take a look out the window."

"My God, sir, that must be Court Square down there," I exclaimed. "Yes, yes, there they are—the fountain, the statues, and the promenades. Just as you described them. You can clearly pick them out in the winter without the leaves. I now see why you call it your favorite spot and the soul of Memphis."

Master Taylor pivoted away from the window, moved toward the back of the room, and said lightheartedly, "Take a seat at your new desk there, and let's review your classes once more before its time to enter the den. You've got a pretty heavy workload, Thomas—two advanced grammar classes with the freshmen, a composition course with the sophomores, and literature classes with the juniors and seniors at the beginning of the day. I believe you'll have our Aaron in the first period. Push on him, Thomas. He's bright, he writes well, and the competition's going to be real steep at the University of the South beginning this fall."

"I'll treat Aaron and his classmates as my mentor, Master Hudson, treated me," I replied. "I'll respectfully challenge every aspect of their rhetoric, question how they put their ideas into words, examine their structure, diction, and tone, analyze form and thought at every level—from word to sentence, sentence to paragraph, and paragraph to overall composition. . . . Believe me, Master Taylor, my goal is to have them all prepared to compete at the next level with the sons of Northern merchants and politicians who've had a habit of ridiculing our culture while slyly sending their children down here to our finest schools."

Master Taylor checked his pocket watch and said, "Well, it's time to head on down to meet the seniors. You ready to go?"

"I'm looking forward to it, sir. Just let me grab my copy of Defoe's *Journal*, and I'll be all set."

Once we entered the classroom, the students' noisy conversations ceased, and their eyes focused first on their headmaster and then on Mr. Karrigan's unknown, untried proxy. Master Taylor walked to the front of the room, wrote my full name on the board, and introduced me to a dozen attentive seniors: "Gentlemen, I would like you to meet Mr. Karrigan's replacement. He grew up around here during the war. So I'm sure y'all will get along just fine. He's reviewed Mr. Karrigan's syllabus and explained he'll be making a few changes. But I'm confident one thing will not change—just as Mr. Karrigan had, Thomas here will be challenging you daily so you'll be prepared for college this fall. Work hard; respect others; and good things will follow. Thomas, the stage is all yours."

As Master Taylor exited, I replied, "Thank you, sir," and then took my place at the head of the class. I paused, surveyed the students, and began. "So let's get to know each other a bit before we start to work. Tell me a little about yourselves and your families." But what I thought would be a safe means to transition from Mr. Karrigan to me quickly became a painful recollection of childhood terror and loss for them. Almost half these boys had lost a father or an older brother in the war, and a good third of the remaining had lost a mother either in childbirth or to some dreadful disease.

The stories seemed to feed on one another, spiraling downward, becoming more horrific by the minute. My first impulse was to panic. Cataclysmic thoughts raced through my mind—"What in God's name were you thinking? This is not how you begin on a positive note. How will you ever dig your way out of this hole? Stop! Just stop! Take a deep breath. . . . Take another. . . . What did Mama always say? 'Find the silver lining. Find the silver lining.'"

When the last senior had completed his fateful history, I inexplicably reached down, grasped Defoe's *Journal*, and responded, "How many of you have read *Robinson Crusoe*? Just as I suspected—all of you. How many of you have read it numerous times? Again, just as I thought—almost all of you. Since y'all are so familiar with *Crusoe*, would anyone object to reading something else by Defoe? Something gripping but less well known? Very good then. So let's begin." For some reason this time I knew precisely when to stop selling and enjoy the sale I'd just made. Given their backgrounds I believed the boys would immediately engage and finish their senior year on a positive note.

I raised the novel and said calmly, "Daniel Defoe published *A Journal of the Plague Year* in March 1722. That's three years after *Crusoe* and only three months after he'd published a second successful novel, *Moll Flanders*. The *Journal* is a semifictional narrative of one Londoner's experiences between 1663 and 1665, when a hundred thousand Englishmen died of the Great Plague. While his friends and peers were racing to the countryside to escape the pestilence, the narrator, H. F., stayed behind and recorded the horror—quacks selling fake medicines and cures; madmen running through the streets; families quarantined in their houses increasing the likelihood of infection; and thousands of rotting corpses stacked in the streets awaiting the burial carts."

I paused, checked my watch, and said, "We only have a few minutes left today. We'll begin reading excerpts aloud in class tomorrow followed by a discussion of what we've read. After we finish Defoe, we'll tackle the pre-Romantic 'Graveyard Poets' and then one of my own additions to the syllabus, William Wordsworth. We'll focus on an idea Wordsworth develops in the *Lyrical Ballads*—the 'real language of men.' For the remainder of the semester, we'll then cross the Atlantic and read some of our own contemporary writers—Irving, Hawthorne, Whitman, and Poe.

"Every two weeks or so, we'll have a short quiz covering our class discussions. While these short tests will make up a third of your total grade, the other two-thirds will be determined by a college-level term paper related in some way to the material we've been covering in class. The outline for your essay will be due six weeks from now. I'll provide feedback to ensure you're on the right track. Are there any questions? Okay then. Class dismissed."

I had already decided before the semester began that the quizzes would not be killers. I would use the tests to confirm the students were retaining the most important points about the authors and their works. On the other hand, the term paper would help calibrate performance and clearly separate the sheep from the goats. In addition, I assumed the detailed outlines would give me an early indication of what to expect from the final product.

Reviewing their outlines six weeks later, I confirmed what I had suspected after spending only a short time with this group of upperclassmen. They were intelligent, skilled, and savvy. They had chosen challenging topics including Teaching the Teacher: Socratic Irony in Plato's Euthyphro; Final Words: Science and Scripture in Galileo's Letter to the Grand Duchess Christina; Striking Differences: Shakespeare's Shylock versus Marlowe's Jew of Malta; Almost Heaven: Dante's Portrayal of Virtuous Pagans in the *Inferno*; and The Voice of Reason in Montaigne's Essay, "Of Cannibals."

While judging the students' intelligence and skill sets was easy, gauging their savvy required a bit more insight. The first thing I noticed was that only three students, Charles, Samuel, and Aaron, had chosen topics related to Defoe and beyond. Charles opted for Irving (Making Success of Failure: Rip Van Winkle as Antihero); Samuel chose Hawthorne's short stories (Guilt and Isolation in *Mosses from an Old Manse*); and Aaron decided to analyze Defoe and Alessandro Manzoni (Sermons in Stone: Spiritual Meaning in *A Journal of the Plague Year* and *The Betrothed*).

So why would most of the boys choose works from the first semester? My initial response was they didn't want to wait until we had studied Irving, Defoe, and Hawthorne before drafting their outlines. Plausible. But I sensed there was more to it than that. After all, don't most students wait until the day before the assignments are due to start their projects? And then a second more likely explanation occurred to me. Playing the odds, these shrewd upperclassmen assumed I would be much more familiar with the authors I had chosen than the one's Mr. Karrigan had covered in the first half of the year. Thus minor slips in facts or errors in analyses might just get by me while I was grading their papers.

I next met with each senior individually to discuss his outline and to offer suggestions on how to strengthen the essay. All the private sessions went well, but my interview with Aaron proved to be the most delicate of all. Master Taylor had told me Aaron was both bright and ambitious and that I should push on him to perform at the highest level. I had now lived in the same household with Aaron for going on two months and completely agreed with Master Taylor's assessment. So expecting a superior product vis-à-vis his peers, I chose to review Aaron's outline last. But when we met, I had to explain my unexpectedly critical assessment of his work. "Speaking bluntly, Aaron, I was disappointed with the results. The topic and the content are okay, but they appear limited in scope. I know you've been sick off and on the last month with the flu and then the pneumonia, but I think you can do much better. Your classmates have set the bar high. You'll need to do a lot more now to increase your overall score."

All the while I was speaking, Aaron kept staring down embarrassedly at the offending outline sitting on his lap. When I paused, he looked up and responded sincerely, "I'm sorry. No excuses. How can I make the paper better?"

"My impression is your outline is only scraping the surface," I replied. "The topic has a lot of potential. You make provocative arguments, but then you usually support them with minimal analyses and a brief quote or two from the works. You'll have to dig deeper, Aaron, and make stronger connections between the texts. How do the authors describe the plagues, which struck their countries thirty years apart? How do the characters react? What lessons do Manzoni and Defoe draw from the catastrophes? And can we apply those lessons to our world today? You understand what I'm saying?"

The creative spark was returning to Aaron's eyes as he answered, "Yes, I understand. You want me digging deeper and making stronger connections between the novels. Is there anything else you can think of to improve it?"

"Yes. This should be an easy fix. While you say your essay is about Manzoni and Defoe, you add Poe and his *Masque of the Red Death* near the end of your outline. I believe your intentions are good—adding Poe, since we'll be discussing him toward the end of the semester—but I honestly don't think Poe adds anything to your comparative analyses. If I were you, I'd drop Poe and focus solely on Manzoni and Defoe. I hope this is helpful."

"I understand—concentrate on the two authors and bolster the support for my arguments. I'll get right on it."

"Just remember, Aaron, there is no grade associated with

the outline. Everything depends on the paper." I then smiled and added, "So you have a real opportunity for redemption."

And when it was finally time to review Aaron's term paper at the end of the semester, I immediately realized he had taken up the challenge and had had enough courage of conviction to draft a tour de force without adhering completely to my earlier feedback. While he had drilled down more deeply into the texts and provided stronger support for his arguments, he had refused to focus solely on Defoe and Manzoni. Instead of drafting a comparative analysis of the two novels, he had expanded the breadth of scope to include works spanning two and a half millennia. During the evenings at home I would see Aaron poring over the extensive collection of books in Master Taylor's study. And now I knew why. He had in essence produced a seminal study on how authors throughout history have viewed physical phenomena in moral and/or psychological terms.

Aaron launched his essay with a quote from the ancient Greek poet, Hesiod, who describes how evil, illness, and disaster first spread about the world and left mankind with a single antidote to combat the onslaught of deadly trouble:

> For ere this [the opening of Pandora's jar] the tribes of men lived on earth remote and free from ills and hard toil and heavy sickness. . . . But the woman took off the great lid of the jar with her hands and scattered all these, and her thought caused sorrow and mischief to men. Only Hope remained there in an unbreakable

home under the rim of the great jar, and did
not fly out at the door. . . . But the rest, countless plagues, wander amongst men; for earth is
full of evils and the sea is full. Of themselves
diseases come upon men continually by day and
by night, bringing mischief to mortals silently.

From this prologue Aaron moved next to Thucydides's fac-
tual account of the Plague of Athens in 430 BC and introduced the first of his major themes—that cataclysmic events
cause significant social, civil, and religious upheaval. In the
History of the Peloponnesian War Thucydides describes a uni-
versal breakdown as the pandemic sweeps across North Afri-
ca into Greece. Since the Athenians are living daily with the
real threat of an excruciating death, they spend their money
indiscriminately, ignore victims lying in the streets, requisi-
tion strangers' pyres to cremate their own deceased, abandon
worship of their useless gods, and defile the temples with the
dying and the decaying dead.

Aaron next turned to Lucretius's philosophical poem,
On the Nature of Things, to illustrate a second major theme—
that from the beginning of recorded history writers have
continually applied spiritual meaning to physical catastrophes. Aaron deftly and painstakingly analyzed how Lucretius adds moral meaning to Thucydides's realistic account
of the Plague of Athens. While Thucydides describes the
fever-stricken citizenry diving into wells and streams to
quench their thirst, Lucretius adds a moral meaning—comparing the diseased to the ambitious seeking to satisfy an in-

satiable thirst for wealth and fame while quelling a nagging fear of losing everything at death.

And then Aaron was on to the Byzantine scholar, Procopius, who describes the social, civil, and religious collapse when the plague overwhelms Constantinople in 542 AD. Procopius reports in his *History of the Wars* that none of the deeply religious could explain why the city had been beset with an epidemic or why "the disease, whether by chance or by some providence, chose out with exactitude the worst men and let them go free." Echoing Thucydides's account a millennium earlier, Procopius reports the social and civil fabric unraveled as the death toll mounted:

> Now in the beginning each man attended to the burial of the dead of his own house, and these they threw even into the tombs of others, either escaping detection or using violence; but afterwards confusion and disorder everywhere became complete. For slaves remained destitute of masters, and men who in former times were very prosperous were deprived of the service of their domestics who were either sick or dead, and many houses became completely destitute of human inhabitants. For this reason it came about that some of the notable men of the city because of the universal destitution remained unburied for many days.

Aaron's supporting examples flowed one after another. From Procopius he moved on to Boccaccio's description of the pestilence in fourteenth-century Florence, next to Dekker's account of the epidemic in Jacobean England, then to Mary Shelley's plague-ridden future world in *The Last Man*, followed by Manzoni's Great Plague of Milan in *The Betrothed* and finally to Defoe's *A Journal of the Plague Year*. Oddly enough, during our in-class discussion of Defoe, Aaron gave no indication either that he was expanding his paper or that he had any profound insight into the *Journal* and its place among centuries of plague literature.

Throughout the essay Aaron focused on the evil, illness, and disaster that was unleashed with the opening of Pandora's jar. Time and time again the plague attacked irrationally, spread relentlessly, and then for some unknown reason faded away spontaneously. It killed without regard either to morality or social status. But in his concluding paragraphs, Aaron turned from the social and civil chaos to the only antidote the gods left us to combat adversity—the hope, which was hiding "under the rim of the great jar."

Despite the death, alienation, and bleakness surrounding them, most Greeks, Romans, Byzantines, Italians, and English remained optimistic that their nightmare would end. Aaron argued that under such daunting pressure this hopeful optimism was transformed into a calm courage—the inexplicable, death-defying courage to act on behalf of others. While on the surface all these works emphasize death and disorder, they also quietly celebrate valor, sacrifice, and an unspeakable love for family, friends, and outright strangers. Aaron then quoted

Defoe's *Journal* to support his final point and conclude an exceptional essay:

> A plague is a formidable enemy, and is armed with terrors that every man is not sufficiently fortified to resist or prepared to stand the shock against. It is very certain that a great many of the clergy who were in circumstances to do it withdrew and fled for the safety of their lives; but 'tis true also that a great many of them stayed, and many of them fell in the calamity and in the discharge of their duty. . . . I cannot but leave it upon record that the civil officers, such as constables, head-boroughs, Lord Mayor's and sheriffs'-men, as also parish officers, whose business it was to take charge of the poor, did their duties in general with as much courage as any. . . . But then it must be added, too, that a great number of them died; indeed it was scarce possible it should be otherwise.

5

THE SIEGE BEGAN as a series of feints and skirmishes followed by the low rumble of advancing thunder. It all began so routinely and so seemingly unrelated to what would happen over the next twelve months. In late July we said farewell to Aaron as he boarded the train for his first term at my alma mater on Sewanee Mountain. And from then until now I don't believe there was a day went by when one of us didn't confess to missing him or reminiscing about something he had said or done while living here. But the pendulum was beginning to swing back now from those bittersweet memories to eager anticipation of his arrival next month for the beginning of a twelve-week winter break.

Amanda, Hannah, and I were in the kitchen just before dinner keeping Mrs. Taylor company while waiting for Master Taylor to return from feeding the horses. "I've just about got all the Christmas presents sewn, so I can begin workin' on Aaron's new uniforms," Mrs. Taylor said while stirring the thick pork gravy. "That'll be twenty-five dollars saved, which can then go toward Aaron's books and incidentals. And I've been collectin' other necessities for him right along—some new sheets, towels, and pillow cases he can take back with him in the spring." She sighed, looked toward me, and said impatiently, "Honey, would you look out the window there and see if Preston's on his way. He said he was just goin' down to feed the horses. . . . I swear he'll be late for his own funeral. He'll dawdle, and the supper'll be ruined. You just wait and see."

I glanced out the window and then announced, "But this is your lucky day, Mrs. Taylor, he's walkin' up the yard right now, and he's movin' real fast."

"Well, Lord help us! This'll be a first for him, showin' up on time for anything," she said grudgingly. "Here, Hannah, put the meat and beans in the bowls there and take them into the dinin' room. Looks like for once we'll be eatin' on time."

Master Taylor appeared in the doorway and said, "Emma, don't hold supper for me. Something's wrong with the horses. Bessie's down, and Nell's hacking. They both have runny noses. I'm going to go get Doc. I hope it's not that horse flu we've been reading about in the newspapers."

Before the week was out everyone was talking about the "Great Epizootic," which had worked its way south from New England and had now taken hold here in Memphis. All the mules and horses had gotten infected and were too sick to carry riders or pull loads. The merchants on Main Street desperately tried to keep their businesses going. Now and again you'd see several of the shopkeepers working together vainly trying to pull a wagon full of goods along the road. And since the firemen couldn't get coal for their locomotives, even the trains stopped running until the horses could recover and the coal deliveries resume.

The following month, after Aaron's return home, we were all sitting in the parlor admiring our Christmas tree and listening to Master Taylor reporting the news from the *Avalanche*. "It says here the horse flu's now peaked and the shops should start opening again soon. But some staples will be in short supply because of the severe freeze. River traffic's suspended. It's solid ice up and downstream for miles. What else can go wrong?" He paused, scanned the paper, and continued, "Oh, listen to this. Dr. Thornton, the physician in charge over at City Hospital, is now saying they've begun admitting patients with the smallpox. I'd heard rumors about this last week over on Main Street. Fred Walker at the general store told me confidentially his next-door neighbor had come down with a fever and vomiting. After ten days or so, a rash spread over his body and then began to blister."

"Excuse me, Master Taylor, why would Mr. Walker speak to you confidentially about his neighbor?" I asked innocently. "Wouldn't he want everyone to know about the smallpox so we could protect ourselves?"

Master Taylor folded his newspaper and placed it on the table beside him. "Speaking bluntly, Thomas, every time the whispers start about a lot of people getting sick, the merchants get scared. If a panic sets in, business dries up. They don't want any public announcements until officials are forced to declare an epidemic to confirm the obvious. There's kind of an unwritten agreement between the shopkeepers and the politicians to wait until the last minute."

Mrs. Taylor looked up from her sewing and asked, "So, Preston, ya think Dr. Thornton's announcement means this outbreak is serious?"

"I do, Emma," the headmaster responded; and then glancing toward me, he added, "And Thomas, after the holidays we'll need to really be on the lookout at the academy for any signs of illness among the boys."

Perhaps by the grace of the gods, vigilance or good luck none of our family and only two of the juniors at the academy contracted the smallpox, which ran rampant for weeks especially along the riverfront. In the middle of March we put Aaron back on the train and went about our lives until during a family hour Master Taylor confirmed rumors that he said had been circulating for some time now. "It says here in the *Avalanche* that some cases of the cholera have made it up the river from the epidemic in New Orleans. The first case they say was April fifteenth—an Irishman who had arrived here a few days before that. The second was the thirtieth—an Italian who keeps an eating house on the river."

"That's gotta be Giovanni!" Mrs. Taylor interjected. "He's the only Italian I know down there servin' food."

Master Taylor looked askance at his wife's interruption, sighed, and patiently continued. "The third was May 1—a railroad conductor, who lives in the same area as the Italian."

Mrs. Taylor couldn't contain her unease. "Preston, ya think this is gonna spread?"

"I don't think so, Emma. The cholera's never taken hold here before in a serious way. We're high up on the Chickasaw Bluffs with a good supply of fresh water from deep wells. And besides, it says here just to be safe the Board of Health has urged the mayor to immediately clean the streets and alleys and has asked the citizens to lime their cellars and any other offensive places. So I think we're going to be okay."

But unfortunately Master Taylor's reassurances evaporated only days after reporting that the railroad conductor had taken ill. The cholera began spreading rapidly, especially in a convict camp close to the railroad tracks. And then I don't know whether it was someone in the mayor's office, the Board of Health, or the Health and Sanitary Committee, but someone recommended for some unknown reason breaking up the infected camp and scattering the inmates throughout the city. So for the first time in Memphis's history the cholera spread, prevailed from May through the middle of August, and killed almost three hundred people.

The good news was folks didn't fear the cholera as much as the smallpox. So they continued shopping, and the merchants turned a steady profit throughout the summer. But how could the gods tolerate this sanguine situation for long? They couldn't; and they didn't. But it wasn't disease this time that undermined the merchants. Over dinner one evening Master Taylor explained, "Damn Grant has done it again. This time he's not only attacked the South but the whole country."

"How so, sir?" I asked.

"Back in February he signed the 'Crime of '73,' which meant we'd no longer back our currency with silver—only with gold now. Can you imagine what that did to the demand and price for silver? Think about what that's done to the silver mines and states out west. On top of that, look what the act has done to the money supply and interest rates. Farmers are really hurting for loans, and investors don't want to touch long-term bonds. In fact, I read in the paper today a major investment bank's teetering on the edge of bankruptcy. Can you imagine what that shock will do to the national banks and the local businesses here in Memphis? Horrible . . . And all because of that damn Grant."

Contrary to everyone's expectations the disturbing news just kept on coming. In fact, after our discussion of Grant and the economy, Mrs. Taylor confided to Amanda and me she no longer looked forward to her husband's reports during family hour. But here we were again sitting in the parlor trying to absorb Master Taylor's latest report from the daily newspapers. "Well, it looks like the rumors are true again. It says here the steam-tug *Bee* dropped a dying deck hand off at Happy Hollow on August 10 and returned the following day from Osceola with the body of the *Bee's* captain. . .They say some of the folks in the Hollow have now gotten ill. The doctors don't know what it is for sure; they're using terms like 'congestive chill,' 'congestion of the brain,' and 'congestion of the stomach.' And the bills of mortality say 'not yellow fever.' The article goes on to say the Board of Health is holding regular meetings and comparing notes, observations, and opinions to get to the bottom of it."

"Are ya sure we can believe that, Preston?" Mrs. Taylor asked and then added, "Remember what they said in the *Appeal* about the men droppin' dead in Shreveport with five more dyin' each and every day after that? Remember how everyone dismissed the reverend who'd taken care of the victims of the yellow fever in Savannah back in '57? He said he knew the symptoms and tried to warn Shreveport they now had a yellow fever epidemic on their hands. And when it got so bad that the gravediggers couldn't keep up with the number of burials, the citizens finally panicked and left in droves, leavin' only about four thousand in the city."

Mrs. Taylor shook her head and then continued, "I had nightmares about it. The steamers unloadin' stacks of coffins from other towns. The rich and the poor alike shoved into the backs of makeshift hearses. And then the hauntin' clatter of hoofs echoin' through the night carryin' the dead to the cemeteries. Oh, I just hope it doesn't happen here, Preston."

"I don't think it will, Emma," Master Taylor responded, trying to relieve his wife's fears. "After all, look at what we've been through already this year."

I'm sure the gods smiled at his reassurances; they relish proving us wrong. By the first of September the disease had spread to the top of the bluff and into the Pinch District, a seedy Irish neighborhood near the river frequented by sailors, gamblers, and prostitutes. True to form the newspapers held out as long as they could before announcing the dreaded truth on the thirteenth—yellow fever had indeed invaded parts of Memphis.

This time Master Taylor didn't wait for dinner or a family hour to tell everyone the news. He asked we all join him in the parlor to discuss "some disturbing developments." He cleared his throat and began, "Today's *Appeal* says the Board of Health has now confirmed yellow fever in the Hollow and the Pinch."

"Lord a' mercy! What'll we do now, Preston?" Mrs. Taylor asked anxiously.

"I'm not sure yet what's best for us," he replied. "And there's not much we can do about it right now anyway."

"Why not, Father?" Amanda asked nervously.

"Once people got their hands on the newspapers this morning the panic set in and the stampede began. Folks are leaving by any means possible. The railroad platforms and the wharves are already piled high with trunks, suitcases, tables, and chairs. People are trampling each other trying to board the trains and boats. You should see it. And forget about escaping by horse or carriage. The streets are clogged with wagons and hordes of frightened people. I even saw a house over on Madison with the door wide open. I climbed the stairs and shouted, 'Anyone home?' But there was nothing but silence. I slowly entered the hallway and shouted again. Still nothing. I got the shock of my life when I reached the dining room. The table was still set with the silverware! They'd packed a bag and run out into the streets leaving their valuables behind."

But it didn't take Master Taylor long to decide a course of action, once Dr. Landrum, his personal physician, had paid a visit to the academy during the third day of the "Panic." Everyone agreed Dr. Landrum was a leader. He looked the part—over six feet tall, muscular, intense brown eyes, and long, dark wavy hair graying at the temples; and he sounded the part—a deep, godlike baritone commanding attention and action. He was born near Lexington, Kentucky, and attended Centre College where he met his lifelong friend, John Breckinridge, who would later become the youngest vice president in American history under Buchanan and then the unsuccessful standard-bearer for the Southern Democrats in the 1860 presidential election facing Lincoln.

After graduation, the classmates chose separate paths.

While Breckinridge studied law at Transylvania in Lexington, Landrum entered the prestigious medical school in Louisville. They would see each other occasionally during the summer months or the Christmas holidays, but the young lawyer and doctor never spent much time together until they joined the Third Regiment of Kentucky Volunteers in '47 during the Mexican-American War. With the signing of the Treaty of Guadalupe Hidalgo the following year, Major Breckinridge and Dr. Landrum began a triumphant journey home to Kentucky with celebratory stops in New Orleans and up river in Memphis.

During the stopover in Tennessee, Dr. Landrum attended a "victory ball;" immediately fell in love with Kate, the stunningly beautiful daughter of the state's junior senator; and then vowed to return to marry her and open a practice in the city. And it was only six months later Dr. Landrum kept his word. He said farewell to his family and his old friend, Breckinridge, and traveled southwest to begin his new life in Memphis.

The evening following his meeting with Dr. Landrum at the academy, Master Taylor gathered all of us in the parlor to announce his decision whether to stay or leave the city. The headmaster began, "Doc Landrum dropped by the office to discuss the yellow fever situation. He said he was shocked with how many citizens had already fled despite the reassurances that the scourge had been confined to the Hollow and the Pinch. I'll tell you upfront that Doc wants me to stay and work with him through the Howard Association."

"Is that the same benevolent group that's earned high praise helping the poor down in New Orleans?" I asked.

"Yes, the same organization. And since the mayor has closed the schools here, Doc believes I could be of value to the group. He thought I could help out with the administration of their programs—dividing Memphis into nursing wards, recruiting physicians and nurses from other states, soliciting donations, writing materials on prevention and developing plans to locate and provide care to the sick in their own homes."

"What'll the rest of us do, Preston?" Mrs. Taylor asked. "Stay here and risk everything or abandon you and let you die of the black vomit?"

"Emma, nothing's going to happen to me. The fever's been limited to the areas closest to the river. I'll be over on Main Street in the Howards' offices far from the fever. . . . It's okay by me for the rest of you to leave. I'll take every precaution. I promise you I'll be safe. Remember, I'll have Doc Landrum around for good advice."

"Preston, I'm frightened for all of us, but I can't leave you here. You know the scripture, 'Whither you go, I'll go; and where you lodge, I'll lodge.'"

Once Master Taylor and his wife announced their decisions, the rest of us spoke up in rapid succession.

"Perhaps I can help out over at the Howards." I said.

"Me too," Hannah suggested.

"And you can also count on me, Father," Amanda said and then added, "Mary Sharp College can wait until the spring semester."

Master Taylor rose from his chair, walked over to where Amanda was standing, cradled her head in his hands, and replied lovingly, "No, no. You've worked too hard, and there will be plenty of us left here to pitch in. When the panic settles down, we're going to put you on the train for Winchester. I'll telegraph President Graves at Mary Sharp; explain the situation and ask him to find you lodging until the fall semester begins."

So once the die was cast and the meeting ended, Master Taylor looked at me, pulled a long thick cigar from his breast pocket, and pointed toward the front of the house. He was signaling his customary invitation to join him on the porch as he participated in what Mrs. Taylor called his "repugnant habit," which she had permanently banned from the residence. After stepping out onto the veranda, Master Taylor quickly cut the cap, struck a match on a porch post, swirled the warm leathery smoke around in his mouth, exhaled, and then began pacing from one end of the veranda to the other. As usual, I tagged along stopping only to embarrassedly offer curious passersby "a very good evening to ya."

Since the sun had set an hour before, it was now getting really dark. And for the first time we spotted an unusual glow on the horizon. Master Taylor stopped suddenly, removed the cigar from his clenched teeth, and said excitedly, "Looks like something's on fire up on North Front Street! Let's take a walk, Thomas, and see what's going on."

As we neared the intersection of Market and Front, we encountered a team of city workers hurriedly digging a trench across Market. Master Taylor walked up to one of the men and said, "Excuse me, sir. I assume this has something to do with the fever?"

The fellow planted his shovel in the loose dirt, wiped his brow with a blue bandana, and replied, "Yep, the Board of Health gave the order this afternoon. This is our fifth pit today. It'll be ready for the coal oil and matches in just a few more minutes. Then we'll have to keep the oil fires burnin' day in and day out. They're supposed to clean the air and keep the fever from spreadin' outside the Hollow and the Pinch."

"Well, we'll let you get back to work now," Master Taylor said and then added pensively, "May God be with you . . . and with all of Memphis too."

"I think he was with us before, sir; but I don't know about now," the laborer replied.

"How so, sir?"

"Look what all's happened to us since the winter—the horses, the smallpox, the cholera, and now the yellow jack. I swear it was the sinning, the damned Mardi Gras that brought his wrath down upon us. Yep, it was the damned Mardi Gras that's done us in."

Master Taylor didn't respond to the man's speculation; he focused on the here and now and said, "Let's pray your oil fires work and the fever doesn't spread over the city."

As he turned to grab his shovel, the worker replied, "Amen to that, sir. I'll say 'Amen' to that."

6

OUR BOYS FOUGHT valiantly to hold the line; but by the first week of October, the fever had spread over a thirty-block area from Poplar Avenue to the Bayou Gayoso, a lower-class tenement district of Irish, Germans, and Jews. During the two-week span between the Board of Health's initial announcement and its latest public update, we managed to put Amanda on the train for Winchester and settle into our new roles battling a ruthless enemy.

While Master Taylor solicited donations and recruited out-of-state doctors and nurses, Hannah and I helped the Howards divide the city into nursing wards and plan home care for the sick and dying. In addition to my work with Hannah, I became the Howard's liaison to our allies in the fight—the Catholic Church, the Hebrew Hospital Relief Association, the German Benevolent Society, the Knights of Pythias, the Masons, and the Citizens Relief Committee, which was charged with receiving and distributing donated materials from all over the United States.

We fell into a routine and worked long hours. Rise at six o'clock; leave the house by seven; and return home some twelve hours later to Mrs. Taylor's fine cooking. So everything was stable and relatively risk-free—that is, until one evening at dinner when Hannah proposed the unthinkable. "Father, you know Thomas and I've been setting up the nursing districts and planning the home care; but the planning's coming to an end now. Thomas still has his work with the Catholics and Jews, but I won't have anything left to do. I want to help."

Master Taylor looked up from his plate and replied, "I know the Relief Committee can use all the help they can get. And, Thomas, I believe you speak with those folks almost every day, don't you?"

"Yes, sir, and I can ask them about Hannah."

"No, Father, that's not what I had in mind. While setting up the nursing districts and the home care, I met some of the volunteers coming in from Missouri, Mississippi, and Illinois . . . and I want to do what they're doing. I'm not afraid, Father."

Becoming increasingly agitated, Mrs. Taylor pushed back from the table and interjected, "Oh my God, Preston, you can't allow her to go to the Pinch or the Bayou! She'll get sick, and it'll be the death of all of us!"

Trying to soothe his wife's concerns, Master Taylor said, "We're not going to do anything rash, Emma. We need to pray on it and ask Doc Landrum what he thinks."

Several evenings later during family hour we learned Master Taylor's decision. "I've been reading the scriptures, praying, and talking to Doc about Hannah's wanting to nurse the sick. Doc spent over an hour explaining the fever. He said there were many theories on what causes yellow jack, but no one really knows for sure how it starts. Perhaps filth in the cities? A putrid atmosphere? A fungus? A germ? Doc then walked over to his bookcase, pulled a journal off the shelf, and explained that one of the most eminent medical men of Great Britain, a Dr. Lyons, had written a convincing treatise on yellow fever as he saw it in Lisbon a few years back. Doc lent me his copy so I could share some passages with you." Master Taylor picked up the thin volume from the side table, opened to a bookmark, and began reading:

> Great numbers of the citizens of Lisbon fled to Cintra and other favorite places of resort; yet no cases of yellow fever can be adduced to show that the disease spread, or was carried by contagion or otherwise from Lisbon to such localities. Cintra was perhaps the place most frequented, and with which much free daily communication was kept up; but I could obtain no reliable evidence that one single case of yellow fever occurred in that town. . . . Little if any apprehension of personal contagion was entertained by those in attendance upon and in daily contact with the sick; and this indifference to exposure to the supposed contagion of the fever was observable in all classes of society, among the lowest as well as the highest.

He closed the journal, placed it on his lap, and continued: "Doc said after reading the treatise, he next corresponded with a colleague in Nashville, who agreed with Dr. Lyons's conclusions about personal contagion based on his own experiences back East after medical school. This associate emphasized there was no more danger in attending a yellow fever patient than a case of intermittent fever. The colleague said he'd walked through the quarantine grounds at Staten Island and conversed with the patients; that he was in the yellow fever haunts below Brooklyn Heights in 1856; and that he was later in the infected district of Philadelphia during a serious outbreak there. And yet, despite the multiple exposures, he said he never had the least fear of catching the disease."

Master Taylor then turned and spoke directly to his wife. "But Doc saved his most convincing argument for last, Emma. He said based on having read Dr. Lyons's treatise and his colleague's letter, he was determined to give their assumptions a full trial when he had a chance. Doc said before the newspapers confirmed the epidemic here in September, he personally went to the Pinch and stayed in the room with a patient all day and night, sleeping in the man's bedroom with the black vomit all around. He said he unpacked the patient's clothes and handled them freely. He touched the patient, nursed him, and held the fellow's head while he vomited. Doc then ended our conversation assuring me yellow fever wasn't contagious and Hannah shouldn't fear contracting yellow jack from those she'd be attending."

Turning back toward his adopted daughter, Master Taylor concluded, "So, Hannah, based on everything I've heard, I'm sure you'll be safe and won't be a threat to any of us here. Tomorrow morning we'll go into the Howards' together and speak with Mr. Johnson, the superintendent of nurses, who's in charge of training and scheduling."

Hannah rose from the settee, enthusiastically hugged Master Taylor, and said, "Thank you, Father! My prayers are answered!" This time Mrs. Taylor didn't object. She just lowered her head and whispered a barely audible twenty-third Psalm.

Hannah's enthusiasm reached a peak the following Friday when her training ended. In less than seventy-two hours, she would begin attending real patients ravaged by the dreaded yellow jack. During dinner that Friday evening, Hannah dominated the conversation describing the content of the last day of training. But to be honest, there was no way Hannah's enthusiasm alone could account for the level of detail she provided describing the precautions the nurses must take to protect themselves and all those around them. And knowing Hannah fairly well now, I was most sure the detail was her way of allaying Mrs. Taylor's lingering fears about the risk of contagion.

Introducing the subject, Hannah said, "Now before you draw any conclusions, Father, I know what Doc said about the likelihood of people catching the fever from their patients, but the Howards want to be extra careful. The instructor reviewed the protocol with us twice today and then asked us for any questions. The teacher said once the disease had run its course, we should burn the patient's clothing, bedding, and, yes, even the carpets. And as far as the patient's valuable articles, they should be disinfected with superheated steam."

Hannah paused, pulled a folded paper from her apron pocket, and summarized the contents. "The Howards recommend we scrub the bare floors, the woodwork, and all the furniture with a solution of carbolic acid in water. Next we clean the walls with a standard lime wash fortified with carbolic acid. Then, after sealing the house as tightly as possible, we burn brimstone for four hours to disinfect the air. And finally, we pour a solution of copperas and crude carbolic acid into the privies and vaults."

She slipped the paper back into her pocket, turned toward Mrs. Taylor, and said reassuringly, "And there's nothing to worry about here, Mother. We won't have to wash any of my uniforms. The Howards want us to change out of our soiled clothes daily so they can boil them before we wear them again."

As I've already noted, that last day of training marked the peak of Hannah's enthusiasm. From that point on her demeanor changed dramatically. Despite our inquiries at dinner, Hannah became increasingly reticent to describe either her feelings or her experiences. In fact, after only her second week on the job, she began finding excuses to avoid dinner altogether. Our once-animated Hannah had become a brooding, ghostly sphinx who entered the house each evening and immediately trudged up the stairs to her sanctuary where she remained until the following morning.

Watching Hannah's transformation from idealist to somber veteran revived an uncomfortable feeling I'd experienced during the war. Mother and Father said I was too young to fight then; and besides, they argued, someone had to stay home to help out with the farm. But every time my older brother sneaked past the bluecoats for a brief visit, I could see the changes—the deepening lines, the graying beard, the sadness in the eyes. Instinctively, I wanted to saddle up and ride off into the night with him every time he came home, become part of the giant force sweeping the South. Yet every time Robert prepared to leave, I'd stand there under our buckeye tree with the rest of the family, embrace him, wish him well, and then watch him disappear into the forest line. But now there were no excuses. I was no longer too young; and there was no longer any acreage to farm. So I was determined to leave my post behind the lines and join brave Hannah on the battlefield.

The following evening after dinner, Master Taylor fortunately signaled me to join him on the porch for a cigar and conversation. I say "fortunately" because I didn't dare announce my decision in Mrs. Taylor's presence. I didn't want to upset her any more than she already was with Hannah's daily exposure to the yellow scourge. I had two objectives for our meeting: first, gain Master Taylor's acceptance, and then plot a way with him to ease the shock when his wife learned another member of the household was joining the fight.

We had lit our cigars and made several round-trips of the veranda before I summoned the courage to reveal my plans. "Excuse me, sir, I've something I need to discuss with you—privately—at least for now."

Master Taylor maintained his usual pace and asked, "What's on your mind, Thomas?"

I surprised even myself when I divulged my secret quickly and clearly in one succinct sentence: "I want to join Hannah on the front lines, sir."

The headmaster stopped abruptly, puffed several times on his cigar, and then responded, "My God, Thomas, are you really sure you want to take that on? You're doing such great work with the Catholics, the Jews, and the Relief Committee.

You've already helped establish the infirmary at the navy yard and the clinic over in the Jewish neighborhood. The Hebrew Hospital Relief Association has even praised you by name in the *Avalanche* for your work on their behalf. Why in God's name, Thomas, would you want to give up strategic successes like these to become a foot soldier in the war? It doesn't make any sense. . . . Look what it's doing to Hannah. . . . Why, Thomas? Why?"

"To be perfectly honest, sir, a sense of duty laden with a great deal of guilt."

"Guilt?"

"My parents said I was too young to serve in the war and they needed me on the farm. So every time I'd watch my brother mount and return to battle, I'd feel intense guilt; but none more severe than when near the end of the war I had to tell my family Robert had been killed in action and wouldn't be coming home any more. So now when I see Hannah climbing the stairs each night, I see my brother and remember the pain I felt."

Master Taylor stared down at the cigar he was rolling between his thumb and forefinger, slowly looked up, and said, "Okay, Thomas, if that's what you want, we'll speak with Mr. Johnson tomorrow about your training and scheduling."

Before Master Taylor could resume his pacing, I placed my hand on his forearm and asked, "How do you think Mrs. Taylor will take to the news?"

"I don't know, Thomas. We'll just have to tell Emma and then remind her what Doc said about the contagion."

"Thanks for helping me out, sir. And I promise you I'll be

back in the classroom teaching when you open Westminster again."

When my training ended the following Friday, I asked and was allowed to join Hannah at the new infirmary on Gayoso Street. I didn't say anything to anyone in the household that weekend about my first assignment. I just wanted to show up on Monday morning, change into my uniform, and then surprise Hannah as she made her rounds.

And that's exactly what I did. I pulled off my plan without a hitch. I entered the three-story frame house at precisely nine o'clock; changed into my uniform; and then began poking my head in and out of rooms looking for Hannah. I finally saw her exiting a patient's room at the far end of the hallway. She was speaking with another nurse with her back to me. Courtesy dictated I wait until she'd finished the conversation before making my move.

When Hannah turned and started back up the aisle, I began walking toward her. She didn't see me; she was reviewing notes I presume about the next patient she'd be attending. When she got within a yard or two, I whispered, "Hannah."

She looked up and gasped. "Thomas? What are you doing here? Why are you in that uniform?"

I smiled and replied, "I've had the training, Hannah, and I've come to fight the battle with you."

She didn't say a word; she just rushed forward and embraced her new comrade-in-arms. And then pulling back and holding me at arm's length, she smiled faintly and repeated over and over, "Thomas . . . Thomas."

Hannah then tugged at my arm and guided me out of the

house onto the front porch. She asked, "Have you met Miss Cook yet?"

"Miss Cook? I haven't met anyone. I kinda sneaked in trying to surprise you. I just spoke with the fellow at the front desk who gave me my uniform and showed me where I could go to change clothes. I then went from room to room looking for you."

"Oh, well, you have to meet Miss Cook. She owns the house. She decided to turn it into a temporary hospital."

"She was living in this big house all alone?"

Hannah smiled and replied, "Well, not exactly. Several ladies were living upstairs."

"So she was running a boardinghouse?"

Hannah continued smiling coyly and said, "Well, not exactly. How should I say? . . . Miss Cook's a purveyor of . . . ah . . . ah . . . commercial affection."

I laughed aloud and responded teasingly, "Oh my God, Hannah, what would Master and Mrs. Taylor think? Their daughter working in one of the twenty or so bordellos flourishing in the city!"

Playing along with my mock dismay, Hannah replied jokingly, "Stop it, Thomas. You know it's a hospital now." And then becoming serious, she said, "Miss Cook has truly sacrificed. She released her girls and spends the day now attending the sick. She's a saint, Thomas. You'll know it when you meet her."

Just as we were about to reenter the house, a tall, attractive, dark-haired nurse pushed the screen door open, walked out onto the porch, and greeted Hannah. "Good mornin', dear. I hope you've had your coffee. Doc says we'll be gettin' three more patients this afternoon."

She paused to light a cigarette and then continued in a syrupy drawl, "Hannah dear, ya haven't introduced me to your handsome young friend here."

"Excuse me, Miss Cook, this is Thomas. He teaches at my father's academy. He was working with the Howards and decided to get more involved with the patients."

Miss Cook extended her hand and said, "Good to see ya, honey. We can use all the extra help we can get. The numbers just keep risin'. It's overwhelmin' sometimes."

"Nice to meet you, ma'am. I'll do everything I can to help."

During the exchange between the three of us, my eyes darted back and forth between the cigarette and Miss Cook's remarkable face. I was witnessing in the flesh what I had only heard of in taverns and read about in magazines—a beautiful madam smoking, elegantly smoking a cigarette. And it was as if she were reading my mind, sensing my youthful pleasure.

She gazed into my eyes, smiled, took several long drags, exhaled, and said pensively, "You know, life's so strange. Chance? Perhaps. . . . I don't know. But now, the second time in a week. First, the tug master who somehow survived long enough in the Pinch for Doc to find him—Hannah, you know, the pleasant fellow we've got up on the second floor at the far end of the hall—he was feelin' so much better the day before yesterday that he began spinnin' stories about grow-in' up along the river in Cincinnati. One tale led to another, and little by little we discovered he and my papa had known each other. Known each other well—in fact, went to the same church and school together. He said he later lost contact with

Papa after takin' a job on the river. Now isn't that somethin'? What are the odds of that happenin' again? And then lo and behold, yesterday, the new fellow, the one with the mild fever, said I looked familiar. And come to find out I'd treated him in Louisville some years ago when he came down with the smallpox. Now aren't those the strangest coincidences?"

"Strange. Absolutely strange," we chimed in.

Miss Cook nodded her approval, took one last long drag off her cigarette, and said, "Well, let's get back inside and help these folks."

And help we did. Long, fourteen-hour shifts. Day in and day out. Rise in the dark and return home after sunset. I'd describe the work as demanding but very rewarding because we could see the results of our labor. As long as Hannah and I worked there, the hospital never lost a patient. In fact, even after we left, I don't recall ever reading or hearing that anyone died at Miss Cook's place. Good fortune? Fate? Coincidence? No. I think it was more a combination of superb care and accepting mostly patients whose fevers had broken and who were already on the road to recovery before arriving at our infirmary. In one sense these were the lucky souls who survived the scourge. But others could equally argue these same patients were the unluckiest of all. Many of them had been found lying helpless in their shuttered homes surrounded by the decaying corpses of their loved ones. And as the biblical Job said some millennia before, only they had escaped to tell their stories.

I believe it was the low-risk, routine nature of the care at Miss Cook's that sparked the unsettling conversation Hannah and I had not long after I began volunteering. It was a Sunday afternoon, our only time off for at least the next two weeks. The Taylors, Hannah, and I had attended Sunday morning services and then enjoyed one of Mrs. Taylor's finest baked ham meals. When an old friend dropped by later that afternoon to visit the parents, I asked Hannah if she'd like to take a walk around Court Square. She unexpectedly agreed to come along. I was surprised because after warming to me when I first showed up at Miss Cook's, she gradually withdrew and treated me as coolly at work as she had at home the past few weeks.

It was difficult reading Hannah, but she appeared to be spiraling downward. Her initial exhaustion appeared now to be overlain with anxiety and agitation. As we walked beneath the cedars, I opened the delicate conversation. "Hannah, something's troubling you. You've been as quiet at work as at home. Did I say or do—"

Hannah interrupted, "No, Thomas, no. It's not you. It's not anyone. It's me. I'm frustrated."

"Frustrated? About what?"

"To be honest, I'm bored. I could be doing so much more."

"How's that, Hannah?"

"We know almost everyone coming to Miss Cook's is gonna survive. They've already seen the worst of the fever. But what about all the others?"

"The others? What others?"

"Well, for instance, what about the patients' families? If I'd been out in the streets, gone in the houses, been on the real front line, perhaps I could have helped save some of the dying. . . . It haunts me, Thomas. I've got to leave Miss Cook's and get out on the front line."

I didn't respond immediately; I just kept walking. A response was clearly fraught with danger. Was Hannah subtly suggesting I should feel the same as she; that I should leave our sanitized version of the war; that I should join her in her gritty streets and houses? But somehow my respect and growing affection for this stunning young woman overcame my doubts, and I responded obliquely, "Borrowing Mrs. Taylor's biblical quote, Hannah, 'Whither you go, I'll go; and where you lodge, I'll lodge.'"

At first she looked at me quizzically but then replied, "So you're willing to leave Miss Cook's and join me on the front line?"

"That's right, Hannah; I'll go with you into the streets, into the houses. We'll fight this scourge together."

As she had at Miss Cook's on my first day, she turned and enthusiastically hugged me. "Yes, Thomas, we're going to fight this plague together!"

I grasped her shoulders, pulled back gently, and cautioned, "We can never mention our new work at home. It's got to remain a secret between you and me. Bravely facing the dangers together . . . working in there alone, without a safety net."

Hannah smiled knowingly, "Yes, Thomas, it'll be our secret. We'll carry it to the grave."

The following morning we reluctantly approached Miss Cook; and after apologizing repeatedly, I tried selling her on our rationale for leaving: "We want to take the fight into the

Hollow, the Pinch, and Gayoso. Treat the critically ill, help save more lives, try to hold the line at the bayou. You know, Miss Cook, most of the folks admitted at your place are going to survive. You know they're the lucky ones. But there are so many more sick and dying down at the river. We just never hear about them until we read the lists in the papers."

I paused and turned toward Hannah, who gave an approving nod. We had no idea how Miss Cook would react to the news; she had displayed no emotion throughout our apology and explanation. And she remained expressionless as she responded. "Well, I'll make no bones about it; it'll be tough losin' the two of you. But we'll make do. They're so many generous people comin' here every day from faraway places to help us out. Yes, we'll make do."

She gazed into our eyes and smiled. "You remind me so much of me when I was younger and fightin' the smallpox in Kentucky. I know exactly what you are feelin' now. Dyin' to get to the front lines, to confront your fears head-on, to feel the exhilaration when you save a soul and wrap yourself in the sweet comfort of knowin' you gave your all when God says, 'I'm sorry, no, not this time.' So no question you're doin' a good thing. Ask the fellow upstairs with the mild fever, who came down with the smallpox years ago in Louisville."

Miss Cook gave us both a big hug and then ordered, "Quick now, be on your way. They need you down in the Hollow and the Pinch. There's a battle ragin' that we've got to win."

As we exited onto the porch, I turned toward Hannah and said, "You're right; Miss Cook's a saint."

7

THE FOLLOWING MORNING Hannah and I pierced the thick, black veil of the fever fires and entered hell. A stifling, deathly silence now trumped the sunrise sounds of wagons we'd heard only seconds before. Taste and smell merged into a single sense heightening the nausea from the unbearable stench of vomit, musk, decay, and cologne. Smoldering heaps of infected mattresses bathed the inferno in a callous gray. Our boots were white with disinfectant. It was hot, and stacks of coffins stood at the corners awaiting Undertaker Jack. Every window of every house was nailed shut against the scourge—some with yellow placards signaling the fever and many with superfluous black cards requesting caskets for the dying and the dead. Superfluous because layers of flies already lined the outside walls, forecasting or announcing death with a whirring as foreboding as that of swarming bees.

I stopped, stared up the hazy avenue, and asked, "My God, Hannah, where do we begin? Look at all the yellow cards hanging from the nails."

Hannah scanned the houses, pointed westward, and replied, "How about that one over there, Thomas? The two-story brick with the watermelon vine climbing up the wall." She didn't mention the child sitting alone on the front stoop; but knowing Hannah, I was just certain the little girl swayed her decision.

I took a deep breath and answered, "Okay by me. Let's get on with it."

As we approached the house, abandoned dogs gathered near the bottom step and began howling the terror of the last judgment. We slowly climbed the stairs and asked the child, "Where's your mama and papa?"

She didn't reply; she just stood up, turned, and led us toward the front door.

"I don't know about you, Hannah," I whispered, "but this scares the hell out of me. Treating the sick on Miss Cook's wards was one thing, but climbing these steps and entering a shuttered house is another."

Hannah, who had lived the horrors of the Hollow and her older brother's death, slid her arm beneath mine, pulled me close, and replied resolutely, "It was meant to be, Thomas. Everything will be okay."

As the child pushed the door back, the pungent smell of rotting silage became overwhelming. I gagged once, twice, and then a third time in rapid succession.

"Breathe through your mouth, Thomas. It helps," Hannah said.

The child guided us down a darkening hallway filled with hot, trapped air. I bumped into an invisible sideboard and said embarrassedly, "God, it's really hard seeing in here with the windows all boarded up. My eyes are having trouble adjusting."

The young girl stopped at the end of the hallway and pointed into the last room on the right. An oil lamp flickered on the mantle, only suggesting the horrors that lay strewn before us. I entered and immediately stumbled over a body lying face up on the floor. I kneeled down to help but announced, "Hannah, we'll need to change the yellow card to black. The father's dead. And he'll need bathing; there's black vomit splattered all over him."

As I was checking on the father, Hannah picked up the oil lamp and moved toward the bed to attend the mother, who was rocking from side to side and shouting deliriously, "God, he's choking! Please, someone help! For God's sake, he's choking!"

Hannah turned up the lamp and placed it on the nightstand. She bravely embraced the woman, stroked her hair, and settled her head back onto the stained pillow. She coolly reported her findings as if she were still working on Miss Cook's wards. "Eyes: sunken, bloodshot; face: waxy; tongue: inflamed, cracked; nose: slight hemorrhaging; skin: moist, clammy." When she pulled the sheet back to check the woman's abdomen and legs, Hannah began shouting, "Oh my God, Thomas, she's miscarried—miscarried a boy! Full-term, dead, covered in afterbirth." And then only seconds later whispered calmly, "I expect Mama will be following along soon afterward, child."

We stayed on in the living crypt until the mother died in the late slant of that September light. While Hannah comforted the dying woman, I took measurements, made the placard, and then scribbled on it with chalk: "3 coffins needed—man, woman, infant—5 ft. 4; 5 ft. 2; 1 ft. 6."

When we'd done all we could, we posted the black card on a nail, sat down on the top step with the little girl between us, and began a veiled conversation about the orphan's fate. "Given the circumstances, what do you think we should do?" Hannah asked. "She's no idea what's just happened."

"Maybe we should speak with Sister Constance," I replied.

"Sister Constance?"

"Mother Superior of Saint Mary's Episcopal."

"Why?

"I learned working with the Howards that Saint Mary's has a place for children in her situation."

"Canfield Asylum?"

"No, not that one. Saint Mary's operates Canfield for Negroes. They have another place for parishioners, but I forget the name."

"What'll we do in the meantime?" she asked.

"Let's coax her back to your father's place. I'm sure he'll take her in until we can talk to Sister Constance. But, Hannah, we'll have to be careful with our story. Master Taylor doesn't know what we've been up to since we left Miss Cook's."

We now began hearing the mortician's call. "Bring out your dead! Bring out your dead!" After spotting a black placard on a house halfway up the street, Undertaker Jack and several Negroes stopped their team of horses, jumped down from the oversized furniture wagon, and entered the abandoned home to retrieve the latest victims.

"For the child's sake, perhaps we should leave and let the card speak for itself," Hannah suggested.

Turning to the little girl, I said, "We have to go now. Mama and Papa are really sick, and these men have come to take good care of 'em."

Sensing something was wrong, the child shook her head and refused to budge. I instinctively grasped her under the arms and carried her down the stairs and out of the Pinch, the young girl kicking and screaming the whole way.

Over the next six weeks, I suspect Hannah and I witnessed the deaths of a third of the two thousand who died before the hard frost mercifully ended the siege in mid-November. I can honestly say there were no easy days. We rose early, moved from the dead to the dying, and walked home every night feeling overwhelmed but willing to rise and continue the good fight the following day. As we'd all observed earlier with Hannah, I too began limiting my interactions with the rest of the family. I too found excuses to avoid dinner and go directly to my room. I now understood what Hannah had been feeling ever since she'd finished her training. It was not that we had negative feelings about the Taylors; it was just that we now had less in common with them. All the Taylors knew about the yellow jack was what they read in the newspapers or heard secondhand on the street. But Hannah and I were making daily round-trips to hell; piercing the acrid veil and encountering scenes that would simultaneously break your heart and make you sick to your stomach.

Ironically, our experience battling the scourge cut two ways. While on the one hand it created distance between the Taylors and us, on the other, it brought Hannah and me closer together. In fact, it was during our second week on the front line that Hannah walked the full length of the moonlit corridor, knocked softly, and glided into my room. In a balletic dance of candlelight the young nurse became goddess with long dark curls flowing down over the shoulders of her full-length robe.

Neither of us spoke as she approached the bed and eased herself in beside me. I instinctively slid my arm around her waist and pulled her up close to my side. There was no need for words. We had both lived it. So that night was a chance for healing and meaning. We gazed out through the starry casement for hours; but there were no answers. Only inscrutable silence with an occasional reassuring glance before turning back to the voiceless firmament again.

When the infections finally began subsiding in November, Hannah returned to my room, silently climbed up into bed, and nestled her head against my shoulder. I thought we'd settle back into our earlier routine; but after a few moments of staring out into the uncaring night, Hannah squeezed my arm and said, "I'm sorry, Thomas, it's been so much harder than I could've imagined. I hope we never have to deal with this again."

I turned toward her and replied, "Hey, you said everything would be okay, and see? You were right. We've survived. The Taylors are healthy and little Amber is safe with Sister Constance over at Saint Mary's."

"But look at all the dead still piling up out at Elmwood."

"We did our best, Hannah. We've saved a lot of people."

"I'm glad you were there, Thomas. It really helped. God, it was so overwhelming."

"I know. And I have to admit that first day was really scary—walking up on the porch and following little Amber into the shuttered house. But with everything beginning to wind down now, I realize I wouldn't have wanted to be any place else but here in Memphis fighting the scourge with you."

Hannah tilted her head up and smiled as tears welled in her eyes.

I stroked the side of her face gently with the back of my hand and said lightheartedly, "Do I see a little rainbow there?"

"Rainbow?" she murmured.

"Your smile. That's what Mama used to say to us children. She'd tease us to make us laugh when we'd be crying about something and then she'd say, 'Do I see a little rainbow?' As we got older, she added another line. She'd say, 'The rainbow takes you to the joy on the far side of sadness.' None of us really understood the meaning until we got a lot older and everyone started dying around us during the war. Finding a way to share a laugh or a smile helped us survive the horrors we saw every day."

She gazed into my eyes and repeated, ". . . the far side of sadness."

I leaned in and lightly touched my lips to hers. Hannah pressed closer and responded to my tentative moves with a resolute "yes." She loosened her belt and slipped the robe off her bare shoulders. I slowly kissed down her neck onto her breasts. Our bodies rose and fell with a tender rhythm. She moaned softly and sighed, "I need you, Thomas." I slipped my legs up over her thighs, arched my body, and then eased down gently into her willing love.

Hannah stayed until first light. She then gently embraced me, lightly brushed her lips along my cheek, and whispered, "Get some rest; we'll go to the Pinch a little later on today.

Things have gotten so much better." As she stepped out into the hallway, she paused, looked back over her shoulder, smiled, and said, "I think we've found the joy your mother was talking about."

I smiled and nodded. "Yes . . . I think so, Hannah."

I lay back on the pillow and tried getting to sleep. It was impossible. Light was beginning to stream in through the lace curtains, and I was thinking of Hannah and what had just happened. Why last night? Perhaps she felt the tide had finally turned, that yellow jack was on the run, and it was fitting to celebrate an imminent victory. We had already had light frosts, and fewer were getting infected and dying. At the peak of the fever, the conditions were daunting. You couldn't help but feel discouraged and afraid the battle would be lost.

And why would this daughter of Master Clary and his slave, Mourning, choose a son of the South and risk the public scourge of scandal and race? Because Hannah knew her mind. She was strong . . . courageous . . . independent. She would never be swayed by what others thought or what they had to say about her. From childhood on, she had heard all the epithets, sensed the contempt for her color, and suffered the inescapable abuse of growing up black in the South.

And despite my family's past, I always thought Hannah my equal in every way. You see, I grew up on a large farm with my parents, grandparents, an older brother, and a younger sister. But there were also two other members of our family, Bella and Israel. When they arrived, Bella was a strong, young woman and Israel her three-month-old son. My grandmother had inherited them along with two hundred acres of real estate from her brother, who had died prematurely of a fever. His last will had valued the land at two thousand dollars and Bella and Israel at fourteen hundred together. But despite my family owning slaves before and during the war, I neither thought in shades of blue and gray nor drew a bright-line distinction between Bella and Israel and me. In fact, everyone living on the farm felt that way. And the terrible irony was that it was black Union soldiers who unjustly executed Israel and left him swinging from our "good luck tree."

No, I believe that night with Hannah was inevitable. Since we'd been through so much together, we had already become one. We had witnessed the suffering, felt the urgent grip of the dying, and watched countless orphans wandering aimlessly through the streets. Our night together was all about acknowledging our feelings, restoring our hearts, and experiencing that rare beauty beyond the awful pain.

Later that morning Hannah and I returned to the Pinch and continued working there until mid-November, when the hard frost finally dealt the scourge a fatal blow. Once the killer frost hit, everyone in Memphis breathed a sigh of relief and became a little less guarded; but mid-November was not the end of the suffering. Folks were still taking to bed with the fever a week after that first hard frost. And I remember thinking the gods were treating these poor souls so cruelly, allowing them to believe they had survived the assault only to let them fall ill, suffer for days on end, and eventually succumb in a most inhumane way.

I had had those same unsettling feelings earlier while

reading accounts of obscure battles fought after Lee's surrender at Appomattox—thousands of casualties at the Battle
of Fort Blakely; a hundred fifty at Girard, Alabama; eighty
at West Point, Georgia; and fifteen at Palmito Ranch near
Brownsville, Texas—almost four thousand young bluecoats
and rebels expecting to be mustered out any day and return
home to their loving wives and children. Expecting to return
home, that is, until the gods smiled and intervened.

Some have asked, "Why did y'all leave the Pinch in mid-November? You'd endured so much; why didn't you just stay there
until the bitter end and the cessation of all the suffering?" Truth
is, we would have stayed; but the gods struck behind our lines,
forcing a quick retreat toward home. It started on Tuesday, the
eighteenth, after Hannah and I had left for the Pinch. When
Master Taylor went downstairs for breakfast, he found Mrs. Taylor sitting at the table with her head in her hands.

"You okay, Emma?" he asked.

"I woke up with a slight chill, and now I'm startin' to get
a headache. Preston, I . . . I hope I don't have the yellow jack."

"Emma, that's not likely. After all, we've had a hard frost,
and you haven't left the yard for over a week or been exposed
to anyone with the scourge. And remember, if you had been
exposed, Doc said it's not contagious. He said he'd been
around a lot of folks infected with the fever and never got
sick. I'm sure you'll be okay. If you'd like, I can stop by Doc's
place and ask him to check in on you."

"Doc's still very busy, Preston. I'll just mix up some sage
and cornmeal and rest awhile. That usually helps with the
headaches."

Returning home from the Pinch that evening, Hannah and I found Master Taylor and Doc Landrum engaged in serious conversation near the front door. Doc was wearing his overcoat and appeared to be on the verge of leaving. As we passed by, we greeted both men briefly and then quickly continued on down the hall to the parlor. Several minutes later Master Taylor entered and explained what had happened during the day.

"Before I left for the Howards this morning, Emma was complaining of a chill and a headache. I offered to get Doc, but she said she wanted to try her sage remedy. By the time I got home late this afternoon, she said the fever and headache had gotten a lot worse despite having taken the sage, McLean's Liver Pills, and some twenty grains of quinine. I immediately sent the Daniels' boy to fetch Doc. After a preliminary exam, he said Emma's pulse was normal and her temperature was 102. He said he didn't think it was serious—most likely just a mild fever we get around here every year with the change of the seasons. He reassured us and promised to stop in tomorrow morning to see how Emma was doing."

"If you'd like, Father, why don't you go on to bed; Thomas and I will look after Mother during the night."

"Yes, sir, please get some rest," I said. "We'll take good care of Mrs. Taylor."

"Well, if you don't mind. . . . But wake me up if there's a problem."

Hannah and I devised a plan where she would take the first shift, wake me, and I would attend Mrs. Taylor the rest of the night. When Master Taylor awoke the following morning, he immediately came down the hallway to check on his wife: "How's she doing, Thomas? Did she have a restful night?"

I looked down and shuffled my feet. I couldn't help it. It was a habit whenever I didn't have good news to report. "Honestly, it wasn't an agreeable night, sir. Mrs. Taylor was restless. She said her headache was making her sick to her stomach; her shoulders and back had begun hurting; and her throat was getting sore. Hannah told me at the end of her shift that Mrs. Taylor was . . . ah . . . having trouble . . . ah . . . emptying her bladder. Despite the pain, she finally fell off to sleep about an hour and a half ago. It's the only rest she's gotten all night."

"Let's just let her sleep then until Doc drops by later this morning," Master Taylor said. And then as he turned to leave the room, he paused and added, "Thanks, Thomas, thanks for looking out for Emma overnight."

"Happy I could help out, sir."

Doc Landrum arrived a little past nine and suggested Hannah join him while he conducted a more thorough examination. About thirty minutes later Doc exited the bedroom, confirmed Mrs. Taylor's condition had indeed worsened, and said he would be dropping by later that afternoon with a highly respected volunteer physician from Charleston, a Dr. Randolph, who would help him corroborate his diagnosis. No more than a minute after Doc left the house, Master Taylor and I descended on poor Hannah hell-bent on gleaning as much information as we could about the examination and Mrs. Taylor's current condition.

Master Taylor launched the interrogation. "Hannah, what did Doc have to say during the physical? Did he offer up a diagnosis?"

"No diagnosis, Father; and he didn't say much durin' the exam either. He only reported findings, which he asked me to record in his notebook."

"You were taking notes?"

"Yes, Father. He said he trusted me because he'd heard good things about my nursing at Miss Cook's."

"Quickly, child, tell us what Doc had you write down."

"I'll try, but I know I won't remember everything."

"Just do your best."

"Doc Landrum first took Mother's temperature and checked her pulse. I wrote down 'pulse 100' and 'temperature 104.' He said, 'skin—hot to touch and dry.' Doc asked Mother if she had passed urine overnight. She responded, and he had me write down, 'urine adequate but passed with pain and straining.' He asked her about discomfort in various parts of her body. She answered, and I recorded, 'severe frontal headache, pain in lumbar, significant aches in lower legs and shoulders.' As Doc moved about the bed, he continued asking questions and making observations, which I quickly recorded in his notebook, 'marked agitation and restlessness; little sleep; face flushed; eyes injected; sensitivity to light; tongue swollen, thinly coated and indentations from teeth; elevated thirst; stomach quiet, sensitive to pressure, and no movements in two days; minimal cinchonism; and administering calomel and quinine.'"

Hannah paused striving to recall the slightest overlooked detail.

"Nothing else?" Master Taylor asked.

"That's all I can remember, Father."

"Well, I guess we'll have to wait until Doc returns this afternoon with the volunteer, Doctor . . . ah . . . Doctor . . ."

"I believe it was Randolph, Father."

"Yes, yes. Dr. Randolph. I hope he can help with a diagnosis."

Doc returned close to six o'clock with the volunteer physician in tow. And after brief introductions, the doctors entered the bedroom and closed the door. Hannah, Master Taylor, and I huddled across the hall anxiously awaiting the verdict. Twenty minutes or so later, the door opened abruptly, and the physicians exited the room. As they approached us, Doc Landrum asked quietly, "Preston, where can we meet to discuss Emma's condition?"

"Let's all go to the parlor. Follow me," Master Taylor replied.

Once we had taken a seat, Doc Landrum reported the results of the joint examination. "Preston, I know you want us to be straight with you. Dr. Randolph and I believe we're unquestionably dealing with the scourge. Emma's putting up a good fight, and her condition is about the same as this morning. And since Emma's been so fearful of catching the fever, we recommend divulging nothing about our diagnosis. At least, not for now."

"My God, Doc, what can we do?" Master Taylor exclaimed.

"Make her as comfortable as you can; she'll need all her strength to wage the battle. Dr. Randolph and I suggest you give her mustard footbaths, sage tea, and frequent sponge baths with lukewarm water and whiskey. We've got to work on getting her temperature down. She's stable for now, but if anything changes during the night, send someone to fetch me. I'll get here right away. Otherwise, I'll see you tomorrow morning at the end of my rounds."

We didn't need to summon Doc during the night; so, as promised, he arrived a little before eleven o'clock the following morning. After Hannah, Master Taylor, and I reported what had transpired overnight, Doc asked Hannah to join him again at Mrs. Taylor's bedside, where he then conducted a follow-up exam. When he exited the bedroom a half hour later, Doc said, "The encouraging thing is Emma's holding her own. I'll drop by again late this afternoon to check her progress. In the meantime, continue the sponge baths and substitute watermelon-seed tea for the sage."

Just as the day before, the minute Doc left the house, Master Taylor began the questioning. "Hannah, were you taking notes again today?"

"Yes, Father," she responded.

"Do you remember what you recorded in Doc's book?"

"Well, just as yesterday, he began by checking Mother's pulse and temperature. I wrote down, 'pulse 92 and temperature 102.' Doc explained to Mother, 'Your temperature's down a bit today, Emma. Looks like the baths are helping.' He then asked her about her sleep, and I recorded 'little sleep and restless.' As he moved about the bed, his observations quickened: 'center of tongue—thick white coating; papillae red and enlarged; edges very red as in scarlet fever; mouth dry; gums ragged and bleeding; lips cracking and bright red; nasal passages dry; and stomach tender and noisy.' Doc then respectfully lowered his voice and asked Mother about her functions. I recorded her responses as 'urine scanty' and 'deep orange.' 'Bowels loose, frequent and tarry.'"

"Can you remember anything else?" Master Taylor asked.

"No, only his explaining to Mother he wanted her to continue the sponge baths and to switch to watermelon-seed tea."

Doc Landrum returned that evening to examine Mrs. Taylor. He said her condition was about the same and he remained cautiously optimistic she would recover. But it seemed the gods were having none of that. During our overnight shifts, Hannah and I both noticed Mrs. Taylor was becoming increasingly restless. It worsened so much during the last of my watch, I was thinking of waking Hannah to summon Doc.

But not long after dawn I heard a muffled knock at the front door. Fortunately, when I answered, Doc Landrum was standing there. He immediately began apologizing for the early visit. I was so relieved to see him I completely ignored his explanation for dropping by so early and launched into what Hannah and I had been observing during the night.

Doc quickly removed his coat and asked me to follow him. After entering the bedroom and greeting Mrs. Taylor, Doc set his bag on the chair, retrieved a pencil and notebook, and asked me to record his findings. Doc began the examination: "pulse 86, temperature 100; decanted urine—minimal without residue; new generalized tremor involving all limbs; lucid and coherent; patient reports hypersensitivity to light and sound; patient reports 'burning up inside'; bleeding from gums, lips, and nose; stomach tender; patient reports diarrhea—loose, tarry stools; patient reports nausea but no vomiting; respiration irregular." Doc paused and then said, "Begin a new paragraph; call it 'prescriptions.' Now write down 'add acetate potassium to watermelon-seed tea' and then say 'apply turpentine poultices to back and abdomen.'" Doc then turned to Mrs. Taylor and said, "I've changed some of the medicines, Emma, to help you feel more comfortable. The best thing you can do is try to rest. I'll be back to see you later this afternoon." After Doc left to finish his rounds, I prepared Mrs. Taylor some of the newly concocted watermelon-seed tea and stayed with her until Master Taylor had risen and come by to check on his wife.

When Doc returned late in the afternoon, Hannah resumed her role as note taker; and once he'd left, Master Taylor again became the interrogator-in-chief, justifiably probing to understand everything that was going on with his wife. Hannah reported the details of the brief examination: "'Pulse 77 and temperature 101. Patient quieter—in and out of sleep; physical findings much as the AM; urine output negligible. And add champagne to the current regimen.'"

Doc appeared the following morning around half past ten. We had some good news to report—Mrs. Taylor's kidneys were functioning a little better. Doc acknowledged this was a good sign and hopefully a precursor to healing. But as Hannah and I had witnessed time and time again, progress in one area usually was accompanied by deterioration in another. After Doc had left, Hannah revealed the results of the latest examination: "'Pulse 80 and temperature 100. Improvement in kidneys—secreted three ounces during the night. Symptoms much as yesterday. Sleeps in fits and starts. Administered sips of champagne. Vomiting within five minutes. Watery mucus with dark flocculi. Revised instructions—nothing by mouth except water and chipped ice.'"

Thankfully, Mrs. Taylor rested most of the morning and into the afternoon. It was the longest stretch of sound sleep she'd enjoyed since the siege began. Master Taylor stayed with his wife, the whole time stroking her arm and reassuring her that everything would be all right. But by the time Doc arrived toward sunset, Mrs. Taylor's condition had worsened. She had been vomiting sporadically throughout the afternoon. And I believe it was the blood in the last bouts of nausea that pushed Mrs. Taylor over the edge. For the first time she grasped the nature, severity, and likely outcome of her disease. She began speaking to apparitions, tearing at her clothes, and trying to escape the bedroom.

Mrs. Taylor turned toward her husband and said, "So you're General Webber? Where'd you get Michael's valise, old man? Do you have somethin' to say? Dead? Impossible!" Abruptly turning to me she commanded, "Come here, Michael, and prove this soldier wrong." She then looked back at Master Taylor and addressed him calmly with the charm and civility of a well-schooled debutante: "General Webber, sir, will you stay for tea? Reverend Forrest will be joinin' us soon. He's bringin' the church orphans here to stay." Now cupping her hands to her ears, she exclaimed, "There, you hear, they're knockin' at the front door. . . . Let go of me! Let go of me! It's my offspring from the Hollow. They mustn't wait."

"Emma, Emma dear, let's get back to bed. We'll answer the door. . . . That's it, Emma, back in the bed. Now stop, Emma; you've got to stay decent. Stop pulling at your gown."

As the delirium deepened, it took all of us to hold Mrs. Taylor down—Master Taylor and Doc holding her legs; Hannah and I pinning her arms to the mattress.

"We can't keep this up for hours on end, Doc. What are we going to do?" Master Taylor asked anxiously.

"Grab that sheet there on the chair. Use your knife and cut some strips. We've no choice but to tie her to the bed. I'll run over to Miss Cook's on my way home and fetch some fabric cuffs. We can trade out the strips for the cuffs tomorrow morning."

Once we had secured Mrs. Taylor to the bed, she began screaming, thrashing about, and trying to yank her arms and legs out of the makeshift cuffs. Red bands quickly appeared on her wrists and ankles. For me, she had become a nightmare memory—my father whistling the cattle into the narrow slaughter pen, the fearful lowing and then the loud thuds of confusion smashing against the reinforced fence.

Doc never left that night. In fact, we all stayed in the room, each taking a turn attending Mrs. Taylor while the others caught an hour or two of restless sleep. During my watch, Mrs. Taylor's arms and legs began to cool. She was retreating from the outside in. And not long before dawn I realized the tautness in the crude restraints had imperceptibly eased over into Mrs. Taylor's lifeless body. She had now and forever found a peace that passes all understanding.

8

AFTER HELPING PREPARE Mrs. Taylor's body for burial, I washed the black flecks of vomit off my face, arms, and hands. These countless specks of her last hours were no match for the lye soap she herself had rendered only days before falling ill. The drops released and flowed easily down my forearms into Michael's white enamel bowl. But it was not the same for Hannah; the stains had set too deeply to be washed away.

"I'll never forgive myself. I was selfish going to work in the Pinch and exposing everyone here to the scourge."

Challenging her theory, I asked, "How can you say that, Hannah? You know you did a lot of good for a lot of people. You saved lives; you didn't kill anyone."

Hannah interrupted, "But Mother hadn't spoken with a soul outside the family for at least a week. She hadn't left the house."

"Hannah, Hannah, remember what Doc said. He doesn't think yellow jack's contagious. After all, you, Doc, and I all worked in the Pinch, and none of us got sick. Ask Doc. Ask your father. No one here believes you're responsible for your mother's death. So promise me you'll push these feelings aside."

"I'll try, Thomas. I'll try."

And over the next several months Hannah kept her promise and worked hard to climb out of her sadness. She was becoming Hannah again. Her smile, her confidence and willingness to converse at dinner were slowly returning. But the steady progress she'd made over weeks and months inexplicably unraveled in a matter of days. The old melancholy had returned and a new, self-imposed isolation had forced this penitent to her room.

After all we'd been through, I couldn't let her suffer alone. I wanted to help or at least share the pain. I knocked lightly at her door. "Hannah." No answer. I tapped again. "Hannah, it's me, Thomas. Please open the door and talk to me." Still no answer. But then I heard the inside bolt slide back inviting me in. I slowly turned the knob, cracked the door, and poked my head into the dim slant of a winter light. Hannah had retreated to the far side of the room beside the slender casements. Her arms were folded and her head bowed. I approached, placed my hands on her shoulders, and gently pulled her to me.

"Hannah, I want to help. Please talk to me. Tell me what's wrong. Is this about your mother's death?"

She shook her head and answered cryptically, "This isn't about death, Thomas. It's about life."

"I don't understand, Hannah. Help me."

She paused and then continued in a flat, unemotional voice, "I'm pregnant, Thomas. I'm going to have our baby."

I didn't respond immediately. I embraced her more tightly, buying time to clear my head.

When I finally replied, I borrowed the disingenuous phrase we'd both used hundreds of times with the dying in the Pinch: "Everything's gonna be all right."

"After all we've experienced, Thomas, do you really believe that?" Hannah retorted. "You know as well as I we were offering false comfort to those poor souls in their final hours. I'm not dying, Thomas. I have to chart a course for living."

"I know, Hannah. I know. But on one level it could be true. Everything could work out okay, if we do the right thing—explain everything to Master Taylor and then plan a wedding."

Hannah took a deep breath and replied, "Maybe there are two rights here, Thomas."

"Two? I don't understand."

"There's your right, Thomas—what many would argue is the moral right: explaining to Father what's happened between us and accepting our fate, which raises great risks—you lose your position at the academy; you no longer stay here in this house; you can't find work in Memphis; and you travel far away looking for a new job. But perhaps there's a second right, which trumps the first—I confirm the pregnancy but refuse to divulge the father's name."

"But think of the pressure we'll bear. What trumps the truth, Hannah?"

"Sacrificing for the innocent, for the helpless. . . . If we confess all, you'll be forced to leave the city, and our baby will never know its father. Lincoln's men made me fatherless at seven. I was old enough to know how it felt to have a father who loved me; and then after they shot him in the head, I learned how hard it was to get along without him. I want our baby to have better than what we had, Thomas. I know you understand. I remember you telling me you'd missed your father after he died when you were a boy. Let's do this for the baby, Thomas. We'll have everything but the wedding." Hannah smiled slightly and added, "I'll find the right moment to speak with Father. And you'll see everything will really be okay this time."

I pulled her close, tilted her chin up, and kissed her softly on the lips. I then whispered, "I love you, Hannah. Everything I have will go to support you and the baby. I promise."

"I love you, Thomas. We've been through so much together already. And we'll get through this too."

Hannah didn't wait long to find the right moment to speak with her father. It was the first day of Lent, the day after a boisterous Mardi Gras signaled Memphis was rising from its knees. Hannah and I met the following afternoon at Court Square to discuss her conversation with Master Taylor.

"What did you say? How'd he react?" I asked.

"I just told him straight out I was pregnant. He sat there in his favorite chair for the longest time staring at Mother's portrait. He finally stood up, walked over, and gave me a firm hug. He then held me out at arm's length and said, 'Honoring your mother's memory, Hannah, we'll manage this the way she would have suggested we handle it. There will be no sermons about the past; we'll move on to the future—you and the baby will always be welcome here, and I'll certainly defend you from any attacks by misguided members of our congregation.'

"He paused and then awkwardly asked, 'Hannah, does the father know . . . know about the baby?' I acknowledged the father knew. He then continued, 'Did he have anything to say about marrying you?' I replied that he had but that I'd refused. He shook his head slowly and repeated my response, trying to absorb the meaning of what he'd just heard. 'He offered to marry you and you turned him down?' I firmly nodded 'yes.'

"'Is he respectable?'

"'Yes, Father.'

"'Temperate?'

"'In every way.'

"'Did he offer support for you and the child?'

"'Yes, Father, he did.'

"He sat back down in his chair, stared wistfully at Mother's picture, and ended our conversation, 'You know, Hannah, once your mother had gotten over the shock, she would have reveled in the birth and nurturing of the baby. Since she's not here to share, I'll do everything I can to make this a happy place before and after the birth of our first grandchild.'"

And almost immediately following Hannah's revelation, Master Taylor's demeanor began to change. He once again became energetic, planned for the future, aggressively defended his daughter against wagging tongues, and proudly arranged public outings to concerts, operas, and plays. Hannah's pregnancy became a cultural whirlwind for the three of us. First, we enjoyed performances by the renowned singers, Christina Nilsson and Adelaide Phillips. Next, we attended sold-out concerts featuring the Swedish violinist, Ole Bull, and the pianist Anton Rubenstein. And interspersed between these recitals, we witnessed fully staged operatic productions of Mozart's *Don Giovanni* and Beethoven's *Fidelio*.

In many ways Master Taylor's revival mirrored the rebirth

of the cordoned city. Residents were returning to the streets now that heavy rains had flushed the ghostly layers of disinfectant into the bayou. Lively commerce steadily replaced the business of death. Citizens strolled the commercial avenues previously stacked with coffins and now lined with untold crates of valuable cotton. Apothecaries, grocers, and banks reopened. And once again trains rumbled into town with passengers and freight. Smoke billowed from the mills. Cotton presses hummed day and night. Mule cars clanged along the tracks; and hammers pounded nails into the frames of a thousand new buildings.

When the Board of Health approved the reopening of the schools, I returned to the academy. Since the scourge had played havoc with the first semester, I had to radically alter the English syllabus—Montaigne's "Cannibals," Galileo's excerpts, and Descartes's *Discourse* would have to go. But Defoe would stay, displacing the Pentateuch as the first reading of the semester. The striking relevance of *A Journal of the Plague Year* far outweighed any consideration of chronology and historical perspective. This was a unique opportunity to engage the students in literature for a lifetime.

And engaged they were. The students avidly read Defoe, drew parallels to their own experiences with the recent scourge, discovered the shadowy line between fiction and reality, and even debated why gods of goodness allow such evil into the world. But unexpectedly for me it was another story. The yellow jack had overwhelmed the narrative. What in the past had seemed so real had now become mere nouns and verbs on the page. The dying and the dead had unalterably changed me. I too was in need of a revival, and Hannah would be the first to know what I planned to do.

After sunrise services and Easter lunch at our history lecturer's house, I asked Hannah to join me for a stroll around Court Square. She cheerfully agreed, pointing to her rounded belly and suggesting it would be good for the baby. As soon as we reached the path encircling the park, I began confessing my feelings. "Hannah, working with you in the Pinch changed me. When I returned to the academy, I quickly realized my zest for teaching had disappeared. I don't know how to describe it, but fiction is no longer real or compelling. The students were excited enough, but I couldn't feel it. I was just putting on a show. I've lost my enthusiasm for finding the truth in words."

"Perhaps you just need more time, more space between you and the Pinch."

"I don't think so, Hannah. It's already been months. It's not getting any better. I've really tried. Believe me; I know there are risks to leaving the academy."

"I don't know how Father will react to your resignation. And what would he do about your staying in the house? You know we've talked about the importance of your being there for the baby."

"I know, I know. I'll offer to help find my replacement and suggest paying a modest rent if he'll let me stay."

"But what'll you do for a living?"

"Practice medicine."

"Become a doctor?"

"Yes. I want to learn the latest techniques. Perhaps I can

do more next time. It was frightening watching people suffer and knowing there wasn't anything I could do."

"How do you propose to do this?"

"I've inquired into the new proprietary medical school—the one between the Board of Health and the Victorian Village. They say it will take two years to complete the course of study: seven or eight hours of lectures a day in anatomy, physiology, therapeutics, chemistry, principles and practice of surgery, theory and practice of medicine, and the diseases of women and children. The curriculum is supposed to be so much better now than in the past—more microscopes, more laboratories and hands-on clinical apprenticeships with local physicians. . . . Doc would be an ideal mentor for me."

"If you're not working, how will you ever pay for all this?"

"I've got the money Mama left me, and I've been saving most of my pay from the academy. That should be enough to cover the two years."

Hannah gazed into my eyes and asked, "You sure this is what you want to do?"

"I'm sure, Hannah. I'm really sure."

She lightly stroked my cheek, ran her fingers up into my hair, and whispered, "I'll be proud to call you 'doctor.'"

I guess the gods had no objection to my change of plans. I openly expressed my feelings to Master Taylor. He graciously accepted my explanation; and since I'd become a part of the family, he insisted on my staying at the house while attending the medical college. I offered to help in the search for a replacement, but Master Taylor said he had a likely candidate in mind.

An old friend, Bishop Quintard, leader of the Episcopal Diocese of Tennessee and vice chancellor of the University of the South at Sewanee, had recently written Master Taylor a personal letter of recommendation for a promising graduate seeking a teaching position in his hometown. Since Master Taylor had worked closely with the bishop in establishing a refuge for the poor near the Pinch, he felt he should take any of the clergyman's recommendations seriously. I quickly agreed and lightheartedly added a supporting rationale for vetting the bishop's candidate—our alma mater on Sewanee Mountain had continually produced highly qualified lecturers in English, history, and the arts.

Knowing this would be my last teaching assignment, I worked hard to finish the second semester with a flourish. I wanted the students to experience the real language of American contemporaries—Hawthorne, Whitman, and Poe. As with Defoe at the beginning of the school year, I now used Poe's "A Descent into the Maelström" and "Masque of the Red Death" to reinforce our earlier discussions about fact and fiction, good and evil, and the unbearable fragility of life. I followed Poe with Hawthorne's "Young Goodman Brown" and *The Scarlet Letter*. I never said anything; I stepped back and allowed the students to identify Hawthorne's themes and then relate them back to Poe and Defoe.

I ended the semester with Whitman to drive home two messages—one academic and the other personal. To demonstrate the close thematic ties between Whitman, Hawthorne, and Poe I chose Whitman's poem "Song of Myself," which depicts a visionary journey encompassing good, evil, life, death, body, and soul. And to subtly convey my personal and final advice to the class, I opted for Whitman's lyric, "When I Heard the Learn'd Astronomer," from the "Songs of Parting" cluster in the most recent edition of *Leaves of Grass*:

> When I heard the learn'd astronomer;
> When the proofs, the figures, were ranged in columns before me;
> When I was shown the charts and the diagrams, to add, divide, and measure them;
> When I, sitting, heard the astronomer, where he lectured with much applause in the lecture-room,
> How soon, unaccountable, I became tired and sick;
> Till rising and gliding out, I wander'd off by myself,
> In the mystical moist night-air, and from time to time,
> Look'd up in perfect silence at the stars.

The class immediately focused on the poet's message that charts, diagrams, scientific observations, and mathematical analyses can't adequately capture the power and mystery of the universe. To sense that spiritual nature we must step out into the "moist night-air" and scan the arc of incalculable stars. I praised the class for their interpretation and then asked them to dig even deeper. "Anything else come to mind? Perhaps something on a personal, an individual level."

Our resident philosopher, Andrew, confidently raised his hand and expressed insight far beyond his years, saying,

"Sometimes we have to separate ourselves from others to find the truth in ourselves."

I eased into my role as Socratic student and asked, "Separation? Physical or mental?"

"Sometimes both," he responded.

"Change direction? Do something unfamiliar, uncomfortable?"

"How better to discover who we are?"

"Move beyond the precision of the classroom to the messy uncertainty of life?"

"Yes, to a jagged imprecision from which dreams are made."

"Give up everything we've trained for and start over again?"

"If that's where the light leads us, yes."

"Leave the academy and treat the sick?"

"If that's where the light takes you, yes."

9

OUR LIL' JIM had not yet turned four when the omens appeared and set the city on edge again. First, a local celebrity who had publicly taken the temperance pledge was inexplicably crushed beneath a trolley in broad daylight during our Independence Day festivities. Several days later a second pillar of the community was struck down by lightning while walking home from work. And then there was a ratcheting up—streetlamps exploded and caught fire, mules died in the fields and a six-foot rattler slithered about the alleyways between Cotton Row and the Peabody Hotel.

But the most ominous occurrence of all hadn't even happened yet. It was the approaching solar eclipse, which Hannah broached at the dinner table in mid-July, two weeks before the actual event. "Everyone's in a tizzy at the market about the streetlights, the snake, and the upcoming eclipse. They see a connection like in '73 when we had the omens—first the horse fever, next the smallpox, and then the cholera, all leading up to the yellow jack that August. People are talking about the omens of '73 and getting scared again."

I quickly joined in supporting Hannah. "Yes, I've been hearing the same thing from my patients. They rattle off the occurrences—the explosions, the mules, the snake—and then quickly move on to what they call the 'special eclipse.' I know people believe eclipses can foreshadow, but my patients are really anxious about this special one at the end of July. I don't know what makes it so special."

Master Taylor smiled and replied, "I know, Thomas. I'd had the same question about the eclipse. So I asked Mr. Greenwood, who replaced Mr. Martin—you know, the instructor in the sciences when you were there at the academy. Mr. Greenwood said the folks have been listening to the astrologers who've told them the eclipse will happen during the constellation Ophiuchus."

"Ophiuchus? I've never heard of it," I interjected.

"The way Mr. Greenwood explained it, Ophiuchus is the serpent bearer and the obscure thirteenth sign of the zodiac." He winked and then added, "So you can see how the snake near the Peabody got connected to the eclipse. But there's more to it than that. Mr. Greenwood said Ophiuchus is the only constellation based on a real person, a doctor, of all people, who lived in of all places ancient Memphis in Egypt. And astrologers over the years have suggested that an eclipse occurring under the doctor's sign foretold disease and a fierce battle between life and death."

Hannah jumped in. "But is there any proof, Father, that any of this has ever happened? An epidemic occurring after a solar eclipse in the doctor's sign?"

"Ah, that's how the astrologers make their interpretations realistic for their followers. They remind the folks that there was indeed a solar eclipse in Philadelphia under the doctor's sign almost a hundred years ago and that that special eclipse was then followed by the deadliest years of yellow fever ever experienced in the new colonies."

Master Taylor paused and then continued reassuringly, "But the newspapers say New Orleans officials have been supplying our leaders here with weekly updates, and New Orleans hasn't reported anything suspicious. So I don't think we have anything to worry about for now." He looked over at me and added as if subtly asking for his own reassurances, "Unless you know something, Thomas, that hasn't been reported publicly. Something you and Doc Landrum learned while advising the Memphis Board of Health."

"Rest assured, sir, if I'd heard anything, you and Hannah would've been the first to know. The newspapers have been reporting accurately; there've been no cases of the fever in New Orleans so far."

But ironically, I never had a chance to forewarn Master Taylor and Hannah of an impending storm because only eleven days later everyone in the country learned the foreboding news at the same time. Every major newspaper across the land published a letter from Dr. Chopin of the New Orleans Board of Health to Dr. Woodworth, the supervising surgeon of Marine Hospitals in Washington, confirming the first death from the fever, the purser on the steamer *Sudder*, which had docked at the New Orleans wharf on the twenty-third of July.

And it didn't take the Memphis Board of Health long to leap into action. The following morning Doc and I received a message from the board president announcing an emergency summit for Saturday evening; and at precisely seven o'clock President Saunders called that meeting to order. All five board members attended—Doctors Saunders, Erskine, and Adams; Mayor Flippin; and Police Chief Athy. The president immediately turned the subject to quarantine. "To limit the rising excitement in town about the fever coming up the river from New Orleans, we've got to take decisive action. We've got to get a quarantine in place immediately. You've had some time to think about it, Phil. What's your plan?"

Chief Athy shuffled through his papers, found his recommendations, and began: "Let me say I've run this by Mayor Flippin. He's given me some ideas, which I've incorporated here. First, we'll establish an armed post at the southern tip of President's Island to intercept river traffic headed north from New Orleans. We'll embargo all the cotton, sugar, and coffee coming our way. Next we'll post armed guards along the tracks at both Whitehaven Station and Germantown. And finally we'll require the railroad and steamboat officials to conduct rigorous surveillance of all passengers and baggage. If y'all agree, I'll make sure the plan gets published in the morning papers to let everyone know we're working hard to avoid a repeat of '73."

And after approving the mayor and chief's plan unanimously, the board agreed to meet every Monday night at eight o'clock and as a contingency authorized Dr. Erskine to purchase barrels of Calvert's Number 5 carbolic acid for use as a disinfectant.

The initial public response to the board's plan published on the twenty-eighth was positive and it tended to have a calming effect on the community. But unfortunately the pot was stirred again the following day, and the levels of anxiety returned to where they had been prior to the plan's publication. The morning of the twenty-ninth broke cloudy, providing some respite from the relentless heat that had plagued the city for almost a month. Unlike most residents, Doc and I went to work that morning. The streets were eerily empty for a Monday. Commerce had practically come to a halt. Everyone in town had made plans for the day—witnessing the total eclipse of the sun that afternoon. But Doc and I felt a need to compromise. We agreed to see patients in the office until two o'clock; hurry back to fetch Hannah, Lil' Jim, and Master Taylor; race out to the bluffs; and then if the clouds cooperated, witness the rare portentous event.

When Doc and I returned home from the office, I rattled off the checklist. "Smoked glass?"

"Packed away in the haversack there," Master Taylor answered. "I even found a pair of Emma's opera glasses to take along."

"Victuals?" I asked. "Doc and I are starved."

"There's Johnnycake, sharp cheddar, and canteens of buttermilk for the two of you," Hannah replied.

"Mares harnessed?"

"An hour ago out back," Master Taylor said.

"Well, let's load the carriage and get going!" I urged. "There'll be thousands out on the bluffs. Looks like the sun's beginning to break through the clouds. We'll need to find some shade. It's got to be well over ninety degrees already."

At precisely 4:28 p.m. by Doc's watch a fellow shouted, "There it is! It's starting!" We all leapt out from under the trees, held our smoked glasses skyward, and watched the moon slowly obliterate the sun. Anticipation turned to awe as unnerving night slowly settled in over the city.

By the next morning, a number of citizens had reached the tipping point and begun anxiously preparing for the worst. Patients told me they could just feel it in their bones. The birds had stopped chirping, and their pets and livestock were breaking through fences and running away. They said they'd seen enough. They were going to shut down their businesses, cash out their bank accounts, and visit distant relatives in faraway places until the first hard frost had killed off the yellow jack for the year.

Despite the omens and the eclipse, the Board of Health meeting the following Monday was mostly about the growing number of fatalities in New Orleans and the tamping down of malicious rumors in Memphis. While no confirmed cases of yellow fever had been reported in the city, Dr. Erskine revealed he had admitted a deckhand from the steamer *Golden Crown* to the quarantine hospital on President's Island three days earlier and unfortunately the fellow had died. He described the case as "highly suspicious," since the sailor had developed the characteristic symptoms—a deep yellow skin with numerous bruises about the body. Dr. Erskine quickly added, however, he had no reason to believe the worker had had significant contact with anyone in the city.

But only eight days later, on the thirteenth, the feared Damoclean sword actually fell. During an emergency meeting early that Tuesday evening, President Saunders disclosed that unbeknown to the board ,the deckhand had indeed been in town. "We've now learned the deceased steamboatman, a

Mr. Warren, had rowed ashore to visit an Italian snack house in the Pinch the evening before he fell ill. We've been able to glean this information because the proprietor of the snack shop got the yellow jack and died earlier today. After learning of the lady's death, I asked Mayor Flippin here to take immediate action to limit the contagion and try to find others who'd eaten there recently besides the deckhand." Dr. Saunders then turned to the mayor and said, "You want to explain what steps you've taken to secure the site?"

"Well, first I ordered the shack closed and quarantined. Next, I supervised the disinfection of all adjacent buildings with Calvert's Number 5. And then reluctantly I requested the dignified burning of Mrs. Bionda's remains. It was the last thing I wanted to do. I'd known her a long time and enjoyed the fish there weekly during my last campaign. She was a friend, and I wanted her to have what we'll all hopefully have someday—a proper funeral and burial in Elmwood Cemetery. But I knew I had to stop the spread. I'm sure Kate'll understand. That's really . . . really all I have for you, Dudley."

"We're all sorry, John," Dr. Saunders said. He then paused out of respect for the mayor's loss, cleared his throat and politely transitioned to another pressing subject. "What should we say to the public? How do we announce Mrs. Bionda's death without alarming everyone?"

"Based on the personal information the mayor's provided, how about something along these lines?" Chief Athy replied. "The sad case of Mrs. Bionda, who left two little children and a grief-stricken husband, doesn't prove necessarily that others will follow. There's no need of a panic or stampede."

"Any objection to Chief Athy's suggestion?" Dr. Saunders asked. "Okay then. That's unanimous. Try to get the word out tonight for the morning papers, Chief."

The news I shared with Hannah and Master Taylor at the dinner table worsened over the next two days—first, that the board would report twenty-two new cases in the morning papers of the fifteenth and, second, that Dr. Saunders would announce thirty-three additional cases in the press on the sixteenth. But this information paled in comparison to what I described to them at dinner the following evening.

"What'd you learn today, Thomas?" Master Taylor asked.

"It's not what I learned, sir, but what I saw. Looks like the dam broke, and the stampede's begun in earnest. Like in '73 but a lot worse this time."

"How's that?"

"I saw panic in the streets today, sir, bedlam like I've never seen before. Courtesy has been kicked to the curb. People were using any means possible to flee the city: carriages, drays, buggies, wagons—even furniture vans. Despite the risk of exposure and quarantine, some chose the steamers. But those who could afford the fares opted for the trains, calling the steamboats 'contagion traps' and 'charnel houses.' And you wouldn't have believed the depots on the Louisville Road—platforms piled high with trunks, boxes, suitcases, and canvas bags. Policemen were overrun by mobs of armed men who'd been denied entry to the passenger cars. The mob vaulted through open windows commandeering entire sections of trains. I suspect half the city—twenty to twenty-five thousand people—are on the run. It's mayhem well beyond the likes of '73."

"We had no idea any of this was happening. Hannah and I haven't been out of the house all day. We've been looking after Lil' Jim."

"What do you think we should do, Father?"

"Nothing just yet, Hannah. Let things settle down a bit before deciding. It's a lot different now than in '73. We've got Lil' Jim, Emma's gone, and Thomas has joined Doc Landrum's practice."

But in less than a week, well before "things had settled down a bit," Master Taylor was back at the dinner table with the general outline of a plan. "Thomas, you've already shared your thoughts with me; I know you're compelled to stay here and fight the scourge. And I've decided to do the same. I'll go back to what I was doing in '73 with the Howard Association—establishing nursing wards, soliciting donations, recruiting physicians and nurses and the like."

"Well, if the two of you plan on helping out, I want to get back to what I was doing, too," Hannah asserted.

While my heart was breaking at the thought of saying good-bye to my love and my child, I knew the right thing to do here was to play devil's advocate. "But what'll you do with Lil' Jim?" I asked. "He can't stay here alone."

"Think about it, Hannah," Master Taylor added. "Thomas is right. You've got to care for Lil' Jim. And besides, Thomas and I agree the city's not the place for him right now. You told me what it was like last time in the bayou and the Pinch. The piles of caskets, the sickening stench, smoky fires, the horrifying screams, and poor souls wandering half-naked through the streets. And the fever seems to be a lot worse this time. The scourge could spread all over Memphis, not just by the river as in '73. You wouldn't want Lil' Jim around all that."

"But we've no choice. We have nowhere else to go," she said.

"I didn't know for sure either, Hannah, until this afternoon."

"What do you mean, Father? What happened today?"

"Father Walsh, the assistant priest at St. Patrick's and president of their Father Mathew Society, dropped by the office to coordinate his efforts with ours at the Howard Association. He explained his organization met last Sunday after mass to discuss the scourge and to possibly organize a corps of nurses to assist member and nonmember families without regard to their race, color, or creed. Father Walsh said he knew his group didn't have the ability to carry out the grand idea. So he politely dissuaded them and suggested an alternative—establishing a camp of refuge and relief some miles outside of Memphis.

"Once he'd gained the members' approval, he conducted a search and found a suitable site on two hundred acres of farmland owned by Messrs. Hill and Fontaine—you know, the prominent merchants down on Cotton Row. Father Walsh said it was the ideal place to erect his Father Mathew Camp— there's a boiling spring flowing through rolling meadows and a grove of forest trees.

"After hearing Father Walsh's description of the site and plans for the camp, I respectfully raised your situation, and he immediately offered to welcome you and Lil' Jim with open arms. I thanked him profusely and said I would respond to his generous offer after speaking with you."

"I really want to stay and fight the fever, Father. . . .But you're right. Lil' Jim's better off in the camp away from here."

So the following week Master Taylor and I loaded Lil' Jim, Hannah, and their belongings into a wagon and rode out to the camp. Father Walsh had instructed Master Taylor to drop Hannah and Lil' Jim off in the "Quarantine Department," where they would stay for a time, after which they would be admitted to the main camp if they remained healthy.

When we arrived at the site, an armed sentry directed us to the quarantined area at the far end of the main avenue. Eight-foot-high canvas tents lined the street on both sides as far as the eye could see. The area was bustling with new arrivals unloading their carts, unpacking their trunks and scolding their dogs and children for wandering about in the road. From our vantage point behind the tents we could see Sacred Heart of Our Divine Lord, a little church on wheels, where Father Walsh celebrated mass every morning before heading off to Memphis to minister to the dying. And just beyond the church, we spotted large tents bearing handmade signs: "Commissary," "Druggist," "Hospital," "Kitchen" and "Dining Hall."

"Look over there," Master Taylor said. "They've even set up a tent for a one-room school. I can't believe how much they've accomplished in such a short time. There must be four to five hundred people here all told." He then added lightheartedly, "Perhaps they ought to call this place 'New Memphis.'" He wrapped his arm around his daughter's shoulder and said caringly, "I think you've made the right decision, Hannah. This will be a good place for you and Lil' Jim."

"I know, Father. But I can't lie. If I had my druthers, I'd be back in Memphis helping out."

"I know you would, Hannah. I know," Master Taylor replied. He paused and reluctantly changed the subject. "I guess we'd better get going. Send us notes by courier. Let us know how you're making out."

After sharing a painful but hopeful good-bye, Master Taylor and I climbed up into the wagon, waved bravely to Hannah and Lil' Jim, and headed home to join the battle beneath the windswept bluffs.

10

BY THE END of the week, volunteers had made good progress turning central Memphis into hell. They had piled deathbed blankets at every corner for burning; covered the avenues, alleys, and sidewalks with ghostly lime; and ignited miles of tarry trenches to drive out spores suspected of infecting the heavy summer air. Stacks of coffins spilled out onto the deserted streets.

The panic was over. In less than ten days thirty thousand residents had fled the city, leaving behind the Negroes and the poor to fend for themselves. You could now walk or ride for miles up Main Street without seeing a half dozen people. The only signs of life were the hearses carrying the dead out to the cemeteries. The sickening howl of abandoned dogs pierced the silence. Shadowy demons danced on the midnight walls. Doc Landrum saw the Last Judgment; I envisioned hell. Our nightmare days were filled with the moans of the dying and the stunned faces of survivors bereft of their families. Our only respite was sharing observations with our brother physicians fighting on the front lines with us.

At the outset of the epidemic President Saunders suggested a weekly exchange of medical ideas following the regularly scheduled Board of Health meetings. During our first session, board member Erskine set the objectives. He proposed we focus on effective treatments rather than on "large-scale" topics such as prevention or the source of infection. "We don't know how the scourge begins and then spreads—whether by animal matter, fungi, and noxious gases in the bayou, or by importation each summer via the trains and the riverboats. But we do know the first heavy frost stops the scourge and that contrary to public opinion, yellow jack is not readily spread through close contact with victims.

"So, gentleman, let's face it. We all know the cow's out of the barn. Discussing prevention through improved sanitation won't help us now. We all know the situation—we have no waterworks and no way to dispose of sewage. When we have downpours, the rainwater runs down the backside of the bluffs into the town, floods the privies, and deposits the filth in the bayou. Even if we had a plan to solve the problem, the town fathers tell us there are no funds to support the project. And discussing additional quarantines now won't help us much either. Some of the blockades worked; others didn't. I don't believe now's the time to ask why. Once the battle's over we'll have plenty of time to debate long-term prevention with sanitation and quarantine.

"So I think the most we can do for the folks still here is find the best possible treatments for the scourge—develop a protocol of best practices and share it with the physicians. Let's start with the basics, and as we get more information, we can make changes to the protocol at our weekly meetings. Dr. Adams, would you please take notes? . . . Now who'd like to begin?"

"I'll get the ball rolling," President Saunders said. "If someone has eaten a full meal two or so hours before contracting the fever, I'd give them a prompt emetic—mustard and salt, a teaspoon each, in a glass of warm water."

Doc Landrum interrupted, "What do you think about a purgative after the vomiting subsides? Clean out the entire digestive tract."

"Yes, I agree. A strong laxative is in order. Ten grains of calomel tends to work within six hours. By the way, this is also when I like to administer ten grains of quinine to fight the scourge."

"Other ideas?" Dr. Erskine asked.

A Dr. Sample from Mississippi spoke up. "I've had success fightin' the fever by gettin' my patients to perspire freely after administerin' the calomel and quinine. I use hot mustard footbaths; I keep the patients wrapped in heavy blankets the whole time. If their temperature rises above 103 Fahrenheit, I sponge their bodies with cool water under the blankets. If the spongin' doesn't reduce the fever and the pulse quickens, I give them Fleming's Tincture of Aconite, five drops every hour until the pulse drops to around ninety. But you have to take great care not to push the sedative effects too far, especially goin' into the third day of an attack."

"Yes, I've read your approach in the literature," Dr. Erskine said. "I believe a few physicians have tried the procedure here in the past. . . . Okay, then. Are there other suggestions for the protocol?"

"Patients on the mend tend to have irritable stomachs," Dr. Adams offered. "I recommend five grains of bismuth in a tablespoon of peppermint or camphor water every hour or two until the symptoms subside."

"Sometimes patients on the mend also have trouble urinating," a Dr. Williams of Kentucky suggested. "I give sweet spirits of nitre in watermelon-seed tea every two to three hours—a teaspoonful to two ounces of tea, cold or hot, makes no difference. A turpentine stupe applied to the abdomen usually helps control the pain associated with the diuretic."

"One of the basics we should place near the top of the protocol is 'no food during paroxysms of fever,'" Doc Landrum emphasized. "We have to prevent choking. But a little cool water or crushed ice is okay."

"We're making good progress. Anything else?" Dr. Erskine asked.

"Once the fever subsides, introduce a little chicken broth, beef tea, or milk," Dr. Adams suggested. "Increase the amounts as the patient progresses. But if a secondary fever appears, I like to continue these nourishments and add some weak whiskey, brandy, or champagne to the diet."

"Very good. What else?" Dr. Erskine probed.

"I've found opiates to be contraindicated during febrile paroxysms," a Dr. Gaither of Arkansas said. "They can be administered cautiously at the termination of the fever to ensure sleep, but only if you've tried bromide of potassium first and it's failed."

"Besides food and medicines, are there any general recommendations?" Dr. Erskine asked.

"After the fever ends, the patient must not be allowed to rise for any purpose for at least five days," a Dr. Leach of

Louisiana offered. "And for a fortnight thereafter, the patient should avoid exposure to the sun or violent exercise."

"Okay. Anything else?"

"In the '73 scourge we didn't change the patient's bedding or clothing until twenty-four hours after the fever subsided," I observed. "And we didn't allow the patient to sit up or help himself either during the changing."

"For the sake of research, all the doctors should record the temperature and pulse at every visit," Dr. Adams interjected. "And the urine should be tested daily for albumen after the second day."

"Is there anything we're missing?" Dr. Erskine asked.

After a short pause, President Saunders took the floor and said, "Okay, then. Thank you, Dr. Erskine. . . . And now if you don't mind, Dr. Adams, would you please edit the recommendations and see they get distributed to all the physicians in the city."

When the meeting adjourned, a number of us stood outside the hall and shared personal stories late into the night. It was a relief just having someone listen to the horrors we were experiencing day in and day out. Many of our colleagues had no one with whom to share their pain; they had selflessly left their homes and families behind to come here to help us out. And this first meeting tonight went a long way in helping us bond as a family, as a band of brothers, fighting the good fight against this inexplicable evil.

I finally tore myself away from the group around midnight and began walking home up Front Street to avoid the smoking trenches on Main. A full moon lit the silvery way, the silence interrupted only by the occasional crunch of the parched limey dust under my boots. When I reached the corner with Exchange, I imagined hearing a low moaning coming from the stoop of one of the brick row houses. There, again and then again, a low groaning. As I neared the steps, I could see a small figure with its thin legs drawn up toward the stomach. I knelt down on the top step and pushed the long curls back from the child's face and whispered, "Boy, you live here?"

The child moved his head slowly from side to side.

"Can you tell me your name, son?"

"Jimmie, sir."

"Your surname, Jimmie?"

"Winters, sir."

"Where are your parents, Jimmie?"

"They're at the camp, sir."

"Camp? Which camp, Jimmie?"

"Williams, sir."

"Camp Williams, Jimmie?"

"Yes, sir."

"How in the world did you get here on this stoop in the middle of the night?"

"My brother, sir."

"Your brother? Where's your brother, Jimmie?"

"I don't know, sir. I'm looking for him."

"Did your brother get separated from your family on the way to camp?"

"Yes, sir."

"Do your parents know you're in Memphis, Jimmie?"

"No, sir. I sneaked away."

The boy closed his eyes and began trembling. I instinctively turned to the street looking for anyone to help get Jimmie to a hospital. I stroked his hair, whispered support, and prayed silently that someone would miraculously appear in the dead of night. I guess this time the gods were listening. First I heard the approaching hoofbeats and then saw the death wagon round the corner onto Exchange.

"Help, sir! Help!" I shouted. "I need to get this boy to a hospital!"

The driver pulled on the reins, jumped down, and helped me get Jimmie up on the wagon bench between us.

"What's the closest hospital?" I asked. "City? Walthall Infirmary near the navy yard?"

"No, no. I know a place about nine blocks east. It has a good reputation."

"Okay, let's get the boy there as fast as possible. He's in the early stages of the fever. There's a chance to save him."

As we rode along the deserted thoroughfare, the unkempt, bearded driver looked over and introduced himself. "Undertaker Jack, Sir."

"Dr. Thomas, Jack," I replied, then added, "I really appreciate what you're doing to help us out here. May I ask where you were headed before you stopped?"

"To pick up four more coffins to add to the nine already there in the back. After that, I was headed out to Elmwood Cemetery with my baker's dozen." Undertaker Jack paused, looked down at Jimmie, and said, "He reminds me of Little Grace. She came down with the fever two weeks ago and has completely recovered. Some of the children heal quickly."

"Grace? Whose Grace?"

"The superintendent's daughter at Elmwood. We call her the 'Graveyard Girl.' She lives on the grounds with her father. Imagine what she's already seen!" He shook his head. "She started keeping a logbook in August—red leather, handwrites the names. Lists the cause of death as 'yellow fever.' That lasted only a few days. She now uses ditto marks to state the cause. Too many entries. Entire families wiped out—husband, wife, and all the children, gone. Besides keeping the ledger, Grace rings the tower bell each time a soul is buried. Think of it. It's the only bell still tolling for the mourners and the dead. All the churches are shut until the frost kills the jack."

We turned the corner onto Gayoso, traveled east a couple of blocks, and stopped in front of Miss Cook's three-story Mansion House where Hannah and I had worked for a short time during the scourge of '73.

"I know this place, Jack."

"What man in Memphis doesn't?" he replied smilingly.

"No, no, not that way. I worked here in '73 when it was one of the best hospitals in the city. All volunteers. So she's closed her establishment and done it again?"

"Unbelievable but true. Let all her girls go again, but several stayed behind to volunteer."

We carried Jimmie up the steps onto the front porch and pounded on the door. A tall, dark-haired attractive woman now in her mid- to late thirties stepped out onto the moonlit porch. I recognized Miss Cook immediately. She was even more beautiful than I had remembered. Without saying a word or looking at either Jack or me, she moved toward the boy and cradled his head in her hands.

"It's the fever. Early stages," I said. "Found him on a stoop. Ran away from camp to find his brother."

"Let's get him inside in the parlor light," Miss Cook urged.

While leading the way into the converted bagnio, Miss Cook called out to one of her tireless nurses. "Anna, prepare a bed quickly on the first floor!" And within fifteen minutes, Miss Cook had little Jimmie tucked into a clean bed receiving care from a team of experienced volunteers. Seeing that Jimmie was now in good hands, I thanked Miss Cook for taking the boy in and promised to find his parents as soon as possible.

As she escorted us to the front door, Miss Cook looked over and said, "I remember your face. You worked here in the last scourge, didn't you?"

"Yes, five years ago, almost to the day."

"You're the one who stayed a short time and left with ah . . . ah . . ."

"Hannah, ma'am."

"Yes, yes, Hannah, who wanted to work on the front line, and you left with her. Is she well?"

"Yes. She's out at Father Mathew Camp with her son."

"And you, ah . . ."

"Thomas, ma'am. I was a teacher at Westminster Academy with Hannah's father. But after working here and on the front line in '73, I decided to study medicine. So to my patients now I'm 'Doc Thomas.'"

"Congratulations, Thomas—er, Doctor."

"If you don't mind, Miss Cook, I'd really like to follow up on the boy."

"You're always welcome here, Doctor."

As Undertaker Jack and I walked down the front stairs, he generously asked, "Where's home, Doc?"

"Uptown near Court Square and the Peabody Hotel."

"Hop aboard. It's on my way to pick up the last four caskets before heading out to Elmwood."

After we'd made the turn off Gayoso onto Main, I resumed our conversation, "Speaking of Elmwood, how are things out there and at the other cemeteries? Pretty much in order?"

"I'd like to say that, Thomas, but I'm a Christian. . . . None of the cemeteries can keep up. I've requisitioned four large furniture wagons to help ferry the dead. Other morticians have done the same. Working day and night, we still have coffins piling up in the streets. The sheer numbers have overwhelmed the cemeteries. Just between you and me, they've resorted to digging shallow graves, sixteen to twenty inches from the surface and laying the coffins side by side in long rows. Looks like deep, ugly gashes where you used to see fine plantings of azaleas and tea roses."

"In all the cemeteries?"

"Yes, sir, every last one of 'em. And later on there's going to be hell to pay."

"How so?"

"You know, families traditionally buy desirable plots—first-class plot, white, about fifteen dollars, and second-class plot, Negro, about twelve. I'm already seeing what's going to be a very big problem once the jack is gone. A few relatives with plot maps in hand are venturing out to the cemeteries to mourn. But to their utter dismay, the deceased are not where they're supposed to be. The mourners search for hours; but even with the help of workers, they can't locate their loved ones' graves.

"But that's not the half of it, Doc. Besides my private engagements, I have a public contract to bury paupers in the potter's field. Paupers in Memphis and all of Shelby County. But it isn't just paupers I'm burying there—no, sir. Many persons of means in high society are handed off to me for burial. No one left to look after their remains. Friends and loved ones already dead. And folks clamor to have the corpses hurried out of their neighborhoods. So the rich end up with me lowering them into a humble, anonymous grave.

"Let's see now, there's already been Dr. Toomey with all his wealth; Thomas Lynch, the respected coffee merchant; William Feder, the cotton speculator; and the Reverend Mister Hollingsworth. All victims of the fever and now, God rest their souls, sleeping eternally in the potter's field."

I was stunned. I didn't respond. But Undertaker Jack needed to keep on talking. "You know, almost every building along this route has a history. See over there? That three-story? Thad Stewart, the cotton factor, got the jack bad last week. High fever. Delirious. Jumped out of the top window there. Broke his neck. Wife died the same day. I drove both of them out to Elmwood the next morning. Grace made the entries and tolled the bell."

He looked to his left and continued: "Four persons died in that little cottage over there in just a day and a half." Next he pointed to the right, "I took nine from that dwelling—four of them children. Took them out to the potter's field and buried each of them separately." Then turning back to the left, "See the little frame house there—the one with the flower boxes and shrubbery? Two weeks ago, a father, mother, and five children lived there happily. They're all now in the potter's field. Lonely, midnight burials. I said a respectful prayer for each before lowering them into a five-foot grave." And finally, looking back to the right, he pointed toward a commercial building, a general store, and said, "Five clerks died on the premises. They succeeded each other rapidly. After the fifth passed, the proprietor couldn't find a sixth willing to replace the last poor fellow. Forced to shutter the place."

Undertaker Jack stopped midstream and pulled hard on the reins. Focusing on the house next to the general store, he screamed, "Halt, you scoundrels! God damn you! Stealing from the dead!" He flung the reins in my lap, jumped down from the wagon, and began chasing the thieves, who quickly disappeared in an alley two doors up from the general store. Several minutes later, Jack reappeared, closed the door on the ransacked house, and stomped back toward the wagon. "It's already begun," he said. "Just like '73. Goes to show you the vermin read the newspapers. They know there're a lot of empty houses around here with most of the rich folk scurrying out of town. Many of the police fled too. Easy pickin's. Just cross the river in the middle of the night, scoop up the valuables, and put them up for sale the next morning. . . . That's the first I've seen of it this time, but I'm sure it's only the beginning. We'll have to report these villains to the Citizens Relief Committee, since most of the city council hightailed it out of town. Couldn't even make a quorum last week, the weasels."

He jumped back up onto the wagon, grasped the reins, and steered the mare toward Court Square. When we reached Master Taylor's house, I extended my hand and said, "Thanks again for helping out with the boy."

"Hope to see ya again soon, Doc."

"Hope it's not too soon, Jack," I replied jokingly.

"I'm so overwhelmed trying to keep up. Would you do me a favor and report this thievery to the Relief Committee?"

"For sure. At their next meeting. You've got my word on it."

"And tell them they've got to replace the missing police."

"Absolutely."

"Good luck, Doc."

"Same to you, Jack. Same to you."

11

As promised, I attended the Citizens Relief Committee meeting the following Monday. The first order of business was updates. And the progress the members had made in so short a time was remarkable—several camps were completely up and running and substantial subscriptions for provisions and money had begun rolling in. The next order of business was a motion to add Negroes to the committee to more accurately reflect the current reality that Negroes outnumbered whites by more than two to one following the mass exodus from the city. The motion was made and carried adding ten Negroes—one Negro for each of the ten wards.

When Chairman Fisher opened the floor for new business, I raised my hand and addressed the members. "Gentlemen, going on a week ago, Undertaker Jack helped me deliver a feverish boy to Miss Cook's mansion hospital on Gayoso Street. On our way back uptown from the hospital, we witnessed several scoundrels running off with goods from a residence next to the general store. Undertaker Jack gave chase but lost them when they ducked into an alley. Since he's so busy right now, he asked me to report the theft and to remind you that the ransacking of houses and commercial establishments became a real problem in '73."

A fellow at the back of the room interrupted. "The need for nurses is well known to the country and that fact has brought upon us the scum of the nation—in fact, an invasion of cutthroats, thieves, and prostitutes as bad as any that have trod the earth! These villains have thrust themselves upon Memphis, and we're going to be at their mercy. These vultures are following the field of battle and swooping down to rob the dead and dying. They're walking out with trunks of jewelry and silverware."

A second voice chimed in: "That's not the half of it. My neighbors lost their horses and buggies to these foreign bandits."

And then a third: "Where are all the police? They seem to have disappeared along with everyone else!"

Chairman Fisher banged his gavel to regain control, turned quickly to Police Chief Athy, and asked, "What's the current condition of the force, Phil? Are you close to full strength?"

"Not quite, Charlie. Two detectives and three patrolmen resigned three days after the first yellow fever death. Four more patrolmen left within the week, and a captain departed two days after that. But the rest of the force, thirty-one of forty-one men, are standing fast."

"The city population's down by more than fifty percent and your force is down by a quarter. Do you think you need more men?"

"You have to take more than the number of people into account, Charlie. Thousands of empty homes are now prey to theft, and we're being called on hourly to aid the sick and dying. I've been working up a plan to present to you and the committee."

"Can you give us an idea what you have in mind, Phil?"

"Well, first let me tell you what I've already done on my own, actions which didn't need the committee's approval. I've reorganized the shift schedule—reassigning a number of my men from the noon to midnight shift to the overnight tour of duty when the city is most vulnerable to burglary. But I'll need the committee's approval to execute the rest of my plan."

"Go on." Chairman Fisher said.

"I know money's tight right now, Charlie, but I want to add twenty-eight new policemen. This'll bring me close to sixty."

"Any objection, Mr. Chase?"

"No, sir."

"How about you, Mr. Goodyear?"

"No, sir."

"Mr. Maccabee?"

"No, sir."

"And you, Mayor Flippin?"

"If the chief says he needs the men, then I say let him have 'em."

"Okay, Phil, that's a unanimous authorization to add twenty-eight new officers to the force."

A lean, graying Negro sitting to my right raised his hand, and Chairman Fisher acknowledged him. "Yes, Mr. Shaw."

"It's not a point of order, sir. More a suggestion. I think I speak for most of the Negroes left in the city, sir. And to a person we're ready to come to the front in this hour of trial and do our whole duty in protecting life and property in the city of Memphis. So, sir, we respectfully request Chief Athy select from among us an equal number of the new policemen."

Another Negro sitting next to this Mr. Shaw asked to be recognized, and Chairman Fisher responded, "Yes, sir, you have something to add?"

"Pastor R. N. Countee, Beale Street Baptist Church. I agree with Mr. Shaw's sentiments. We would just as soon die in Memphis as anywhere else. We are here in her prosperity and don't care to forsake her in this time of adversity."

There was an awkward silence as committee members stared at one another. But Mayor Flippin weighed in eloquently, saving the day, "The white man and the Negro are sharing this painful experience. We're in the same boat, on the same stream; and sharing responsibilities in a common suffering should weld us together now and even long after this unfortunate dispensation of Providence has passed."

Chairman Fisher turned to Chief Athy. "You have any problems with what Mr. Shaw and Pastor Countee are suggesting?"

"No, sir, fourteen Negroes and fourteen whites—all of good character, muscle, and pluck. Every one of them will make good and efficient officers."

"Okay, let's put it to a vote. A show of hands please." Chairman Fisher paused, surveyed the panel, and declared, "It's unanimous; the motion carries."

A spontaneous applause erupted in the room—perhaps out of the relief of having resolved an uncomfortable situation and then again perhaps out of recognition they had accomplished a significant human achievement.

When the meeting adjourned, I hurried home to see if there was any word from Hannah. Master Taylor had already returned from his job at the Howard Association. He was sitting at the dining room table relishing a piece of fried chicken.

"Any word from Hannah and Lil' Jim?" I asked.

"Nothing yet," Master Taylor responded.

"You think everything's okay?"

"Hannah's probably still settling in. I'm sure we'll hear something fairly soon, once they get past the quarantine. . . . Want some chicken and corn? There's plenty here. Mrs. Edmondson brought it over to the association this afternoon."

"I'm starved. I skipped lunch to attend the Citizens Relief Committee meeting to let them know the thieves are coming to town."

Master Taylor reached into his breast pocket and pulled out a long, thick cigar. He cut the cap, struck a match on the underside of the table, and took several long, enjoyable puffs. He looked up toward the ceiling and whispered, "Forgive me, Emma." He looked over toward me, smiled faintly, and continued, "You know, it's strange, but I've heard other widows and widowers say the same thing. The traits that annoyed them most about their spouses became endearing once they were gone. I miss Emma's nagging about—what did she call it—my 'repugnant habit' and her insistence I leave the house to enjoy a good cigar."

He pointed to the chicken and corn on the cob and said, "I'm sorry. Here, you have the rest. . . . So, tell me about the Relief Committee meeting this afternoon. What did they have to say about the ruffians breaking into houses? Did they decide to do anything?"

"Well, after I explained what I'd seen, several folk spoke up in support of my testimony saying jewelry, silverware, horses, and buggies had begun disappearing from their neighbors' properties. This led another fellow to ask why there were no longer any policemen patrolling the streets. The police chief admitted ten or so officers had resigned at the beginning of the scourge and recommended hiring about thirty new men. The Relief Committee unanimously approved the chief's request. And then something happened that should make us all proud."

"What's that, Thomas?

"Two Negroes spoke up recommending their folk comprise half the new policemen."

"How'd the committee react?"

"Well, after some hemming and hawing, the members unanimously approved the request. . . . So, ah, Master Taylor, just curious, do you know anything about a Pastor Countee and a Mr. Shaw?"

"Why's that?"

"They're the two Negroes who spoke up about adding their folk to the force."

"I don't know much about Pastor Countee. He's the new minister over at the Beale Street Baptist Church. Took over last year when the founder, Reverend Henderson, died."

"What about Shaw? I didn't catch a first name."

Master Taylor smiled and replied, "Has to be Edward. I count him among my friends. Says he was born in Kentucky. Came here in the 1850s. A freeman. After the war, he opened a saloon and gambling house. Used his money to become a lawyer. First I heard of him was when he got into politics and pushed for mixing the schools and for Negro rights. Great orator. Couldn't scare him off, either. I remember one of his political rallies in '69. The Klan showed up and started firing. He and his men didn't run. They stayed and returned fire!

"Before you came to town, he served on the city council, the Shelby County Commission, and was elected wharf master. Last time I talked to him he said he was beginning to dabble in newspapers. Yes, sir, old Ed's a force to be reckoned with. First Negro to run for Congress from these parts."

"While attending the meeting, I had the feeling all the members knew who he was. I now understand why."

"You had enough to eat?"

"Yes, yes. Delicious. Please pass my compliments on to Mrs. Edmondson."

Master Taylor nodded and replied, "She'll be happy to hear all was left was cobs and bones."

The following morning I rose early and headed downtown to Gayoso Street to check on the Winters boy. "How's little Jimmie doing today, Anna?"

"A light case, sir. It looks like he's going to be okay. The fever's down; but he keeps on asking if we found his brother."

Jimmie didn't notice when Anna and I entered the room. He was captivated by a gray squirrel sitting on the ledge staring in through the window. "Jimmie, Jimmie," Anna whispered. He turned his head. "Jimmie, this is Dr. Thomas. He's the man who brought you here the other night. He's come by to see how you're doing."

"Did you find my brother?"

"No, Jimmie, we're still looking. But I have some good

news. The Howard Association found your parents at the Williams Camp. They know you're here in good hands and will return to them once you're well."

Since I could see he was recovering nicely, I conducted a cursory examination. "His pulse and temperature are normal. Lungs clear. Have you been checking his urine for albumen, Anna?"

"Every day, sir. It's been negative."

"Tell Miss Cook I think he can return to the camp in five more days. Just make sure he stays in bed and gets plenty of rest until then."

"You know how hard it is to keep a boy like this down once they're on the mend?"

"Jimmie, you mind Miss Anna now. You hear?" I gave his hair a tousle, pointed to the squirrel, and said, "Looks like your friend's waiting for you there."

As we exited into the hallway, Anna tugged at my arm. "Doctor, I'm really worried."

"Worried about what, Anna?"

"Miss Cook. I saw her this morning, looking exhausted, sitting on the divan rubbing her temples. I asked her if she had taken ill. She said it was just a headache, nothing more."

"Where is she?"

"Up on the second floor tending patients."

"Let's go find her."

We climbed the stairs, searched several rooms, and finally located her at the far end of the hallway tending to a Mr. Thompson, one of the editors of the *Avalanche* newspaper. He was unconscious and appeared to be suffering from a lethal case of the fever. Miss Cook was sitting at his bedside holding his hand and reciting a familiar passage from Saint John: "Let not your heart be troubled: ye believe in God, believe also in me. In my Father's house are many mansions. I go to prepare a place for you. I'll come again and receive you; that where I am, there ye may be also."

"Excuse me, Miss Cook," I whispered.

She turned and responded, "Doctor."

"Came to check on the Winters boy. The Howards found his parents. He's looking much better. You've done a great job."

Miss Cook glanced at the dying man and then back at me. "The child's an exception. We're not as lucky at the Mansion House this time around. Remember, we didn't lose a soul in '73. But now it's different. We're doing everything we can, and we're still losing two out of three. The fever's so much stronger than before."

When Miss Cook turned toward Mr. Thompson, I signaled Anna to leave the room.

"Anna's worried," I said.

"About what?"

"Your health. She said you look very tired and have a bad headache."

"It's nothing. Just slight. Will be gone by sundown."

"Why don't you take a break. Let's go outside and have a cigarette."

Miss Cook swung around in the chair, hesitated for a moment, and then started to rise. It seemed to take a great deal of effort. When she became upright, her left leg buckled. She grasped the back of the chair and then slowly eased herself down onto the floor.

As I rushed to her side, I called out, "Anna, Anna, come quick!" I braced Miss Cook against the back wall, pulled out my pocket watch, and measured her pulse. It was down, way down in the forties. She was semiconscious. Her forehead was on fire.

"Anna, you need to give Miss Cook a cold bath and get her to bed. Fetch one of the male nurses to help me. We'll lift her back into the chair and carry her to her room."

By the time we got across the hallway, several nurses had already made up her mattress with fresh linens. The male nurse and I set the chair down and hooked our arms up under hers. As we raised her out of the seat, she moaned, "No. No. Not there. Please, a pallet on the floor."

I knew what she was thinking. "Save the bed for someone else. If I die, you'll have to burn it." So following her wishes, the burly nurse and I lowered Miss Cook onto the floor.

Unlike many of the lucky folk, who fell into a stupor and died quickly, Miss Cook suffered mightily for days. First there was the high fever, next the jaundice, then the hemorrhaging, convulsions, the kidney failure, and finally the projectile black vomit. During her struggle, I remember only one real respite from pain. It was toward the end. I had decided to stay the night. She and I were alone. I was dozing but subconsciously aware of her rhythmic moaning.

In the dead of night, she bolted upright and spoke clearly to ghostly gentlemen entering the room. "Welcome again to the Mansion House, Reverend Berryman. Absolutely, your regular honey, Angel, is waiting for you upstairs. . . . And good to see you again, Father Stewart. Yes, the voluptuous Black

Beauty is down the hallway there, third room on the right. . . . And nice to see you again too, Rabbi Alterman. Velvet should be here shortly. In the meantime let's share a whiskey or two." She waved her right arm out in a welcoming gesture, closed her eyes, and slumped back onto her blood-spattered pillow. Silence. By dawn, Miss Cook was dead.

That same afternoon we held a brief, informal service in the parlor at the Mansion House with Reverend Berryman officiating. There were only six mourners in the room to hear the minister's sermon—two of Miss Cook's inmates turned nurses, Undertaker Jack, Anna, a recuperating reporter from the *Memphis Appeal* newspaper, and me. The six of us sat facing the sealed wooden coffin. Reverend Berryman stood before us next to the simple casket and began, "We read today from the Gospel according to John, Chapter 20:

> On the first day of the week cometh Mary Magdalene early unto the sepulcher, when it was yet dark, and seeth the stone taken away. She stood weeping: and as she wept, she stooped down, and looked in, and seeth two angels in white sitting, the one at the head, and the other at the feet, where the body of Jesus had lain. And they say unto her, "Woman, why weepest thou?" She saith unto them, "Because they have taken away my Lord, and I know not where they have laid him." And when she had thus said, she turned herself back, and saw Jesus standing, and knew not that it was Jesus. He saith unto her, "Wom-

an, why weepest thou? Whom seekest thou?"
She, supposing him to be the gardener, saith
unto him, "Sir, if thou have borne him hence,
tell me where thou hast laid him, and I will take
him away." Jesus saith unto her, "Mary." She
turned herself, and saith unto him, "Rabboni;"
which is to say, Master.

"This Mary Magdalene, who was the first person to see our
Savior after His resurrection, was according to the Gospels of
Matthew and Mark the only disciple who attended the cruci-
fixion, witnessed the burial, and then spoke with Jesus after
His resurrection.

"Who was this woman who could testify to all three major events? The holiest of the holiest? No. . . no. Mary Magdalene was anything but a saint with an unblemished past. According to the Gospels she had been a prostitute out of whom
Jesus had cast seven demons. So what lessons can we draw
from Mary's life? I would suggest she teaches us that through
self-sacrifice and repentance we too can enjoy salvation. She
was a penitent who devoted her remaining life to Christ and
acted as the apostle to the apostles.

"And in this here and now I believe Miss Cook has
followed a like path and become the Mary Magdalene of
Memphis. Whatever her sins, she vanquished them with her
sacrifice. Didn't our Savior promise as much when he said,
'For as much as you did it unto the least of these, ye did it
also unto me?' Out of sin, Miss Cook, in all the tenderness
and fullness of her womanhood, merged, transfigured and

purified, to become the healer. Surely the sins of this woman must have been forgiven her, for her faith has made her whole—made her one with the loving Christ, whose example she followed in giving her life that others might live. She is now at peace with the Lord."

After the service, Jack and I carried Miss Cook's coffin out to the street and loaded it onto the back of one of his wagons piled high with at least a half dozen other caskets. Out of respect for Miss Cook and her unselfish deeds I decided to accompany Jack to the graveyard and help him with her burial. We waved to the mourners standing at the top of the steps and turned the mares eastward toward the cemetery. When we arrived at Elmwood, we stopped at the gatehouse, where Jack introduced me to Little Grace, the Graveyard Girl. Jack pulled a piece of paper from his vest pocket and read off the names as Little Grace recorded the entries in her red leather logbook: "Kelley, Jane; Garland, Charles; Milden, Jennie; Anderson, Richard; Austin, William; Fischer, Patrick; and Cook, Annie."

As the sun eased behind a row of ancient magnolias, we dug the last of the seven graves. I had suggested we bury Miss Cook last and in a separate special place. When we had shoveled down at least five feet into the red clay, we climbed out, slid our ropes beneath her coffin, and lowered Miss Cook into the ground. Undertaker Jack offered up a few final words: "In the sure hope of the resurrection to eternal life through our Lord Jesus Christ, we commit Miss Cook to the earth. The Lord bless her and keep her; the Lord make his face to shine upon her and be gracious unto her; the Lord lift up his countenance upon her and give her peace, both now and forevermore. Amen."

Jack and I painted names on makeshift crosses, stowed our shovels, and then headed back toward the main gate. As we approached the entrance, Little Grace ran out from the gatehouse, waved, and tolled her bell seven times.

"Remarkable girl," Jack said.

"I'd say."

We then became lost in our own thoughts and rode silently for more than a mile.

Jack finally broke the silence. "The reverend did a good job on short notice, didn't he?"

"Yes, and especially when he called Miss Cook the Mary Magdalene of Memphis. I really liked that."

After another brief silence, I broached the subject of Miss Cook's final hours. "Jack, I want your take on something."

"Sure, go ahead."

"You know how things can look so different in the wee hours of the morning, especially as a life winds down. Well, several hours before Miss Cook died, she sat upright, stared out through the door, and welcomed back three spirits who had come a calling again on her girls, Angel, Velvet, and Black Beauty."

"Nothing odd about that. Hell, half the men in Memphis have experienced at least one of those three."

"But it wasn't just any three men."

"Well, who then?"

"Reverend Berryman, Father Stewart, and Rabbi Alterman."

"Just a feverish dream. Nothing more."

"My first impression too. I reasoned she must have known the reverend. The church is just down the street. And you know how clergymen are always on the lookout for sinners. The Mansion House would surely have been a prime target. And his church being close by—that's why we asked the reverend to officiate her funeral today. But I'm not so sure about the other two. How would she have ever known Rabbi Alterman or Father Stewart, if the premise of her delirium were not true—that is, if they weren't Mansion House regulars? And if I'm not mistaken, they're both fairly new to Memphis, and the Catholic church and synagogue are both on the far side of town. So in a strange way her hallucination makes a lot of sense."

"But it just may be the turtle on the fence post, Thomas. Your assumption he climbed up there may be wrong. But you know one thing you have to keep in mind here when weighing the scales—these fellows sent their congregants and loved ones to the camps or to other cities to get them out of harm's way. The reverend, the rabbi, and the priest stayed behind to comfort the dying, and they're paying the price. I buried the rabbi day before yesterday, and the priest's fighting for his life at the Walthal Infirmary, dying there among the poor whom he'd gone to see. So all three are heroes in my book."

"I have to give you that, Jack. I have to give you that."

We pulled up in front of Master Taylor's house. I climbed down, thanked Jack again for helping out, and trudged up the front steps. The house was pitch black. It was past nine o'clock; and as usual, Master Taylor had already gone to bed. I devoured some johnnie cakes and molasses and then went straight up to my room. I knew tomorrow would be another tough day.

As I lay in the dark at the edge of sleep, a blasphemous notion crossed my mind—Miss Cook had suffered unspeakably for six days while Jesus endured only six hours on the cross to save the world.

12

AFTER THE FIRST hectic weeks of eighteen-hour days, Master Taylor and I settled into a routine—rising early, working hard, and then sharing information over dinner every night. With chaos swirling about us, it was comforting to follow a pattern. We even subconsciously developed a blueprint for our conversations: first, updates from Hannah and Lil' Jim, and then newspaper accounts from the *Appeal* and the *Avalanche* interspersed with remarkable incidents we'd experienced during the day.

As the carnage mounted, Master Taylor became King Henry intoning the dead at Agincourt. "It says here in the *Avalanche* that during the first week of the epidemic back in mid-August the Board of Health recorded fifteen hundred taken ill with ten dying every day. . . . Let's see. The second week, three thousand cases and fifty deaths a day. . . . My God, the numbers keep rising. Here are the latest totals— only estimates—ten thousand sick with considerably more than two hundred deaths per day. That's half the people left in town taken to bed. When you're in the middle of the battle, you know a lot of people are falling, but it doesn't strike you until you hear the numbers. I've never seen anything like it."

"You just have to keep your head down and keep fighting," I replied. "Otherwise, it's overwhelming."

"Especially when you know the White House has turned a deaf ear to our requests for help. I remember Mayor Flippin expressing his frustrations privately about the president. The mayor said he telegraphed an urgent appeal in mid-August as the bodies began piling up. Hayes responded in a personal letter saying he suspected the, ah—how'd he get it off?—'the Memphis sorrow,' was greatly exaggerated by the panic-stricken people. But in any event, they'd do all they could for our relief. But when nothing happened, the mayor said he telegraphed the president again. I don't know if there ever was a response. I didn't hear any more about it after the mayor came down with the scourge himself. My guess is if the president responded, it was probably with more of the same. One thing's for sure, I don't recall ever seeing any help coming from Washington. Do you?"

"I heard somewhere the secretary of war was supposedly sending rations for two thousand people for twenty days because the public charities couldn't keep up. But that's all I know. Maybe there's something about Hayes in that stack of backlogged newspapers there we haven't read yet."

"Okay, let's see what they're reporting. . . . My God, first thing here. Dr. Watson was buried on the thirty-first."

"K.P.?" I asked. "Damn, I worked with him in '73. He was a good man. I saw him at the first physicians' advisory meeting. Said he was gonna work down in the Pinch again as last time. Asked if I wanted to join him. Never complained. Took the risks. Treated everybody. The meeting was the last time I ever saw him."

Master Taylor glanced back down at the newspaper and began summarizing. "Says here apparently no one missed him. I guess everyone thought he was back in the Pinch helping the poor. Just happenstance they found him. Says a Sergeant McElroy of the Signal Service was walking down Second Street and was told of a possible body in number 56. Seeing the house was boarded up, he immediately kicked the door in and found K.P.'s decomposing corpse lying on a mattress on the floor in an otherwise empty room. The sergeant sent for the undertaker and then asked neighbors if they knew why the doctor was there or when he entered the building. No one had seen him or could explain why he was there."

"Most likely during the delirium he crawled in the place and lingered for days," I suggested. "We've seen that before. Really sad. . . . Never any answers for these things. Fellow spends his life attending the sick and helping the poor, so now he dies alone, unattended by physician or nurse. Why? It's a damn waste."

Master Taylor slowly shook his head and returned to summarizing the updates. "It doesn't get any better, Thomas. Says here they found a poor woman in a makeshift hut on Main Street near the depot. Stiff, naked, sitting on a chair—a dead infant hanging by the nipple of her mother's left breast, another child breathing its last on a pallet, and black vomit and excreta covering everything in the room. Buried the mother and the children in the same box."

As I listened to that story, a recent memory swept over me. "I wasn't gonna say anything more about missing dinner last Wednesday night," I said. "I explained then I was taking care of a patient. But there was more to it than that. I had something similar happen—similar to the lady in the hut. I'd finished my rounds and had actually started walking home. It was a bright blue moon. Streets deserted as usual. A stark silver beauty glazed the truth. I imagined the whispers of my mother's voice singing a favorite lullaby:

> Darkness falls and man calls
> Go to sleep my little baby.
> When you wake, you shall have
> All the pretty ponies.

"I instinctively followed the melody to a well-kept cottage. I peered through the open window into the lamplight and saw a young mother clutching her infant while pacing about the room. She was singing my mother's lullaby. I crossed the lane and climbed the front stairs. I knocked once, twice, and even a third time. The lyric continued. I turned the knob, slowly opened the door, and eased my head in. 'I'm sorry, ma'am,' I called, 'I just wanted to tell you my mother sang that song to me as a child. You render it beautifully.' She continued pacing, gazing at the infant and singing the lullaby.

"When she reached the wall and turned, I realized something was terribly wrong. Disheveled hair. Soiled dress. A vacant stare. My first thought was to rescue the child. I approached the woman and whispered several times, 'It's okay. . . . It's okay. I'm a doctor, miss, please let me see your baby. . . . It's okay, miss.' I slowly gained her trust—enough to where she let me pull back the blanket covering the child's face.

"Despite all the training I've had, I recoiled in horror. The infant was already decomposing. As I tried coaxing the mother to leave the house, a familiar face stepped into the room and asked, 'Is everything okay here, Doc? I was patrolling the neighborhood and saw the door wide open.' It was Officer Hadly from across town. I explained the child was dead and the mother deranged. After summoning help, Hadly, his partner, and I gently separated the mother from the infant, drove her to the asylum, and prepared the baby's body for burial."

"Oh my heavens, Thomas. That must have been brutal."

"It truly was, Master Taylor. It truly was. And not just for me. When I met Officer Hadly on the street several days later, he asked if I had visited the lady. I said I had. I found her in a happy state of mind—cradling a blanket, pacing the ward, and singing my mother's lullaby. Hadly shook his head and said, 'I just don't understand how these things happen. I knew the family. They were members of my church, the Second Presbyterian. Her husband had died just a few days before you found her. And before that her family had been carried out one after the other to the trenches. She watched her last hope die with that youngest child. Her mind could bear no more and cracked. The poor family. The poor woman. Why, Doc? Why?'"

I paused and breathed deeply, trying to quiet my mind. "The first time you see something like this, Master Taylor, you go outside to vomit. Then, after a while, you learn to tolerate it; but you never really get used to it. Got sick to my stomach the first time I saw this kind of thing in '73, and this time, I did the same thing again—retched all over Reverend Tanner's porch. It's a combination of the shock and the stench. Even as a physician, seeing a pile of bones steeped in a green puddle of rotting fluids makes you shudder. Ugh!"

"People outside Memphis don't know the sacrifice you're all making on the front line, Thomas. The nurses and physicians dying at their posts; priests, ministers, rabbis, and the good sisters succumbing quickly after comforting the dying. Some day they'll praise all of you, Thomas, all of you who stayed and fought."

"There was never a question of staying, Master Taylor."

"That's what I don't understand—why some of the professionals hunkered down and others ran away to far-off cities. Now, here's an example of professionals doing their job. People are saying the newspapers may have to shut down because everyone's getting the jack. The *Appeal* has only three left on staff while the *Avalanche* is down to one employee. Looks like the fellow's getting some help from the agent at the Associated Press. Despite all the setbacks in the publishing offices, they've managed to keep the news flowing so far.

"But for every one of you heroes, there are at least two that beat a fast retreat. Where are the city magistrates? You can't get anything done. The legal system's ground to a halt. Thank God for the Relief Committee. And the druggists? They're nowhere to be found. You know how hard it is now to get the medicines you need. . . . And remember Hannah's letter the other day about that damn councilman out at the camp? His wife gets the fever. Hannah helps out the best she can, but the wife gets progressively worse. For the sake of the women and children in the compound, the camp doctor orders her moved to City Hospital. Hannah said she was there in the room as the physician attempted persuading the councilman to accompany his wife. Hannah said the more the doctor cajoled, the more the politician demurred without explanation. When the physician finally asked him point-blank why he shouldn't go to the hospital with her, he hemmed and hawed, finally pointed to his dog, and said, 'Whose going to take care of him?' In my book, that man should've been shot on the spot."

"It's human nature to fear the unknown." I suggested. "Folks read the newspapers. They hear the whispers. They see a coffin coming out of a neighbor's house. One fellow panics and then another. Terror ratchets up, becomes an epidemic like the jack. They don't have the training or the childhood experiences to give them perspective. As a boy during the war, I saw a lot of suffering and dying. Battles swirled all around our farm. Ironically, none of my family was shot or killed in action. But one by one they all died—old age, accidents, or senseless dueling. Father, mother, grandfather, brother. Death was an unknown that quickly lost its novelty."

Master Taylor glanced away toward a daguerreotype of Emma hanging on the wall and mused, "I guess we should try to focus on the heroes streaming into Memphis. Heed Shakespeare's words: 'There's some soul of goodness in things evil would men observingly distil it out.'" He leaned over and picked up another newspaper from the pile. "Well, we're making good progress this evening with the backlog of papers," he said. "Here's the *Appeal* from the twentieth. Says the Relief Committee sent a telegram to be read at the Booth

Theatre in New York the following evening. It quotes the text of the message:

> Deaths to date, 2,250; number sick now, about 3,000 of 19,000 remaining in city; and average deaths, 60% of the sick. We're feeding some 10,000 in the camps and the city. Memphis is a hospital. Fifteen volunteer physicians have died; twenty others are sick. Countless numbers of nurses have died—many that had had the fever before and thought themselves safe. Fever is abating some today perhaps for want of material. We're praying for frost—it's our only hope. A thousand thanks to the generous people of New York who have sent money, food and supplies.

"So it's good the Relief Committee's beginning to get the word out about what's happening here. But you and I know, Thomas, there's a lot more to be done. There's more to the suffering than the sick and dying. Industry and commerce have ceased. The stores are shuttered, the factories vacant, the wharves deserted, the depots silent—nothing moving in or out. So if you're healthy, there's no way to earn a living. There are thousands with nothing to live on. But even if they have money, they don't have a way to spend it. There are no provisions to buy; the farmers and factors have stopped coming to town."

Master Taylor picked up another copy of the *Appeal* and began scanning the pages. "Speaking of the Relief Committee, Thomas, there's news; but it ain't good. The chairman, Charlie Fisher, died on the twenty-seventh. Had you heard? Says it was a combination of overwork and the scourge. On duty twenty-four hours a day at home, at the office, and in the streets. Praises him here for quietly taking the sick into his home and nursing them back to health."

"That's really discouraging." I said. "He seemed like a pleasant enough fellow. You know I spoke with him briefly before the Relief Committee's regular meeting—the one where I raised the issue of the thieves near the general store."

"Sad to say, Thomas, most of the men you saw on the Relief Committee are no longer with us. In the death notice it says the chairman's the fifteenth member of the committee to succumb to the scourge. I believe I read the original makeup was twenty members. . . . Think of it; fifteen out of the first twenty dead in a little over a month."

"It's as if the gods were using sharpshooters to degrade the committee's response."

"Oh, I don't know about that, Thomas. I gave up a long time ago trying to understand God's motives. The mystery for me is how we could have so many heroes and villains in the same state at the same time. On the one hand we have doctors, nurses, and administrators fighting and sacrificing, while on the other hand we have cowards who've fled the city and now prey on others out of fear or greed. Take this recent article in the *Advocate*—says here a young boy orphaned by the yellow jack fled Memphis to join his grandfather in Mason. Knowing the townsfolk had imposed a strict quarantine on 'refugees,' the grandfather rented an isolated cabin and hired a Negro woman to stay with the boy until his quarantine expired.

"Their first night in the wilderness was a nightmare. Fearing a spread of the scourge, some locals rode out to the cabin, brickbatted it, set fire to it, and drove the boy out into the dark. They fired shot after shot as he ran off into the woods. Says here the youth spent the night alone in the forest shivering in the early October chill and expecting to be killed at any moment. The following morning the boy sneaked back to his grandfather's house and explained what had happened. After hearing of the brutality, the grandfather chose to violate the regulation and hide the child in his home until the quarantine period had ended."

"Ignorance makes cowards of us all," I responded and added, "Since it was family, I believe I would have done what the grandfather did. Action trumps fear every time."

Master Taylor reached down and chose a final paper from the dwindling stack. "One more *Advocate* and then we'll call it a night. Let's see . . . Oh boy, looks like there are more and more of these stories every day. But this one has a twist; shows the good and the bad at the same time. Well, I believe you know John Rawls, the druggist over by the Peabody. Says here his wife died last week and he, the children, and the undertaker drove the body out to the Evergreen Cemetery. Arrived a little past five o'clock—Evergreen officially closes at six. That's when they usher the mourners out, and the gravediggers stop working. Well, just as Mr. Rawls arrived at the grave site, the cemetery foreman appeared leading a team of Negroes with shovels. Apparently this supervisor wanted to leave early; and to discourage the diggers, he reminded them he wouldn't pay them extra for work they did after six o'clock.

"You know what the Negroes did? Right there in front of the widower and children, they told the boss that sometimes they worked for friendship and then started digging the grave. How about that! Brutality and bravery in an instant. But it got even worse. As the diggers lowered the coffin into the ground, the supervisor approached them and, surely in earshot of Mr. Rawls and his children, declared, 'You've worked after quitting hour, and you'll receive nothing for it! From now on, ya hear, no work'll be done after six o'clock no matter how many damned carcasses are brought out here for burial.' Says here that after a painful silence, the mourners turned away and quietly exited the grounds. You know, that bastard needs to be fired."

As I pushed back from the table, I assured him, "I wouldn't worry about that, Master Taylor. Since it got in the papers, I'm sure there'll be sufficient outrage, and justice will be done."

13

WE DIDN'T HAVE to read the newspapers to know the siege was over. Near the end of October we awoke to a glistening crust coating the fields and killing the scourge. And within minutes of that autumnal surprise, hopeful messages flashed over the wires to loved ones everywhere: "We've survived, and it's now time to come home."

The following morning we received a telegram from Hannah and Lil' Jim inviting us out to the camp for a thanksgiving mass and a solemn procession back to town. Early on All Saints' Day Master Taylor and I hitched the mares to the wagon, drove out to the grounds, and began searching for Hannah and Lil' Jim. In an earlier message Hannah explained their tent was off the main street near Sacred Heart of Our Divine Lord, the little church on wheels. We thought it would be easy to find them, but half the Memphis survivors and all the members of the camp had gravitated toward the small church to celebrate mass and partake of Holy Communion.

We weaved through the multitude and finally found them staring out from their tent toward the makeshift altar only a few feet away. We approached unnoticed until Master Taylor spontaneously shouted, "Hannah! Lil' Jim!" Daughter and grandson turned, recognized us, and began running. As Hannah raced into her father's arms, Lil' Jim clutched my legs, jumped up and down, and yelled, "Thomas! Thomas!" In the middle of this reunion dance, we changed partners. Lil' Jim ran over to his grandfather, who immediately picked him up and tossed him playfully into the air. Hannah gazed into my eyes and moved slowly toward me. We instinctively embraced to share a passionate kiss. But at the last instant, she slid her head off to the side and buried our secret in my beard.

After celebrating a mass thanking God for sparing the camp, Father Walsh instructed the congregants to pull up stakes, move the ark from the altar to its traveling cart, and prepare to break camp. The somber procession formed as follows: first, the ark guarded by members of the Father Mathew Total Abstinence Society; next, carriages containing all the camp inhabitants; then the priests and other dignitaries of the Catholic Church; and lastly, the wagons containing the tents, luggage, and remaining supplies.

Out of respect for the dead and bereaved, we paraded silently without a band leading the procession. Our first stop in Memphis was Saint Brigid's, where the celebrated orator, Reverend J. T. Webb, offered a thanksgiving discourse followed by the Gregorian *Te Deum* by an all-male choir. As evening approached, the members disbanded and traveled the few remaining blocks home to face the memories and the loss.

But as the one struggle ended, another began. The challenge now—to breathe life back into a shattered city. Thirty thousand heard the message and began heading home to pick up the pieces, comfort survivors, and mourn five thousand dead. The wharves and depots were quickly filling with prodigal sons and daughters wearing black and wandering about in a dazed bustle.

During our first dinner together after Hannah and Lil' Jim returned, Master Taylor observed, "The order of today is sorrow tinged with a trace of hope. But what I learned full well after Emma's death is that we all have mighty reservoirs of resilience. We're flexible subjects; and the order of tomorrow will be guarded hope tinged with a trace of sadness. The wheels of commerce have already begun to turn. You can see it in the newspapers, the shops, and streets. The *Appeal* and *Avalanche* are publishing ads for 'new supplies at rock bottom prices' and 'all your mourning needs—crepe, cloth and black-border stationary.'

"The markets are reopening with storefront signs touting fresh oysters, potatoes, souse meat, and greens. Bales of cotton are stacking up again on the sidewalks and spilling out into the streets at the Exchange. Pass by any restaurant; smell the catfish frying. Stop before any tavern; inhale the sweet blend of malted barley and cigar smoke. Take a seat in Court Square; welcome back the cacophony of streetcars, calliopes, and rail yard whistles. Or take a stroll up Beale Street again to the cadence of spirituals, field hollers, and chants. Yes, sir. Memphis has already dragged itself up to its knees."

"Yes, you can feel the spirits lifting a bit," I responded. "We've all got a lot to be thankful for."

"Speaking of that, Thomas, General Humes stopped by the Howard's office today. Said he's heading up a committee to host a ceremony at the Greenlaw Opera House on the twenty-eighth, Thanksgiving Day. Said the mayor and the council want to publicly express the city's gratitude to the North and South for supporting Memphis with money, people, and goods during the scourge. It looks like it's going to be a big-time affair. Judge Smith, Colonel Stewart, ex-Chancellor Morgan, and Reverend Stainback are also serving on the committee, and General Humes has already tapped Colton Greene to design stage decorations. He's the fellow, you know, who's run every one of our Memphis Mardi Gras celebrations. And you know what? When the general dropped by today, he asked me to coordinate the florists who'd be designing the arrangements to complement Mr. Greene's staging."

"We'll all go to the Opera House, Father?" Hannah asked.

"Of course. All of us, including Amanda, who'll be coming home to stay. I think it's our duty." And then Master Taylor added humorously, "I'd really be hurt if you didn't go just to see my floral handiwork." He smiled at Hannah and looked around the table. "So we'll get up early, head to church, attend the Greenlaw ceremony, and then hurry back here for a hearty Thanksgiving dinner."

"It'll really be good seeing Amanda." I said. "She's all grown up, gotten her degree and coming back home now to teach."

"That's if her interview with Miss Conway goes well," Master Taylor emphasized.

"Miss Conway? Who's Miss Conway, Father?"

"Emma and I met her some years ago. She was principal of the Market Street School. Left there last year to start a college preparatory for women. Told me a few weeks ago she'd be up to fifty students when her school reopens next month. Started the school alone; but with the growing number of parents wanting to send their daughters off to Vassar and Wellesley, she said she'd be expanding the faculty at the beginning of the year.

"I explained Amanda had finished her course work at Mary Sharp and would be coming home to look for a teaching position. Miss Conway encouraged me to speak with Amanda about the opening. Amanda tells me they've corresponded and agreed to meet over the Thanksgiving holiday. You never know about these things; but I feel confident she'll get the job. She's studied a wide range of disciplines, from trigonometry to philosophy and astronomy. And another thing she has on her side is a letter of recommendation from my friend, President Graves, at Mary Sharp."

"It's too bad Aaron won't be with us here for Thanksgiving, Father."

"I know. But he's promised to come home for Christmas with 'some big news.' Apparently about landing a job. That's all I know; he didn't say any more than that."

"I can't wait for Christmas!" Hannah exclaimed. "It's been a long time since we've all been together as a family."

"Everyone but Emma," Master Taylor sighed.

"I'm sorry, Father," Hannah responded. "I didn't mean . . ."

"I know, dear," Master Taylor interjected and then added almost as an aside, "After all, if God gave us everything we wanted on earth, would there be any need for a heaven?"

On the day before Thanksgiving, we all climbed into the carriage and headed out to the depot to welcome Amanda home for good. When her train rounded the final bend and blasted its warning whistle, Lil' Jim began running back and forth waving excitedly at the engineer leaning out of the cab window. The passenger cars began to hiss and screech. And when the coaches finally clanged to a stop, the conductor hopped down from the last car and raced toward the front of the train to happily assist young ladies stepping down onto the platform. With so many years of practice, the middle-aged trainman had polished his assistance into a balletic pas-de-deux. He would extend his arm gracefully into the doorway and magically retrieve the gloved hand of a stylish debutante.

Amanda was his third partner of the day. She glided down the steps, curtsied a thank you, and turned to look for us. She was wearing a burgundy lace-trimmed, ruffled dress, a lined jacket with puff sleeves, and a matching lace and floral-trimmed hat resting atop her auburn curls. As she approached the depot, I whispered to Lil' Jim, "That's your Aunt Amanda there, boy. Go say hello." Lil' Jim began running and shouting, "Auntie! Auntie!"

Amanda extended her arms inviting a big hug. "Lil' Jim, is that you? You look just like your mother."

Master Taylor embraced his daughter and said, "It's really good having you home."

"It's really good being back in Memphis, Father," she replied. "I missed y'all a lot. It was so hard being away knowing what troubles you had here."

We loaded her luggage into the carriage and drove back to the Taylor home, where we spent the rest of the day sharing the good times of the last four years and excitedly planning for Thanksgiving Day. After everyone else had retired for the night, I grabbed my jacket and stepped out onto the porch to enjoy a cigar. I remembered the day we put Amanda on the train for Mary Sharp just as the first wave of scourge rolled over the Hollow and the Pinch in '73. She was so young, so innocent. She protested Master Taylor's decision to send her off to Winchester weeks before school would begin. She wanted to stay here to help us out. How could she have known? In fact, how could any of us have known the hell we were about to face?

And now the ingénue returns home the sophisticate educated in the ways of Galileo, Hegel, and Sir Thomas More, prepared now to share her knowledge with a new generation of Wellesley aspirants. Wisdom through experience? No, traditional knowledge gained through years of formal training. Optimism unburdened by the sight and stench of rotting corpses and choking fever fires. In a matter of weeks all of the misery had disappeared from the streets of Memphis, and the rain had washed the lime away. Nothing was left of the horror to validate the heroism and the sacrifice.

Long before dawn Master Taylor tapped lightly on my door. I had agreed to help him prepare an early breakfast before we all left for church. While I got the fire going and ground the coffee, Master Taylor sawed some thick slices off the hickory-smoked ham and cracked a dozen fresh eggs into a bowl. After browning the first slices, Master Taylor signaled it was time to rouse everyone and get them downstairs for breakfast before rushing off to morning services.

And rush we did. There was one thing for sure about Master Taylor—he hated arriving late for even the most trivial of social functions. And this morning he drove the mares as if certifiably possessed, barely missing a pedestrian, a farmer's wagon, and a dying mule. But thanks be to God, we arrived in one piece and slid into our seats as the choral director stepped before the choir to lead the opening hymn, "The Search for Truth":

> Oh, darkly on the path of life
> The pilgrim holds his course in strife;
> His wandering vision strives in vain
> The distant prospect to attain;
> And prejudice will arise between,
> And doubt's dark clouds enfold the scene.

I must concede Reverend Woodburn's Thanksgiving sermon didn't open auspiciously. He read scripture after scripture driving home the linkage between pestilence and the sin of disobedience. "If ye walk contrary to me, I will send the pestilence among you" (Leviticus); "Because of the wickedness of thy doings, the Lord shall make the pestilence cleave unto thee until he has consumed thee off the face of the land" (Deuteronomy); "When they fast I will not hear them cry . . . but I will consume them by the sword, and by the famine and by the pestilence" (Jeremiah); and "Nation shall rise up against nation, and kingdom against kingdom; and there shall be famines, pestilences, and earthquakes in diverse places. All these are the beginning of sorrows" (Matthew).

The pastor then focused on the malignant nature of the scourge with one death out of every two sickened; on the unprecedented scope of infection, from New Orleans to Memphis to Savannah; and on the abnormally high death rate among children, a higher mortality for the boys and girls than for any other age group. I remember anticipating what would follow next—an unassailable syllogism: if sin causes pestilence, and if the scourge in Memphis was virulent, then the level of disobedience to God's laws here must have been scandalous. But to the reverend's credit, he pivoted away from the jaded rhetorical device to focus on the physical rather than the spiritual; on the good as opposed to the evil; and on the future rather than on the past: "From August until now we've suffered unspeakable tragedies; but I believe, instead of focusing on these horrific times, it's better we learn lessons for the common good.

"First, Newton tells us there's a law of cause and effect and that for every action there is an equal and opposite reaction. The inspired teachings declare cleanliness is next to godliness. And scientists agree with the scriptures explaining cleanliness is a requirement for good health. So what is the lesson to be drawn from our experience with the scourge? The city fathers must focus their attention first and foremost on the drainage and sewage of the city. Now I know none of us likes handing over our money to pay taxes; but it's better to pay our dues in money rather than in the lives, tears, and suffering of our fellow citizens. 'Render therefore unto Caesar the things which are Caesar's; and unto God the things that are God's.'

"Secondly, there are baffling revelations of character in war and in epidemics. While you expected resolve, patience, and sacrifice during the recent scourge, instead you were shocked by instances of human frailty, panic, and crime. While you assumed everyone would treat their fellow men with love and compassion, instead you witnessed husbands abandoning wives, wives leaving husbands, and children deserting parents. But just when you thought you would never witness another noble deed, you watched strangers come to town and die one after another while serving the public good. Priests, nuns, reverends, doctors, and nurses from the North and the South traveled here to do the Lord's work. Heroism was the rule; neglect and desertion the exception. This noble army of martyrs widely separated by birth, circumstances, education, livelihood, and experience strengthened the weak and offered hope to the downtrodden. These heroes had heard the Lord's promise, 'He that loveth his life shall lose it, and he that hateth his life in this world shall keep it unto life eternal.'

"And then thirdly, as Jesus teaches, we are not to judge our neighbors' actions: 'Judge not, that ye be not judged. For with what judgment ye judge, ye shall be judged: and with what measure ye mete, it shall be measured to you again. And why beholdest thou the mote that is in thy brother's eye, but considerest not the beam that is in thine own eye?' Why would the Lord teach this? I'd submit it's to emphasize we're incapable of knowing our brothers' motives and personal situations driving their behavior.

"And now two final thoughts. First, we should not let these strangers die in vain. We should follow their example and continually provide support for the sick, the weak, and the poor. And secondly, as Saint Paul wrote in his inspired letter to the Thessalonians, we will see the dead again: 'I would not have you to be ignorant, brethren, concerning them which are asleep, that ye sorrow not, even as others who have no hope. For if we believe that Jesus died and rose again, even so also them which sleep in Jesus will God bring with him when he returns.'"

Reverend Woodburn slowly closed the Bible and bowed his head, signaling the transition from lesson to song:

> Abide with me; fast falls the eventide;
> The darkness deepens; Lord with me abide.
> When other helpers fail and comforts flee,
> Help of the helpless, O abide with me.

During the singing of this closing hymn, the pastor made his way to the vestibule where he greeted us as we left the building. And I must confess it was one of the few times, if not the only time, I praised a sermon for style and substance and truly meant it.

When we reached the bottom of the front steps, I lifted Lil' Jim up onto my shoulders, and we all walked the short distance from the church to the Greenlaw Opera House, where the mass-meeting of gratitude would begin at twelve o'clock sharp. This brick Romanesque "Temple of Drama" had two four-story wings and a central structure rising ninety feet above the street with a façade containing massive front doors, sixty windows, and a pediment decorated with scrolls and lyres. Once inside the building, we climbed the grand staircase to the first-floor lobby where six doors gave access to the opera hall itself. The sweep of the fifty-foot-high ceiling featured wide cornices arcing toward a large skylight surrounded by a galaxy of smaller oblate windows.

Since we'd arrived early, Master Taylor led us down the center aisle to the stage where he proudly unveiled his floral handiwork. "If I must say so, I think the florists did a great job with the festoons and floor arrangements."

"So what do we have here, Master Taylor?" I asked. "Let's see, there's pine and cedar for the festoons and I believe it's— correct me if I'm wrong—azaleas, begonias, orchids, ferns, and palms."

"You're right on all counts, Thomas," Master Taylor replied. "The idea was to have the flowers augment Mr. Greene's pharaoh-themed props. You know, he's a very resourceful fellow. Saved the city some money. He salvaged the staging here from the last Mardi Gras celebration before the scourge." Master Taylor paused and pulled out his pocket watch. "We've got about ten minutes before the ceremony begins. Might as well take our seats. Follow me. They're right over here in the reserved section on the aisle. I'll hold Lil' Jim on my lap. I know it's been a long day for him already. If he gets restless, I'll be able to get up and move to the back of the auditorium."

At precisely noon General Humes led an army of Memphis luminaries onto the stage, including among others, Mayor Flippin, Colonel Townsend, Judge Holman, and Mr. Agelasto. After a local reverend led us in a brief opening prayer, General Humes strode to the lectern, surveyed the standing-room-only crowd, and began speaking.

"The sentiments of gratitude and admiration, which have called together this crowded assemblage of the people of Memphis, are as sincere, profound, and enduring as the heroic, noble, and beneficent gestures of the peoples of the North and South toward our stricken city. . . ."

By the close of his address, the audience was on its feet giving the general a loud and prolonged ovation.

As he acknowledged the crowd's enthusiastic applause, Mr. Kellar, chairman of the Resolution Committee, took the floor to present his committee's twenty-one resolutions. He waited patiently for the attendees to settle back into their seats and then opened the proposal with a preamble: "Whereas, we the citizens of Memphis mindful of the individual heroism displayed on behalf of our deeply afflicted people, and of the generosity, consideration, and aid extended to them by a sympathetic world, desire to testify our appreciation to . . .."

He then listed twenty-one people, institutions, and associations for whom his committee was grateful, including the president of the United States, the Howard Association, the Memphis police and firemen, the railroad and steamship lines, and the Western Union Telegraph Company. Loud applause erupted after the reading of each of the twenty-one resolutions.

The chairman paused until the cheering died down and then continued speaking in a much more solemn tone. "To the martyred dead we feel, but cannot express our gratitude, yet in all days to come shall their memories be kept green and their names go down in the annals of our city, honored, revered, and blessed. To do justice to the memory of any one of a hundred whose names might be suggested would occupy more time than is now at your disposal. Hence we restrain our inclination to mention names, and leave to you the sacred privilege of recalling the pleasant memories that cluster around your own hallowed dead."

Mr. Kellar moved to the side of the lectern and asked the attendees for a motion to put the resolutions to a vote. The outcome was never in doubt, and the motion carried unanimously on a single voice vote. General Humes then asked everyone to stand, and he led the gathering in a brief closing prayer. This man of war first thanked the Prince of Peace for all his blessings and then fervently (some might say ironically) asked that he spare us from further suffering. When the general concluded his prayer, we all spontaneously added an emphatic, "Amen," and then headed home to a bittersweet Thanksgiving.

14

THE TIME BETWEEN the holidays had flown by quickly. Here we were already at Monday the twenty-third, and it was time to return to the depot to meet Aaron's five o'clock train. During the past few weeks the mood in the household had been on the upswing. And there was certainly real cause for optimism. We had celebrated Master Taylor's birthday; Amanda had secured the job at Miss Conway's new school; and for the first time, Lil' Jim helped us decorate the Douglas fir with popcorn garland and homemade fabric ornaments.

By the time Master Taylor, Lil' Jim, and I returned from fetching Aaron, Amanda and Hannah had finished preparing their brother's favorite meal—fried pork chops, boiled potatoes, turnip greens, and bread pudding for dessert. Master Taylor sat at the head of the table proudly acting as the master of ceremonies. I had never seen him happier or more animated. My mama would have said it was as if he had died and gone to heaven.

The closest we came to discussing the latest assault on the city was Aaron's question about my changing careers and becoming a doctor. Master Taylor used Aaron's query as a segue to finally ask the one question we'd all wanted answered but had avoided out of deference to Master Taylor. "Speaking of careers, son, you mentioned in one of your last letters you had big news, something about landing a job. We're all ears; tell us about it."

"Well, I've accepted a position in the new administration. I'll be stationed in Nashville, but I'll be coming out here to Memphis more than you can imagine! Every other week or so."

"That's great news, son! And just know you'll always have a place to stay when you're working out here. But tell us; how in the world did you end up in the incoming administration?"

Aaron turned to Amanda and asked, "Do you want to explain, or do you want me to?"

Amanda smiled and said, "How about I start and you finish the tale."

Aaron laughed and said, "Okay, go ahead."

And so Amanda launched into the narrative. "Well, I'd been at Mary Sharp a few months when the faculty announced a holiday social. Since Winchester was close to Sewanee, I wrote Aaron asking if he'd like to attend and meet some of my new friends from the town and the college. He accepted, and I introduced him to a number of acquaintances, one of whom was the son of the future governor. . . . Why don't you take over now, Aaron, and finish the story?"

"Well, over the next three years, the governor's son and I became close friends," Aaron said, his pride apparent to all. "He often invited me to spend weekends at his father's plantation estate in Winchester. During our senior year, we often relived the past and dreaded the future. He'd most likely stay in Winchester, and I'd find a job in Memphis. But after his father won the election this year, my dear friend announced he had a potential solution to our dilemma: he'd speak to his father about my working in the new administration. And during my next visit to the estate, the governor-elect proposed an ideal position."

"What'll you be doing?" Master Taylor asked.

"Well, what I have to say now is highly confidential and doesn't leave the room. Agreed?"

As Aaron looked around the table, everyone nodded their heads and murmured, "Agreed."

"Father, I know you've been reading the newspapers. There've been reports about the city's chronic debt—a long-standing problem worsened by the epidemics, this one and the one back in '73. I hear the number's now north of eight hundred thousand dollars. Everyone believes sanitation is the key to stopping the fever—installing sewers, picking up the garbage, inspecting buildings, cleaning up the streets, and the like."

"The newspaper editors praise Mayor Flippin and the council for wanting to do the right thing," Master Taylor interjected.

"That's right. But they don't have the money to tackle the projects on a grand scale, and the creditors have swamped the city with writs of mandamus."

"Writs of mandamus?" I asked.

"They're court orders requiring Mayor Flippin and the council to impose new taxes to pay specific debts."

"Are the politicians working on anything to solve the problem?" I inquired.

"In Nashville we're hearing the council's going to offer

the creditors fifty cents on the dollar. If they accept, then everything will go on as usual."

"And if they don't?"

"If they don't—which, by the way, is the most likely outcome—Mayor Flippin and the council would surrender the city's charter. This would put Memphis under state supervision and protect it from its creditors. Make it a taxing district under state control. All of this would have to be approved by the Tennessee legislature and signed by the governor."

"Sounds pretty undemocratic if you ask me," Master Taylor said. "Looks like they're destroying home rule and pushing people back another step from political power. But I guess when the wolves are at the door, you haven't got much choice but to wipe the slate clean. . . . But tell me; how would all this work? Who would be in charge of running the city, levying taxes, supervising projects and the like?"

"Well, the latest plan goes something like this. The state legislature approves bills repealing the Memphis charter and instituting commission government. After the governor signs the bills, Mayor Flippin and the city councilmen resign their posts and adjourn the council meeting *sine die*, or without assigning a day for the next meeting. This would make a clean break between the old administration with its debt and the new government, which would be created when the governor signed the bills into law."

"Okay so far; but how does it work?" Master Taylor probed. "What's the structure?"

"Hold on. I'm getting there. So you see, with the complete break of the old from the new, the commission government would then be protected from the prior debt because it would now be an agency of the state. As I said earlier, Memphis would become a taxing district. It would be governed by a board of three salaried fire and police commissioners, an unpaid board of five public works supervisors, a legislative council composed of the two boards, and a permanent Board of Health. All these local government officials would be agents of the state. And to ensure state control, two of the three paid commissioners would be appointed by the governor with state Senate approval and the remaining commissioner by the residents of the taxing district."

Aaron sat back, sighed, and rubbed his palms together. "So those are the plans; and if all this pans out, the governor-elect wants me to act as liaison between his office and the legislative council. I would be coming to Memphis regularly to meet with the council, review proposed and existing contracts, and then personally report back my findings to the governor. He told me he wanted to have one of his own men on the ground here keeping an eye on things. Didn't want things spinning out of control. Chuckled and said he planned on shaking things up in Memphis. He was determined to choose nonpoliticians to fill his vacancies on the council and board of public works. He believes the only way to change things dramatically is to make a complete break with the old way of doing business. I really believe he intends to follow through on this." Aaron glanced about the room and concluded, "So there you have it. All the latest news, which hasn't yet reached the newspapers."

"Congratulations, son, you make us all proud," Master Taylor said. "It'll be great having you home on a regular basis." He pushed back from the table and asked, "Where's Lil' Jim?"

Hannah laughed and responded, "Where else would he be? He's in the parlor with the tree."

"Well, let's join him," Master Taylor said. "Let's make some memories and perhaps start a family tradition or two."

None of us had any idea what Master Taylor had in mind. We all rose from the dining room table and followed him into the parlor. Lil' Jim was sitting on a thick oval rug staring up at the massive tree filled with the popcorn garland, homemade ornaments, and a large blue star on top. After suggesting we all take a seat, Master Taylor stooped down and swept Lil' Jim up from the floor. "Sit here on my lap, boy, and let Granddad read you a story about Christmas."

Master Taylor grasped a thin volume lying on the table next to his chair, held it up for all to see and announced, "It's Irving's *Sketchbook*. Some of my favorite pieces are in here, especially the tales describing an old-fashioned Christmas celebration at a manor house in England. A squire invites the local peasants into his home for the holiday. I thought we could read one of the tales tonight, one tomorrow night on Christmas Eve, and then finish the last two on Christmas Day and Christmas Night. They're all short, and we know how much Lil' Jim loves to hear stories." He smiled a broad smile.

"So, boy, tonight we'll learn how an English gentleman, Mr. Geoffrey Crayon, meets an old friend, Frank Bracebridge, at a stagecoach inn and winds up celebrating Christmas with him at the Bracebridge castle. This sketch is called 'The Stage Coach.'"

Lil' Jim settled back against his grandfather's chest as Master Taylor began reading: "'In the course of a December tour in Yorkshire, I rode for a long distance in one of the public coaches on the day preceding Christmas. The coach was crowded, both inside and out, with passengers who, by their talk, seemed principally bound to the mansions of relations or friends to eat the Christmas dinner. . . .'"

The next evening, Christmas Eve, we all returned to the parlor where Master Taylor continued reading the Irving *Sketches* aloud. The narrative tonight was appropriately called "Christmas Eve." Lil' Jim was wide-awake from beginning to end; and when Master Taylor finished reading the sketch, Lil' Jim clamored for more. "Please, Grandpa. Another story, please."

"We'll keep the other two tales for Christmas Day and Christmas Night. But before we go to bed, I'll read you a special poem." Master Taylor pulled a folded paper from his vest pocket and began, "'Twas the night before Christmas, when all through the house / Not a creature was stirring, not even a mouse; / The stockings were hung by the chimney with care, / In hopes that St. Nicholas soon would be there. . . .'"

When he had finished reading the last lines of Moore's "Visit from Saint Nick," Master Taylor preempted any further appeals from Lil' Jim, saying, "Boy, now it's time to get to bed so Saint Nick can come with his bundle of toys."

Lil' Jim hesitated only briefly to consider the options; and then deciding it was in his interest to follow his granddad's advice, he gave us all a big hug and followed his mother upstairs to his room. Once the pair had reached the top of the steps, Amanda, Aaron, Master Taylor, and I headed off to retrieve treasures stashed in every corner of the house for my dear son, whom I loved so much from afar.

Upon entering the parlor Christmas morning we discovered Saint Nick had indeed visited during the night. There were gifts for everyone beneath the tree. For the adults—knitted sweaters, hats, handkerchiefs, and scarves. And for Lil' Jim—fruits, nuts, sweets, and hand-crafted toys, including a rocking horse, a box of alphabet blocks, a spinning top, and a wooden pull train with engine, coal tender, circus car, and caboose.

After exchanging gifts and allowing Lil' Jim to play for the better part of an hour, Master Taylor reminded us, "We've got an hour and a half to dress and get to church for Christmas services."

"Do we really have to, Father?" Hannah asked. "Can't we just stay here today, enjoy each other's company and let Lil' Jim play? After all we've been through, surely the Lord would understand."

Aaron chimed in, "Perhaps this once, Father, given the circumstances."

"Children, your mother must be rolling over in her grave right now," Master Taylor responded gently. "You all know what Emma would do. She'd quote Saint Paul's letter to the Hebrews: 'Not forsaking the assembling of ourselves together, as the manner of some is; but exhorting one another: and so much the more, as ye see the day approaching.' She'd say it's not a chore but a duty. In honor of her memory, children, let's keep the tradition alive." Master Taylor's heartfelt appeal to his wife's memory silenced their objections and easily carried the day. And within an hour, we were all dressed and on our way to Wednesday morning services.

In hindsight, regardless of the rationale, it was helpful for all of us to hear Reverend Woodburn's special Christmas message. It was as filled with surprises as his sermon a month earlier on Thanksgiving Day. As he read his Christmas text, I often asked, "Now where could he be going with that?" Out of the sixty-six books in the Bible, Reverend Woodburn had chosen the same epistle Master Taylor had quoted earlier that morning, Paul's letter to the Hebrews. But Hebrews for Christmas Day? Where were the standard accounts of Christ's birth from Matthew and Luke: "And the angel said unto them, Fear not: for, behold, I bring you good tidings of great joy.... For unto you is born this day in the city of David, a Savior, which is Christ the Lord." But no, none of that from this counterintuitive pastor, who read from the sixth chapter of Hebrews:

> For when God made promise to Abraham, because He could swear by no greater, He swear by Himself, saying, surely blessing I will bless thee, and multiplying I will multiply thee. And so, after Abraham had patiently endured, he obtained the promise. For men verily swear by the greater: and an oath for confirmation is to them an end of all strife. Wherein God, willing more abundantly to show unto the heirs of promise the immutability of His counsel, confirmed

it by an oath: that by two immutable things, in which it was impossible for God to lie, we might have a strong consolation . . . to lay hold upon the hope set before us, which hope we have as an anchor of the soul.

When we returned home from services, Lil' Jim made a bee-line for the parlor. Since Master Taylor and Aaron were resuming their talk about politics, I politely excused myself and joined Hannah and Amanda in the kitchen. "What can I do to help?" I asked.

"How about you getting the fire going in the stove and then shucking the oysters," Hannah said and then admonished, "Be sure to get the muck off the edge of the shells. Otherwise, we'll hear Father's story again about chipping his tooth at the Maxwell House in Nashville. While you're doing that, Amanda and I will get the stuffing ready for the turkey and then get to work on the sweet potatoes and the string beans."

"What's for dessert? I asked.

"One of Father's favorites, of course, lady cake," Hannah responded with a grin.

"You can tell things are starting to come back. . . . You got enough oranges for the batter and the icing?" I asked.

"More than enough," Hannah replied. "And just in time for Christmas."

Following our luncheon we gathered in the parlor to hear the next installment in the Irving series, "Christmas Day." Lil' Jim knew his place. He grabbed his wooden engine and jumped up on his granddad's lap. Unlike his previous performances, Master Taylor didn't offer a preview of what we were about to hear. He would allow the text and the rise and fall of his voice to deliver the message of his homily. After a few opening paragraphs, Master Taylor's voice rose: "I had scarcely dressed myself when a servant appeared to invite me to family prayers. He showed me the way to a small chapel in the old wing of the house, where I found the principal part of the family already assembled."

Falling back to a normal volume and then rising again, he read, "I afterwards understood that early morning service was read on every Sunday and saint's day throughout the year. . . . It was once almost universally the case at the seats of the nobility and gentry of England, and it is much to be regretted that the custom is falling into neglect; for the dullest observer must be sensible of the order and serenity prevalent in those households where the occasional exercise of a beautiful form of worship in the morning gives, as it were, the keynote to every temper for the day and attunes every spirit to harmony."

His voice falling and then rising again, he read on. "While we were talking we heard the distant toll of the village bell, and I was told that the squire was a little particular in having his household at church on a Christmas morning, considering it a day of pouring out of thanks and rejoicing." Falling back again and then rising once more: "I have seldom known a sermon attended apparently with more immediate effects, for on leaving the church the congregation seemed one and all possessed with the gaiety of spirit so earnestly enjoined by their pastor." And every time Master Taylor's voice would rise, his audience would turn, wink, and smile at each other, acknowledging their father's subterranean humor and the irony that most of Irving's sketch supported Master Taylor's conviction of attending church on Christmas Day.

After an eagerly anticipated dinner of tasty leftovers, we returned to the parlor to enjoy the final Irving sketch, "The Christmas Dinner." Lil' Jim jumped up on his grandfather's lap, we claimed our usual places, and Master Taylor began reading. "The dinner was served up in the great hall, where the squire always held his Christmas banquet. A blazing crackling fire of logs had been heaped on to warm the spacious apartment, and the flame went sparkling and wreathing up the wide-mouthed chimney...." Master Taylor next described a sumptuous banquet of boar's head, sirloin, and pheasant pies decorated with peacock feathers. He then dealt out "strange accounts of the popular superstitions and legends of the surrounding country," including the lively effigy of a crusader, who rose from the tomb by the church altar and haunted the village on stormy nights.

Up to the midpoint of the narrative, Master Taylor presented a straightforward rendering of Irving's sketch. But when he began reading Irving's comparison of the host squire to his old school chum, the parson, Master Taylor employed his old trick again—modulating his voice for emphasis:

> The squire told several long stories of early college pranks and adventures, in some of which the parson had been a sharer, though in looking at the latter it required some effort of imagination to figure such a little dark anatomy of a

man into the perpetrator of a madcap gambol. Indeed, the two college chums presented pictures of what men may be made by their different lots in life. The squire had left the university to live lustily on his paternal domains in the vigorous enjoyment of prosperity and sunshine, and had flourished on to a hearty and florid old age; whilst the poor parson, on the contrary, had dried and withered away among dusty tomes in the silence and shadows of his study.

His voice fell back and continued in a regular tone until he reached the final lines of the Irving piece:

> But enough of Christmas and its gambols; it is time for me to pause. . . . Methinks I hear the questions asked by my graver readers, 'To what purpose is all this? How is the world to be made wiser by this talk?' What, after all, is the mite of wisdom that I could throw into the mass of knowledge! But in writing to amuse, if I fail the only evil is in my own disappointment. If, however, I can by any lucky chance, in these days of evil, rub out one wrinkle from the brow of care or beguile the heavy heart of one moment of sorrow . . . surely, surely, I shall not then have written entirely in vain.

When Master Taylor finished reading this final sketch, we all applauded softly because Lil' Jim had fallen asleep, having succumbed to a grown-up narrative and a stomach full of sweets. We smiled affectionately as Master Taylor cradled Lil' Jim in his arms, eased out of his chair, and carried the boy upstairs to tuck him in for the night.

We waited in the parlor until the doting grandfather returned. Amanda, Hannah, and Aaron then excused themselves, explaining they had had enough excitement for one day. They gave us both a big hug, thanked us for a memorable time, and wished us a good night. After they had departed, Master Taylor suggested we end the day observing one last tradition—pulling on our coats, stepping out onto the porch, and lighting a cigar to the future.

Lying in the dark staring out into the spangled night, I focused on Reverend Woodburn's unusual Christmas sermon. The pastor did his parishioners a good deed that day. At the beginning I didn't know where he was going. Hebrews 6 as a text for a Christmas message? I suspect few clergymen have risked that before. So I wished I'd done right by the pastor that day—thanked him for the sermon and praised his courage. He was on the right track. The passage haunted me. I repeated it over and over in my mind all day: "Lay hold upon the hope set before us, which hope we have as an anchor of the soul."

And I also accepted the message Master Taylor was conveying. Comparing the lusty squire to the parson—what was it he called the minister?—"the little dark anatomy of a man." Irving presenting two paths, one flourishing in prosperity and sunshine, the other withering among dusty tomes in silence and the shadows. Opposite points of view—day and night. Master Taylor was pointing us to the light with his rising voice at the end of Irving's sketch, saying, "If, however, I can by any lucky chance, in these days of evil, rub out one wrinkle from the brow of care or beguile the heavy heart of one moment of sorrow . . . surely, surely, I shall not then have written entirely in vain."

I suspect Master Taylor had drawn the same conclusion as the reverend. He was echoing the message in Hebrews 6, "Lay hold upon the hope set before us, which hope we have as an anchor of the soul." So I was not alone. I had been preaching that gospel in my office since the beginning of November. Things had changed, but in some ways they stayed the same—I no longer made the daily rounds trying desperately to treat the yellow jack. No. I spent most of my time in the office treating broken hearts. Just as daunting a task as the yellow jack, just as lethal, and all I had to offer them was hope.

15

Once the holidays had passed the living buried themselves in work to ease the pain. And it was no different for the Taylors. After Aaron left for Nashville and Amanda started her new job, Master Taylor eagerly returned to his beloved academy and Hannah spent her waking hours running the household and caring for Lil' Jim. But it was different for me. There was no way to escape the unrelenting sadness of the past few months. My patients were there every day to remind me of their suffering and loss.

Believing there's truth to the proverb, "Physician, heal thyself," I made a New Year's resolution to "live in the sunshine" and "rub out the wrinkles in my brow." I would live as if I knew I was dying. I made it a point to set an example for my patients and get involved in as many outside activities as I could—attending everything from operas and concerts to lectures and political speeches. But it wasn't always about something edifying or enlightening. I also had the sweet diversions of Mardi Gras, the German Fest, vaudeville, and the minstrel shows.

And I must confess every time Aaron came to town, we spent our evenings at Assembly Hall attending the touring girlie shows—three in the first four months of the year. Two can-cans and one classical statuary production. How could I ever forget the performances—*Naughty Blondes, Forbidden Pleasures*, and *Female Bathers*? Or forget the casts—the Parisian Red Stocking Blondes and the New York Statuary Troupe, which had to get a court order to continue performing? But having experienced the troupe's questionable show before legal notice was served, Aaron and I vehemently disagreed with the police board's decision to deem their presentation "vulgar."

Conversations around the dinner table also helped us climb out of the past. "I was down at the wharves under the bluffs today," Master Taylor said. "You should see how private business is picking up despite the financial mess looming in the city. The river's full of boats and barges piled high with freight and cotton. And hundreds of drays and wagons are waiting at dockside to carry all the goods inland."

"No wonder," I responded. "I've heard the cotton exchange has reopened with very brisk trading, and the iron and leather works are really starting to hum again."

"There's another sign too," Hannah suggested. "Humor's returning to the newspapers. The *Avalanche* has resumed printing 'The Matinee.'"

"'The Matinee'?" I asked.

"It's a daily column reporting the afternoon sessions of the police court. I tell you, there are a lot of strange things happening in Memphis. And, Father, I know you've read recent editorials in the *Avalanche*. They're back up on their hobbyhorse decrying the 'tramp nuisance.'"

"I don't know why they keep that up," Master Taylor replied. "The floating class isn't going to just get up and go away. The more they fight the drifters, the more they dig in. It's just human nature. Even the fever couldn't drive the tramps away. They might as well face it. New Orleans and Memphis have become resort destinations for the country's vagabonds.

"Oh, by the way, Thomas, there's a real twist of irony in *The Appeal* today. I'll just label it 'humor' to stay within the bounds of the current conversation. But *The Appeal* is quoting the Hartford papers saying the major life insurance companies won't be taking huge losses here after all."

"How could that be with over five thousand dead?" Amanda asked.

"While the poor folk stayed and died, the rich with the life insurance policies fled the city and lived," Master Taylor explained. "So no death, no claim, and thus no losses for the insurance companies. I guess in an odd way it's good news all the way around . . . except for the poor."

"Yes, except for all the poor we buried in potter's fields," I thought. "Hidden away en masse outside the city before the respectable rich returned."

As spring eased into summer, our dinner conversations became more relaxed—less about the scourge and its impact and more about simple everyday life. "I left the academy early this afternoon," Master Taylor said. "You and Lil' Jim weren't here when I got home. I guess the two of you were out gallivanting about."

"Father, just try to guess what we were up to?"

"I haven't the faintest idea. What'd you do?"

"Well, Thomas saw his last patient at noon. He came

home, and we took Lil' Jim to a baseball game. A first for all of us."

"It was Aaron's idea," I interjected. "When he was here last time, he suggested we go. Said it was all the rage back East."

"Who was playing?"

"Our new team, the Memphis Reds, was hosting the Indianapolis Blues. Both teams are in the new Alliance League."

"Well, that sounds like fun. Where do they play?" Master Taylor asked.

"Central Park," Hannah responded. "And we were so close to the players. Lil' Jim even got to talk with some of 'em. They were just as nice as could be."

"Not surprising when the boy has a pretty mother," I said smilingly.

"Now, Thomas, flattery will get you everywhere," she laughed. "But seriously, do you remember any of the names?"

"I just remember a Doc Kennedy and a Billy Redmond, I think it was. Hard to get all their names. None of 'em were locals. They were from everywhere—Brooklyn, Saint Louis, Charleston, Holyoke."

"I couldn't believe they were catching that ball with their bare hands," Hannah said. "It must have really stung."

"I believe a few of them had fingerless leather gloves," I said. "But you're right; most of them were using their bare hands. And the ball was really flying off the bats. And you should have seen those bats, Master Taylor. Every shape imaginable—cylindrical, flat, long, short, thick, thin. They were trying anything and everything to get an edge."

"How'd Lil' Jim like baseball?" Master Taylor asked. His eyes were bright with excitement.

"You know how he is when he's outside, Father. He couldn't stay still. He wanted to move around. So we just let him run about nearby. He would stop by for a play or two, and then he'd be back off to the races."

"Well, I guess I should ask the most important question. Who won?"

"We did!" Hannah exclaimed. "I believe it was five runs to four. It really got exciting toward the end."

Hannah excused herself a minute so she could bring out the chess pie she made that morning. After she served us each a large piece of pie, Amanda picked up the thread of the conversation. "So, Father, you said you came home early today from the academy. What were you up to?"

"Oh, spending a few quiet hours preparing for Emma's birthday tomorrow. I feel a bit closer to her when I'm tending her gardenias and four o'clocks. She loved being out there in her 'Garden of Eden.' She said the fragrance and color brought her a little closer to heaven. So I've always imagined that by tending the flowers, it brings me a bit closer to her. And with the rough weather we've had this past winter, the perfume and colors are so much more intense than usual. Perhaps a harbinger of good things to come."

"Let's pray so," Amanda said. "Let's really pray so."

But it wouldn't be long before we realized our prayers would go unanswered. The Memphis Reds would announce they were suspending their season, and the stench of the fever fires would once again overwhelm the heady scent of Mrs. Taylor's Eden. This time there would be no omen and no frontal assault. It would all start so quietly—sharpshooters targeting individuals within households and picking off specific families within neighborhoods—guerrillas choosing their targets carefully.

Our relaxed dinner discussions ended abruptly in early July just before the word got out and the real panic set in again. During our customary evening meal, Master Taylor described a conversation he'd just had with a Howard Association official and a prominent member of the Board of Health. Master Taylor's foreboding words sent shivers through us. "What I'm about to tell you is not to frighten you but to help you prepare for what may be coming. But remember, nothing's for sure yet."

"Sounds ominous, Father," Hannah said. "What is it?"

"Well, after finishing up at the academy this afternoon, I dropped by the Howard office to visit old friends. As it turned out, Vice President Smith was the only person there. After chatting a few minutes, Dr. Burton from the Board of Health stopped in to ask the association to begin planning for contingencies. The doctor explained they had received a report on the eighth that a cobbler had come down with a fever."

"Where'd the fellow live?" I asked.

"Believe he said DeSoto Street in the Sixth Ward."

"How's the cobbler doing now, Father?" Amanda asked.

"Dr. Burton said, unfortunately, the poor man died the following day."

"Let's not jump to conclusions," I said, trying to ease everyone's fears. "It may have been something other than the jack. With the filthy conditions around here, it could have been almost anything."

"I wish that were the case, Thomas; but Dr. Burton said he and several colleagues immediately performed an autopsy. They determined it was the scourge without question. They concluded the cobbler must've taken ill sometime around the fourth."

"That's only one infected," I soothed. "And that could be the end of it."

And for a second time Master Taylor politely debunked my optimism. "I wish that were the case, Thomas. But Dr. Burton said they've now received five additional reports of the fever. So that makes a total of six cases in various locations in three different wards. As I said, the cobbler was on DeSoto in the Sixth Ward. Three more people were in one house on Wellington in the Tenth Ward. Those two houses are both in South Memphis. There were also two patients on Bradford Street in the Eighth Ward, which is in the most northeastern part of the city. Dr. Burton said the Bradford Street house is at least a mile away from the other two residences. None of these five new cases was reported before today because the attending physicians weren't sure of their diagnoses and they were unaware of the newly infected households in the other wards."

"Could these people have worked at the same place?" I asked. "Met at church or during a social function?"

"Smith and I asked that very question. Dr. Burton said they'd uncovered no known interaction between any of these people—neither commercially nor socially. And while they all appeared to have been infected at the same time, there was no indication they'd been infected by the same agent in the same location. Dr. Burton said they even looked at the remote possibility that the attending physicians spread the disease. But each of the households had a different doctor, and none of the physicians had had any physical communication with any of the others.

"Dr. Burton said he agreed to speak with the *Avalanche* yesterday evening. He and his colleagues on the Board of Heath had two objectives for the interview: first, to rightfully inform the public of the cobbler's death, and secondly, to tamp down the wave of anxiety the doctors expected would flood Memphis and beyond."

"With what the city's endured in the past year, tamping down the anxiety sounds like a tall order to me," I said. "I sure wouldn't want that job. Did the doctor say how they proposed to relieve people's fears?"

"Dr. Burton said he and his colleagues prepared a fact sheet overnight to help the reporter with the breaking news for this afternoon's paper. The briefing document supposedly indicated the Board of Health had performed an autopsy on the cobbler and had concluded it was probably a 'sporadic' case caused by germs, which had overwintered in some old clothing. The cobbler had apparently taken some clothes from his in-laws' house after they'd died during the scourge last September. In addition, the doctors theorized that the weakened "sporads" were unlikely to reproduce and cause another widespread epidemic."

"But how could they say that knowing they were already dealing with five more cases?" Hannah asked.

"It turns out Dr. Burton and his colleagues were unaware of the five new infections when they drafted the briefing document and Dr. Burton gave the interview to the newspaper. They just learned about the five new cases today."

"What do you think we should do, Father?" Amanda asked.

"I don't think we're nearly to the point of doing anything. But I'll keep my ear to the ground. I'll drop by the Howard office every day, and I promise to keep y'all posted. I won't keep anything from you."

By the morning of the eleventh the word had spread about the five new cases in the eighth and tenth wards, thus nullifying Dr. Burton's reassurances published on the tenth. Knowing strict quarantines would be imposed once the news had reached surrounding towns, anxious citizens immediately surged for the exits, clogging streets, swarming wharves, and overloading outbound trains.

Master Taylor kept his promise and reported daily at dinner; but ironically, he had nothing new to report until almost a week later, when he revealed, "They had word at the association this afternoon that some cases of fever have cropped up on the outskirts."

"Any connection with the cases reported earlier in the month?" I inquired.

"Not that they know of, Thomas. According to the Howards, these folk pretty much stayed to themselves."

"But how could this be, Father?" Amanda asked. "How

can the scourge be spreading, if none of these people have come into contact with each other?"

"No one knows for sure. According to the Howards, the only clue they have is that all these houses were infected last year."

"But how could these people be getting infected when the fever died out eight or nine months ago?"

"To be honest, Amanda, no one knows for sure," Master Taylor replied. "There's all kinds of speculation. Some of the experts believe the germs wintered over in the furniture, the carpets, or in the walls. But all the homeowners claim their houses were thoroughly ventilated and exposed to the harsh weather of last winter. And they claim they also used artificial means of disinfection on top of the standard ventilation. On the other hand, there are others who think the answer lies in the bedding or clothing. They argue that the house theory loses some credibility because, for example, the houses on DeSoto, Wellington, and Bradford Streets were unoccupied during the epidemic. So it's hard to pin the cause on house infection. They contend it has something to do with clothing or bedding."

"That gets us back to the cobbler theory and the in-laws' infected clothing," Amanda said, frustrated.

"From what I can gather the preponderance of evidence points more toward the bedding than the clothing," Master Taylor responded. "Apparently several of the infected households purchased secondhand bedding after returning home safely from the camps. But regardless of its origin, I hope the jack doesn't eventually cause a full-blown panic like last year, which shut the city down for over three months. I believe that's what finally broke the camel's back and pushed Memphis over the bluffs into bankruptcy."

"Well, after the initial exodus on the eleventh, things have settled down a bit," I said and then suggested, "I guess it was the lack of new infections after the tenth that helped calm folks down."

"And don't forget my friends at the Howards," Master Taylor added. "They've been doing a good job helping the newspapers quash rumors that could lead to panic. There was an article in the *Avalanche* yesterday in which the superintendent of the municipal cemetery denied allegations that politicians were pressuring him to sneak scourge victims into his graveyard after dark to ease public anxiety and help save the business district from further ruin."

"I sure hope these new cases in the suburbs don't wreck everything now," I said. "You never know what's gonna tip the scale."

But toward the end of the month, we realized the scales had tipped when Master Taylor returned home from the Howards and joined us for dinner. We knew even before he'd uttered a word. His shoulders were slumped, his face drained of color, and his usual optimistic demeanor had disappeared.

"Father, what's wrong?" Hannah asked. "Tell us."

"I'm sorry, children. The news isn't good. . . . Dr. Burton dropped by the Howard office this morning. Said the Board of Health had reports of fifty new cases of jack scattered all around the city. Dr. Burton also had a friend with him from the wire services. And after the doctor had finished with the details, his journalist friend piled on with one negative editorial after another from out-of-town newspapers. So it's pretty clear that once the citizens learn about the new cases and read what the big-city editors are saying, it'll be Katy bar the door."

"What are the foreign papers saying, Father?" Amanda asked.

"Too much," Master Taylor said. "Dr. Burton's friend whipped out his notebook and reeled off a number of quotes. I can't remember all of them or precisely what they said, but I remember things like 'citizens of Memphis should drop their theories and run for the hills' and 'imagine the commercial ruin that will follow in the wake of terror, disease and death' and 'the yellow fever germ has become "naturalized" in Memphis, and this trouble of quarantining the city will have to be continued from year to year.' And if those weren't bad enough, other papers wrote 'Memphis is bankrupt in purse; about the only thing left for the citizens to do is desert the city' and 'Memphis is doomed. Yellow fever is there and means to stay there. There's nothing for the people to do but leave.'"

With those words hanging in the air, Master Taylor glanced over at Amanda and Hannah and then delicately segued into the painful discussion of leaving Memphis and returning to the camps. "Over at the Howards this afternoon I heard they're opening up several new encampments. What do you think, Hannah, about taking Lil' Jim and going out to one of the new sites? The Howards told me they're in perfect locations—lots of shade, plenty of soft spring water, good drainage, and very near a supply depot and the trains."

Hannah didn't hesitate and responded decisively, "No. Not this time, Father. Not this time. All the while I was in the camp last summer I regretted not being here to help out as I had in '73. I had a lot of experience treating the jack, and there I was sitting out there sipping coffee and feeling useless. No. Not this time."

Trying to play devil's advocate delicately, Master Taylor responded calmly, "If you're out of the house nursing patients, who's gonna take care of Lil' Jim? I'm pretty sure Thomas will be out treating people, and I'll be back at the Howard office working my usual hours."

Before Hannah could respond, Amanda jumped in, "I'll take care of Lil' Jim during the day and work at the Howards' distribution depot at night. Back before I went away to Mary Sharp in '73, I offered to stay home and help out until the spring semester. But being the loving father you are, you insisted on putting me on the first train to Winchester. . . . None of you can imagine the guilt I felt reading the dispatches coming out of Memphis. I was living the safe, comfortable life of a student, while all of you were here risking everything to fight the scourge."

After these spontaneous revelations of raw truth, everyone at the table retreated to introspection and an awkward silence. Trying to ease the palpable tension in the room, I observed lightly, "Well, Master Taylor, it looks like we have a plan. That sure didn't take long." As I glanced around the dinner table smiling nervously, I whispered to myself, "The die is cast. Please keep 'em all safe from harm."

16

WE WERE LIVING out the Lord's prophecy that the poor would always be with us. As Master Taylor had predicted, once the newspapers reported the fifty new cases and printed the foreign editors' advice, the well heeled who hadn't fled during the first wave of panic flocked to the wharves and the rails. According to the Superintendent of Camps' published report, there were forty thousand inhabitants before the scourge began; and by the end of July, only thirteen thousand of the poorest of the poor remained behind in Memphis.

Having never experienced our hell on earth, Amanda had the most difficulty adjusting to the empty streets, the stench, the blood-curdling screams, and the thick, choking fires. At first she teetered on the edge of despair. All we could do was encourage her to focus on the depot and Lil' Jim and reassure her that the anxiety, the nausea, and the nightmares would gradually disappear.

And we practiced what we preached. We buried ourselves in our assignments. It was as if we'd never been away. The instinctive words, thoughts, and movements were all still there in the mind and in the muscles. But while Master Taylor and I had resumed our medical and administrative duties, Hannah had branched out into a new career.

Only days after our watershed conversation at dinner, Hannah slipped out of the house and walked up Gayoso Street, climbed the stairs of the familiar three-story Mansion House, and knocked on the heavy door. She asked to speak with Anna, who had inherited Miss Cook's enterprise to become the "sole proprietor and purveyor" of the "best services east of the Mississippi." After reminiscing several minutes about Miss Cook's courage, Hannah eased the conversation into a proposal. She argued that because of this latest scourge, the bagnio's revenues would quickly dry up; that Anna could buy a lot of goodwill temporarily converting the establishment into a hospital; and that if Miss Cook were alive today, she would most certainly follow the path she'd taken in both '73 and '78.

Within minutes Hannah convinced the madam "to do the right thing." And when Anna admitted she and her "associates" would stick to the nursing and leave "running the operation" to someone else, Hannah immediately stepped in, offered to assume a leadership role, and willingly became Miss Cook's successor as the second director of the Mansion House Hospital on Gayoso Street.

Dinner that evening was as if we were playing a hand of pinochle or euchre. Each of us had a story to tell, and each of us trumped the last tale told. Master Taylor played the first card of the hand. "Over at the Howards, we're getting strong commitments from out-of-state doctors and nurses just like last year. And the pledges of money and goods are substantial as well. Shows people outside Memphis haven't forgotten us."

Next, Amanda corroborated Master Taylor's observation

and moved the conversation from theory to fact. "Yes, we're already seeing the fulfillment of those pledges at the depot. Over sixty thousand dollars in donations so far, from everywhere—Illinois, New York, Louisiana—and from everyone—individuals, volunteer fire companies, breweries. And the contributions of food, clothing, and medical supplies have been overwhelming. To be honest with y'all, I didn't know whether I'd like the work at the distribution center; but once the goods started rolling in, I realized we were surely doing the Lord's work, doing our best to relieve the suffering."

After a brief pause, Master Taylor prompted Hannah to play her card. "You were up and out of the house mighty early this morning, my dear," Master Taylor observed. And based on years of interaction with Master Taylor, everyone at the table knew his observation was actually a veiled question, "Hannah, what in the world are you up to now?"

Her lips curved into an ambiguous smile. Was she reacting to her father's artful question? Acknowledging she was holding a high card? Or was she signaling both? Well, knowing Hannah, I predicted both; and as she began responding, a wave of smug self-satisfaction spread over me. I instinctively knew where this was going as she replied, "I walked up to Gayoso Street, up to Miss Cook's old place."

"My God, Hannah, I hear it's a brothel again!" Master Taylor exclaimed.

"No, Father. It's the Mansion House Hospital again."

"How do you know that for sure? I've spoken with a lot of Howard physicians, and none has mentioned a conversion. When did this supposedly happen?"

Hannah and I knowingly smiled at each other as she replied, "Today, Father."

"Okay, so who told you?"

"The new director."

"And who might that be? What's his name?"

Hannah's widening smile broke into rare laughter as she paused, allowing the suspense to build.

Still skeptical, Master Taylor repeated his question, "Well, child, what's the new director's name?"

"It's Hannah, Father. Hannah Taylor." She then proceeded to explain to her stunned sister and father how in less than an hour, she had become director of one of the most respected fever hospitals in Memphis.

Once Hannah had played her memorable jack of hearts, everyone looked my way as if silently challenging me to top the last card played. I knew it would be difficult. What I had to play was certainly newsworthy but not the kind of good news the others had offered. So I opened hesitantly, "When I went to the office this morning, Doc Landrum said he had disturbing information from some of the towns east of Memphis. Explained an old brother in arms, Colonel Miller, another physician in Johnston's Army of the Mississippi, had telegraphed him from Warfield. Described a worsening situation there—so far, nine houses and thirty-five cases of fever in Warfield; twenty-eight cases in McGill; and seven in the hamlet of Hurricane Creek. Colonel Miller's telegram was an urgent appeal for help. They need a physician with experience treating the fever to help school the towns' doctors. Doc said he felt compelled to honor the colonel's request; after all, he had been through the worst with his soldier friend at Shiloh, Chickamauga, and Cold Harbor.

"But we all know Doc's getting up in age and is in constant pain with his back and knees . . . so I offered to go in his place. Let Doc stay here and break in some of the out-of-state volunteers. But to be honest, it's also kind of personal for me. I still have distant relatives out that way and most of my immediate family is buried near Warfield. Mother, father, brother . . . I know what they'd want me to do—help the family and our old friends."

A quick look around the table convinced me I'd won the hand. But I could tell immediately it was a pyrrhic victory. Their expressions betrayed their reactions to my plans—surprise, confusion, a sense of abandonment, a premonition, and even a genuine fear for my safety. They saw a lose-lose proposition: I was leaving them here to fight their battle, while racing off to face a potent new scourge with an army of poorly trained doctors and nurses. But to their credit, they quickly came around, accepted my decision, and praised my willingness to help those in need.

The evening before leaving Memphis, I spent two precious hours alone with my beautiful Hannah. Well, not exactly alone. It's true we were outside the house away from the family. But we spent most of the time in the carriage traveling from the Mansion House Hospital to the Nashville & Northwestern depot and then slowly circling back again, taking the long route home while whispering our love for each other and for our dear son, our Lil' Jim.

We could thank the Tennessee Board of Health for making our public tryst possible. Early on in that year's epidemic, the regulators had struck a compromise with the business community. The health officials agreed to restore train service between Memphis and other municipalities but in return insisted on implementing a complex system of inspections and train relays to protect passengers and citizens in towns beyond the city. One of the board's restrictions required me to drop off my valise and doctor's bag at the disinfecting station at least twelve hours before my train departed.

The following morning, Master Taylor hitched up the mares and drove the whole family to the depot, where I purchased a ticket and learned I couldn't board the train for another half hour. The agent said the Nashville & Northwestern was following the spirit and the letter of the law. The Board of Heath demanded the railroads scrupulously fumigate all the passenger cars with sulfur and then seal them up tightly for at least six hours before stowing the baggage and loading the passengers.

So as Mama used to say, "Just in case something happens to one of us," we spent that last half hour on an almost empty platform superstitiously and nervously tying up loose ends and saying our good-byes. I first turned to Master Taylor. "As we discussed last night, you'll see to it that a healthy number of Howard volunteers show up to help Doc with the extra load?"

"Rest assured, Thomas, I won't let Doc down. I'll make sure he gets some of the best volunteer doctors and nurses. You just concern yourself with getting back home safely. No chances, Thomas, you hear? The word's out; the scourge out that way is virulent."

Glancing around the small arc of relatives, lover, and friends, I replied smilingly, "No chances, Master Taylor, I promise. There's so much to live for right here."

I next turned to Amanda with some brotherly advice. "No matter how bad it gets here, persevere. There's no denying how tough it is at the beginning. But keep reminding yourself of all the good you're doing. Keep telling yourself 'everything will soon be back to normal and I'll be teaching the girls at Miss Conway's again.'"

I then reached down, picked Lil' Jim up, and straddled him on my hip. "Boy, you take care of your mama, your grandpa, and Aunt Amanda. When I get back home I promise we'll go see the Memphis Reds again." There was so much more a father should say. But how could I say it without betraying Hannah, confusing Lil' Jim, enraging Master Taylor, and permanently driving myself out of the family? As I lowered my son back down, I hugged him tightly and whispered, "I love you, boy."

He murmured back quickly in a boyish tone, "I love you too, Thomas."

Hannah and I pushed our inevitable good-bye off until the trainman called the "All aboard." As we hugged, I slipped my mother's locket into her hand and murmured its hidden inscription, "My heart's where my home is." I held her out discreetly at arm's length for only a second or two, but long enough to gaze into her eyes and silently convey, "So long. Stay safe. And pray for an early frost."

The conductor walked toward the rear of the train shouting, "All aboard! Last call!" I reluctantly turned away, climbed the steps, and chose a seat on the platform side of the car. I waved to the Taylors huddling as if they were posing for a portrait. I centered them within my mind's eye and snapped the shutter. More daguerreotype than photograph. The sulfur disinfectant had coated the windowpane blurring their lines and producing a copper patina. As the brakes released and the wheels began turning, I remember thinking, "There. I have it now—an unyielding memento, a whisper in thunder, till the day of our dying."

17

WE RAN THE gauntlet to Warfield. Only five miles out of Memphis the brakes screeched and the bunching cars produced a loud wave of clanking. As we slowed to a stop, the conductor passed through our car instructing us to collect our belongings, exit the coach, and submit to interviews by sanitary inspectors. Once we had been thoroughly interrogated about where we had been, where we were going. and the status of our general health, we were permitted to climb aboard a second set of "clean" cars parked on the siding. After finishing our interviews, the health officials then spent the better part of an hour combing through the stowed freight and baggage, which they felt posed the greater threat of infection.

Believing we had finally escaped the board's strict regulations, we settled into sleeping, reading, or conversing with fellow passengers until we heard the screeching of the brakes as we approached a second transfer point fifty miles east in the middle of nowhere. Our apologetic conductor passed through the coach again and promised emphatically this would be the final checkpoint before reaching Warfield.

This inspection went so much more quickly than the last. There were far fewer questions, and I would describe the examination of the freight as "cursory" at best. The emphasis this time appeared to be on the transfer part of the process. Out of an abundance of caution with little regard for scheduling, the state officials decreed passengers should board a third set of "clean" cars to complete their journey. So thirty minutes after boarding for a third time, we rolled off the siding and once again steamed toward my old hometown.

When the conductor moved through the coach announcing "Warfield, five minutes, Warfield," I pulled the piece of paper from my vest pocket on which Doc had scribbled the names of my hosts, a Reverend William Emmett and his wife, Clara. Doc explained they resided in a spacious parsonage ideally situated in Hurricane Creek equidistant from Warfield and McGill. Since Doc assured me the reverend would be on the platform to greet me, I spent those last five minutes rehearsing a sincere apology for arriving almost two hours late.

I stepped off the train, retrieved my baggage, and began walking toward the familiar terminal with my doctor's bag in one hand and my valise in the other. As I approached the depot, a tall, bearded fifty-year-old moved out of the shadows and extended his hand to help me with my luggage, "Doc Thomas?"

And before I could inquire how he knew who I was, he anticipated my question, smiled, and pointed to my black leather bag. We shared a laugh and then he said, "Here, let me help you with your suitcase. Follow me. We'll go through the depot. The missus and I have been waiting for you there."

"I'm sorry we're so late," I interjected. "The Board of Health set up two checkpoints outside Memphis. Changed trains twice, one inspection at five miles and another at fifty."

Reverend Emmett patted me on the shoulder and replied, "Don't fret yourself, Thomas. The missus and I took advantage of the opportunity and discussed the gospel with several folk in the waiting room. And Lord willing, I think Clara and I have at least two converts to our church—the local ticket agent and a McGill undertaker, who'd come to greet a new recruit. Sorry to say, morticians are in great demand here just now." He lowered his voice and continued, "And God forgive me for saying this, but since the scourge hit hard around Warfield, bringing people to Jesus has been pretty easy. People are willing to listen to the scriptures when death's knocking on all the doors around them."

I followed the reverend into the waiting room, where we found a noticeably younger Clara sharing the gospel with a handsome fellow and his equally striking friend. One look at these attentive bucks eagerly conversing with this beautiful woman told me their interest was far more about sinning than salvation. And understandably so; her beauty was indeed breathtaking. She was about five and a half feet tall with blue-gray almond-shaped eyes and long, chestnut-brown curls cascading down over her shoulders. She was wearing a chocolate-brown taffeta bustle gown with a matching bonnet firmly positioned at the back of her head with thick silk ties.

Sensing either a threat to his marriage or a waste of his wife's time, Reverend Emmett politely interrupted the conversation, introduced me to Clara, and suggested we leave immediately for the parsonage. When we reached the open carriage, the reverend helped Clara get settled in the backseat and then signaled I should join him up on the driver's bench for the ride out to Hurricane Creek. He unhitched the mare and then climbed aboard.

Once we'd reached the outskirts where the mare could have free rein, the reverend turned and expressed his thanks on behalf of the surrounding communities. "Let me say right up front, Doc, we all really appreciate your offering to come out and help train the local doctors. And I mean that's every-body—everybody from Warfield to McGill and from Cam-den to Hurricane Creek."

"It's nothing, Reverend. I'm happy to oblige. I grew up out this way. . . . I have distant relatives still farming east of here on the Nashville highway, and my immediate family's all buried there on my cousins' farm."

"Well then, welcome home, Doc. Welcome home." He paused for several seconds signaling a change of subject. "Just so you'll know the immediate plans, we've called a general meeting for nine o'clock tomorrow morning with all the phy-sicians in a twenty-mile radius of here. It'll be out at our church next to the parsonage. We'll introduce you, have you describe your past, and then get the physicians' ideas on how best to tap your experience. I'm sure you'll have a lot of knowledge to impart, having battled the scourge—what did Doc Landrum say?—in '73, '78, and now again for the past month this year? I guess you've seen everything there is to see."

Fearing I might frighten him or undercut my credibility I deflected his question. "There was a lot to see. But, Reverend, I think we need to focus on the conditions here. What's the latest total you have on the sick and the dead? That'll give me a better idea how to respond to questions at the meeting tomorrow morning."

"Well, today's paper said we're now up to seventy-seven cases in Warfield, forty-three in McGill, and twelve in Hurricane Creek. The numbers seem to be growing daily."

"Deaths?"

"I believe the number was twenty-three up to now. It's hard to keep up with the news. I've been going from morning to night, comforting the sick, burying the dead, and consoling the bereaved. In our church alone we've had something like twenty come down with the fever, and I know four of our brothers and sisters have died. It's awfully hard sharing the suffering, but I'm sure you know there's more to it. Living with the fear that any day you or a loved one will come down with the scourge. You've lived it, being in the houses of the sick and dying every day. And on top of all that, Clara and I have to think about the orphanages."

"The orphanages?"

"Yes, we and our sister churches sponsor three asylums, one in northeast Memphis, another in Jackson, and one in nearby Camden. They've been a real challenge for us, especially beginning last year. . . . Well, you know how it was in Memphis. We quickly ran out of space. It was heartbreaking. We first tried placing recent orphans with the other Memphis asylums, but they were all facing the same situation we were. I believe St. Peter's was up to a hundred children. Leath Asylum and St. Mary's each had seventy in their care, and the Hebrew orphanage had quickly reached its maximum of forty. So what to do? . . . We knew we couldn't abandon the children.

So one of our elders came up with the idea of moving the overflow out to Jackson. That worked for a month or so, until Jackson was filled with Memphis orphans. So we brought the remainder of the children out here to nearby Camden. And I'm proud to say by the end of last year we'd found space for every one of the orphans we knew about and still had a few beds to spare.

"But the question we're going to have to face now is, how can we continue bringing Memphis orphans out to Camden when we can expect to see an increase in the number of orphans from around Warfield, McGill, and Hurricane Creek? With all the traveling I've been doing since the fever hit, I've had to depend on Clara to keep me posted on what's happening over at the Camden Asylum. She's been going over there almost every day to help out."

He glanced back toward his wife, smiled, and added, "She's even been talking about bringing several of the children home to live with us permanently at the parsonage. She says she wants a few of the orphans to live out the promises of Jeremiah. It's a favorite passage she quotes frequently: 'For I know the plans I have for you . . . plans to prosper you and not to harm you, plans to give you hope and a future.'

"I tell ya, we've been lucky so far. Our problem's always been finding space for the Memphis orphans. We've never had to deal with the fever at our asylums."

"That's been pretty much the case with all the orphanages in Memphis too," I said. "Very little yellow jack even among the fever orphans. I can only think of one orphanage, and I knew the doctor who was involved there. Canfield Asylum.

Served mainly Negro children run by the Anglican sisters. I believe they took in around forty children, bathed them in a carbolic acid solution and dressed them in clean clothes. For some reason two of the children got the scourge, and then one after another the sisters and the children fell victim to the jack. I believe all but four of the orphans became ill, and twenty-two of them died. Sad to say most of the volunteer sisters from New York died too. But rest assured the Canfield Asylum was a rarity. Never heard of anything else like it around Memphis."

"I guess all we can do is put our faith in the Lord's promise, 'Whoever receives one such child in my name receives me.'"

"No argument from me about that, Reverend. You and your wife are doing the Lord's work. You've received hundreds in his name."

During our meeting the following morning, the local doctors suggested we assemble once more during the week to complete the yellow fever overview. And then after that, they believed I should be on call to accompany them to their patients' homes to consult on the most difficult cases. Ironically, once we implemented the physicians' plan, I rarely saw my hosts. In fact, over the next two weeks I moved across the territory from patient to patient and stayed at the parsonage only once.

But everything changed in mid-September when I received the reverend's urgent message to return to Hurricane Creek as soon as possible. When I arrived back at the parsonage, Reverend Emmett relayed the disturbing news. "When

Clara was last here she mentioned a volunteer nurse at the asylum had come down with the fever. She said it seemed like a mild case. Probably infected before starting work at the orphanage. Clara then wrote late last week saying a second nurse had taken ill and that four of the children were now showing signs."

"Did she describe the symptoms?"

"Clara said it was different for each of them. While the nurses and the children all had a fever, some had a headache and vomiting and others had seizures, red eyes, and bloody noses."

"I need to get over to Camden as soon as possible. Do you have a fresh mare I can borrow?"

"Absolutely. Anything else?"

"No. Just saddle the mare while I pack some clean clothes."

When I met the reverend at the barn after packing, he confided, "I'm really worried about Clara, Doc. She's been staying day in and day out at the asylum. I'm afraid she's more likely to get sick because of the increased exposure."

"Not necessarily the case, Reverend. Look at me. I've been at this since '73. And so far so good. But, Reverend, I'll do everything I can to keep her safe. No unnecessary chances. If I can persuade her . . ."

"Knowing my Clara, don't waste your time, Doc. I'll depend on faith and prayer to protect her."

"Not bad antidotes for our fears, Reverend." I climbed up into the saddle and added, "And stay busy doing the Lord's work."

I pulled on the reins and sped west toward Camden.

When I got to the asylum, I hitched the mare and rushed into the building. The hallways were empty. I began moving from door to door on the first floor trying to find a doctor or a nurse. There was no one to be found. I discovered a stairwell, quickly climbed the steps, and opened the door to chaos. My senses were immediately assaulted. There were children lying in the hallway writhing. The taste and stench of fresh vomit permeated the air. Shrill screams and loud moans echoed along the corridors. The children's dormitory had become a madhouse.

After absorbing the shock, I resumed my search; and when I popped my head into the third room, I found a young volunteer lying diagonally across a child's bed, suffering from the jack.

"Miss, miss. Can you hear me? I'm a doctor. I've come here to help. I'm looking for a volunteer from Hurricane Creek. Clara, a Clara Emmett. Have you seen her today? Do you know where she is?"

The woman was obviously in a great deal of pain. She had pulled her knees up near her chest. She was moaning.

"If you can hear me, please tell me if you know where Clara Emmett is. I promise you I will come back to help you. I just need to speak with Ms. Emmett."

The moaning ceased. The nurse raised her head from the pillow and tried speaking. I leaned closer to hear, but her words were unintelligible.

I tried again. "I'm sorry. Do you know where Clara Emmett is?"

She partially opened her eyes, mumbled, and then slowly pointed skyward.

A surge of adrenalin raced through me as I first interpreted her signal to mean Clara was in heaven. But when I remembered seeing a third floor on the building, I quickly realized she was conveying a less profound but highly useful message.

"Clara's upstairs, miss?"

The young woman nodded.

As I turned to exit the room, I assured her, "I'll be back to treat you. I promise."

I raced down the corridor, found the staircase, and climbed the steps to the third floor. Unlike the hell I'd just passed through, the scene on the top level was eerily peaceful. There was still an acrid odor, but it was quiet, and there were no children lying in the hallways. I turned to my right and headed for the first room. I looked in and found a child sleeping peacefully. When I turned to move on to the next door, a voice rang out from across the corridor. "Doc Thomas, is that you?"

Clara was standing in the doorway holding some soiled bed linens.

"Thank God! I've been looking for you everywhere. Why don't you finish what you're doing, and then let's step outside for a few minutes to talk. I'll be waiting for you out front after I attend to a young nurse on the second floor."

Thirty minutes later Clara found me sitting on a log bench overlooking the rolling front lawn. As she approached, I instinctively rose and embraced her.

"Thank God you've come, Doc. This is as close to hell as it gets on earth. We're doing as much as we can; but the nurses and the children are all getting sick and dying. We're overwhelmed. We haven't slept in days."

"I'll be here to help you until the frost breaks the siege. Tell me what's been going on so I can get us some reinforcements? How many children do you have here right now?"

"We've lost some, Doc. . . . We're down to around fifty-four."

"How many have the fever now?"

"Close to half."

"How many healthy nurses?"

"I believe around six."

"Doctors?"

"They get here at most twice a week. You know they're besieged, Doc. Everyone in the county needs them right now."

"The second floor . . ."

"I know, Doc; as I said, we're overwhelmed."

"No offense, Clara. I wasn't being critical. Just trying to get the lay of the land so I can get to work on more volunteers."

"What are you going to do?"

"Wire a close friend at the Howard Association, see if Memphis can free up some doctors and nurses to help us out. The fever hasn't been as widespread there this year. In the meantime, we'll have to make do. But it'd sure be nice to get some experienced volunteers from the Howards. While I'm at the telegraph office, I'll wire the reverend, let him know you're safe and sound."

Clara sighed and flashed a half-smile. "Don't trouble yourself, Doc. I'm sure William will be dropping by in the next day or two."

And she was right about that. The reverend rode over to Camden the second day I was there. We got to tell him the good news that the Howards would be sending a large contingent of doctors and nurses to help us with the orphanage and patients in the surrounding towns. After spending most of the day with us visiting the children, the reverend led Clara and me in a special prayer and then took his leave, promising to return much more often than he had in the past.

Over the next two weeks, the volunteers arrived, the fever peaked, and we gradually gained control of the scourge. With the unrelenting pressure now off of us, Clara and I found at least an hour every other day or so to sit on the outdoor bench, sip coffee, and speak on a wide range of subjects, including our lives outside the asylum.

"You've done a remarkable job here, Doc, with the children and the staff. I never asked how you came to be a physician."

"The fever of '73 convinced me medicine was my calling."

"What were you doing before '73? A student?"

"Yes, and then I lectured English at the Westminster Academy in Memphis."

"Born there?"

I smiled and replied, "No, not in Memphis. As I told the reverend on the trip out to the parsonage, ironically, I was born on a farm east of Warfield. I still have distant cousins farming the land over there. All my folks are buried in the family graveyard, except my brother, Robert. He's buried in the soldier cemetery at Grave's Bend on the Duck River south of Warfield."

"So you live in the city now?"

"Yes, right in the center of town, near Court Square. Master Taylor, the headmaster of the academy, had space in his house and offered to let me stay there with his wife, a daughter, Amanda, and their two adopted children, Hannah and Aaron. Mrs. Taylor died in the '73 fever. . . . You know, helplessly watching her die helped convince me to change professions. After her death, we didn't stay a family of five for long. Within months we were back up to six."

"Take on another lecturer?"

"No, much more—how should I say it?—much more complicated than that."

"Complicated?"

"Master Taylor's adopted daughter announced she was pregnant."

"And the father? A neighborhood boy, I suppose."

I paused and then replied, "She didn't say."

"The girl wouldn't divulge the truth to her father? He must've threatened to banish her from his house."

"No. No. He's not like that. He's resilient . . . and forgiving to boot. Thank God he didn't do anything rash. The little boy's been a godsend to his grandfather, who'd just lost his wife months before. We all love Lil' Jim. He's smart and looks just like his mother: intense blue eyes, long, curly hair, full of life, full of love. His mother, Hannah, says you can feel and see the love because God marked him."

"See the love? Marked him?"

"Yes, Lil' Jim has a distinct birthmark on his right forearm in the shape of a heart. Hannah says it's a divine symbol."

"Where are they all now? In Memphis riding out the storm?"

"They're all doing their part fighting the scourge. Master

Taylor works at the Howard Relief Association. He's the fellow I contacted to get our volunteer doctors and nurses. Hannah's running a small fever hospital in Memphis. The daughter, Amanda, takes care of Lil' Jim during the day and works at the Howard's distribution depot at night. The adopted son, Aaron, is in Nashville—has an important liaison position in the governor's office working with the Legislative Council in Memphis. Comes back home every two weeks or so."

"Sounds like you lost one family and found another."

"That's a good way to put it. I love 'em, and I think they've grown to respect me too." I checked my watch and said teasingly, "I'd just love going on about myself, but I think the patients need us."

A few days later, during one of our talks, I broached the subject of Clara's past. "Well, I've told you almost everything there is to know about me, but I've heard precious little about you. Why don't you raise the veil a bit?"

"There's really not much to say. I was born in Corinth, Mississippi, some twenty miles south of Shiloh. My father's still a minister there. I have two brothers and a sister. Paul and Jack have moved out to the Indian Territory. My sister, Miriam, is married, has two children and lives in the next town over from my mother and father.

"I married my childhood sweetheart in '62. Later that year Tad joined the Confederate cavalry while I moved back to the parsonage and bore him twin sons, which he saw only twice, briefly, in three years. Saw a lot of action with Pickett. Ne'er a scratch until the Battle of Five Forks. Sheridan's men killed him. . . . Killed him just eight days before Lee surrendered. Never sent Tad home. They say he's buried somewhere southwest of Petersburg on White Oak Road. . . . Funny how you remember the tiniest of details."

"I'm sorry for your loss, Clara," I responded and then politely transitioned, "So . . . ah, the reverend came into your life later on?"

"Yes, William was a traveling evangelist—a lot of preaching in Georgia, Texas, Louisiana, and Mississippi. My father heard about him and thought it would be a good idea to raise the spirits of our church. Invited him for a two-week summer tent revival. Great success—lots of praise and twenty new members. William came again the following year and unbeknownst to me, how should I say, began courting my father. Returned later that year and with my father's blessing, asked me to marry him. Didn't refuse him outright—told William I needed to think on it. My father was upset I hadn't accepted. He argued that despite William's age, he would make a good, God-fearing husband and father. He said I was getting on up in age and had two children, which can be anchors that sink the possibility of other proposals, especially from younger men. . . . To be honest, Doc, I wasn't strongly in love with William, but he would provide stability and shelter for my boys, so I accepted."

"Where are the children now?"

Clara looked down, swallowed hard, and said, "They're gone, Doc. Gone."

"Gone?"

"Only months after the marriage, the boys—my boys, Doc. . . . It was the cholera."

I instinctively put my arm around her shoulder to offer condolences I couldn't express in words. She leaned her head on my shoulder.

"Do you want to go back in now?"

"No. Just hold me for a minute. I have other things I need to say. Things I've never shared. But seeing all the good you've done here, I know I can trust you. I just need to say some things."

I thought it best I let her take the lead and waited for her to continue the conversation when she was ready.

"We've been married going on ten years now. . . . William gave up the traveling evangelism. As you can see, we settled in Hurricane Creek to serve families there as well as Warfield and McGill. We spend most of our time convincing others to join the church."

"Despite all the tragedy in your life, Clara, it seems like things have balanced out now."

"To be honest, Doc, things aren't as they seem. I know William provides . . . but he limits me."

"Limits you? How? You seem to be doing what you want to do."

"Since he's so much older, he's suspicious of everything and everybody."

"To be honest, I haven't seen that while I've been here."

"You have, Doc, but you didn't recognize it for what it is. You remember what happened when you and William came into the depot the day we picked you up?"

"Ah, yes. You were speaking to some fellows about the Bible."

"Do you remember what William did? He rushed into the middle of my conversation with the young men, introduced me to you, and then announced we had to be going. And what did he do when we got out to the carriage? He helped me into the backseat and suggested you ride up on the bench with him. Isn't there something odd about that? And what happened when you showed up at the asylum?"

"The reverend came over to visit the sick."

"Do you think he'd ever been here before that? No. He was too busy comforting the wealthy members of the congregation who ensure his job."

"And the reason he started coming over regularly?"

"Pure and simple. Because you are here, Doc."

"Me? What'd I do?"

"Nothing. That's my point. You see the pattern now? It's been like that for years. He doesn't hit me but says vile things and berates me. If only the members knew. . . . But I put on a good show. Everything *seems* okay between him and me. That's what everyone thinks. But 'seems' can be a very evil word."

I sat there motionless, stunned, absorbing the words without judging plaintiff or defendant.

She then gazed into my eyes and murmured, "And I did this mostly for the boys."

Our discussions continued until the third week of October, when it became clear my services were no longer needed and I could pack up and return to Memphis. We had one last conversation at what had become our outdoor confessional. I searched for an appropriate opening.

"Thank God the volunteer doctors and nurses got everything under control," I said, trying to sound upbeat.

"Modesty will get you nowhere, Doc. You were a godsend. None of us could have done this without your having been here. But I guess you're happy about going home now."

"Some ways yes and some ways no. I miss my other family as you call 'em; and I know this sounds crazy, but I'll also miss the eighteen- to twenty-hour days, miss pulling patients back from the edge, and miss my candid conversations with you. Battling these epidemics is something like fighting a war. . . . My brother, Robert, was a Confederate horseman like your first husband. He'd come home to visit from time to time. But you could tell after a day or two he was getting anxious, wanting to get back into the thick of it. I remember his telling me once that war was ninety-nine percent boredom and one percent sheer terror. But oddly, it was the terror that drew him back to the battlefield to risk everything for his 'brothers.' That's the way it is with the fever too. Everything's routine until you're fighting to save a life, especially a child's. And you, Clara, were the comrade always there struggling along side of me. No bones about it, I'll miss the battle, and I'll miss you too."

"I feel the same, Doc. God forgive me, but now that the scourge is almost over and you're leaving, what'll I do with my life? Go back to the proselytizing, to the abuse and living the lie? When I think about it, I get this hollow feeling in the pit of my stomach, an unbearable emptiness. God, I'll miss the fight, and I'll miss you."

"Perhaps you can continue volunteering at the asylum. I'm sure they can always put you to good use."

"I don't know if William would ever allow it. He wants me close by where he can keep an eye on me."

"I don't know about that. He had no problem with you being over here in Camden alone."

"But that was different. It was a crisis. What would the members think if we didn't pitch in? And before you came here to help, William had no interest in working with these poor children."

"When do you plan on leaving for the parsonage, Clara?"

"Tomorrow, early morning. And I believe you said you were headed back to Memphis on Sunday, day after tomorrow."

"Yes. I have to finish up the report for the state Board of Health."

"What time's your train?"

"Three o'clock."

"Then I insist you come by for Sunday lunch. You know it's only a stone's throw from Hurricane Creek to the Warfield depot." Clara smiled and added, "Besides, you have to return our mare."

I laughed and replied, "Okay. You've got me there. A deal—Sunday lunch and a ride over to the train?"

"Sunday lunch it is and a ride over to Warfield."

As I knocked on the front door of the parsonage, I just knew. Clara hadn't said anything, and I hadn't framed the scene in my head. But I just knew. She answered the door, gave me a brief hug, and invited me in. The breathtaking beauty I'd first seen at the depot had now returned. She was wearing a black, cut-velvet gown with ivory lace at the cuffs and around the low square neckline. She smiled warmly and pointed to an upholstered chair. "Why don't you put your coat over there and come on back to the dining room with me."

"Where's the reverend?" I asked. "I'd like to say hello."

"Oh, I was going to tell you. William was called out to preach. Spur of the moment thing. After I got home late Saturday morning, an elder from over in Centerville came by with an urgent request. They needed a minister for Sunday services, said their regular preacher had taken ill. Doctor had diagnosed it as the ague and not the yellow fever. Knew William had an assistant who could fill in but thought it better the assistant preach here, locally, rather than putting the pressure on the young man to travel and speak to a meeting house full of strangers. William agreed, packed an overnight bag, and left Saturday afternoon. He asked me to go along . . . but I explained I'd just gotten home and honestly looked forward to sleeping in my own bed for a change."

"Well, I'm sorry to miss seeing the reverend again before I have to leave."

As we entered the dining room, Clara pointed to the table and said, "Take a seat, Doc. I'll get the roast and vegetables from the kitchen and be right back."

"I'm not helpless. Here, let me help."

Once we had arranged the overflowing dishes of beef, potatoes, and beans on the table, we sat down in our assigned seats—I at the head of the table and she immediately to my right. Next came what in the past had always been an awkward moment for me—being asked to lead the dinner prayer. But over the years this believing nonbeliever had learned a few tricks. Reciting the Lord's Prayer was always acceptable to everyone.

I began my recitation. But since I felt so comfortable with Clara, I boldly dropped the line "and lead us not into temptation but deliver us from evil," and inserted instead a sincere request that Clara find peace for all the love she had shown others. And as I returned to the standard text, Clara slid her hand over onto mine, and we recited the final lines in unison, "For thine is the kingdom, the power, and the glory forever and ever. Amen."

Neither of us said or ate much during the meal. The subtext was not in the words but in the silence and the gazes. We had already said all there was to say at our confessional on the lawn one week earlier. The echoes still reverberated through us: "And you were the comrade always there struggling along side of me. No bones about it, I'll miss the battle, and I'll miss you." "I feel the same, Doc. God forgive me, but now that the scourge is almost over and you're leaving, what'll I do with my life?" An easy calm had come over us. We knew and willingly accepted what was about to happen—a commemoration of sacrifice, devotion, and bonding that only warriors could comprehend. A celebration without commitment, without judgment, and without guilt. Forever and ever. Amen.

18

I DIDN'T WIRE ahead to ask "my other family" to meet me at the Memphis terminal. I wanted to surprise them. Knock on the door. Embrace Hannah. And watch Lil' Jim run down the hallway screaming, "Thomas! Thomas!" and then have him jump up into my arms. And it was a good thing I hadn't forewarned them. The train was late leaving Nashville, and the Board of Health had still not lifted its onerous "transfer" policy. So it was after dark when we finally rolled into the depot. But I wasn't really worried about getting a ride home. With the scourge now purportedly limited to small pockets of the city I knew there would be some friendly chaps visiting outside the station. And I suspected at least one of them would be looking to earn a little extra money.

As I had envisioned, several fellows were smoking cigars and chatting quietly as I exited the station. "Excuse me, gentlemen. I just came in on the train from Warfield and I'm looking for a ride home. Any of you have an interest in helping me out? I'll pay you fairly."

The tallest of the group asked, "Where you headed?"

"Not far from Court Square."

They surveyed each other and silently appointed the gangling speaker to chauffeur me home. He extended his arm and said, "Here, let me take that valise. I live up that way, and I need to get going. If I don't show up for dinner on time, the wife'll have the police out looking for me. . . . Follow me, sir. My wagon's parked around the side there."

He unhitched his horse, jumped up on the bench beside me, and offered his hand. "My name's J.P. And I didn't catch yours."

"Thomas."

"Well, Thomas. It's nice to meet you."

"Likewise, J.P."

"You a doctor?"

"Yeah." And then I asked him lightheartedly, "My bag give it away?"

"Sure did. Very good, Doc. So you said you'd been to Warfield? Been helping them out with the scourge? Heard they got hit pretty hard out there."

"They sure did. Especially the children. How about around here?"

"Not as bad as last year, Doc. Didn't hit everywhere and everybody. Just certain neighborhoods and then sometimes just a single family on a street. Strange. Still not over. But it's getting a lot better. We think it's peaked. But no frost yet. Everyone's praying for the cold weather, you know."

"That seems to be the key, J.P."

"Okay, Doc. We're coming up on Court Square. Where do we go from here?"

"Take a right and follow your nose to the end of the street."

"Where now?"

"Take a left, and it's just up there. The third on the right."

As we neared our destination, J.P. let out an audible gasp and exclaimed, "Not there, Doc! Please not there!" I didn't respond. I just stared ahead trying to make out details in the dark.

When J.P. stopped in front of the house, I jumped down and ran up the lawn. I could now see the door was open, the windows gone, and tongues of soot blackened the bricks above the window frames. An oppressive smell of smoke lingered in the still, moist air. I quickly turned toward J.P. and shouted, "Do ya know what happened here?"

"Yes, Doc. There was a fire this morning, a little past midnight. As I said, I live just a few streets over. Heard the fire bell, threw on some clothes, and came running. I'm in the hook and ladder company, ya know. Easy to spot the fire. Flames lit up the clouds."

"A man, two young women, and a little boy live here. Did you see anybody? Get anybody out?"

"Only found two."

"Two?"

"A man and a woman."

"Where are they?"

The fireman lowered his head and replied, "I'm sorry, Doc. They're with the undertaker. Looks like the smoke got 'em. As for the other woman and the boy, I suspect they're in there under the timbers. The roof caved in. . . . We ran out of light. Plan on sifting though the place again in the morning. But honestly, Doc, no one could have survived. The fire burned really fast and hot."

"How could this have happened?" I was anguished. Confused. I desperately needed this virtual stranger to answer the unanswerable.

He looked me in the eye and said, "Spoke with a neighbor afterwards. He blamed it on the fever."

"The jack?"

"Yeah, the jack. He thought something could be wrong. Hadn't seen anybody in several days. Saturday night he told his wife he was going to check in on them after services Sunday morning. Fire chief suspects someone in their delirium could have knocked over a lamp, torching the curtains or something. . . . She sure went up fast."

"So no signs of the other woman and the boy?"

"No signs. But I wouldn't hold out hope, Doc. The inside is just piles of ashes and broken timbers."

I sat down on the front step and buried by head in my hands.

"Doc, it looks like you don't have a place to stay. My wife and I have plenty of room. Spend the night with us, and I'll walk back over here with you in the morning."

"Thanks, J.P. But I think I'd rather just stay here."

"So be it, Doc. But keep my lantern. I'll pick it up tomorrow morning."

I looked up and replied, "Thanks again for everything, J.P. . . . Oh, let me pay you."

"Forget it, Doc. That should be the least of your worries. I'll get your things out of the back and get going."

After J. P.'s wagon disappeared around the corner, I picked up the lantern and stepped over the empty threshold. His description was accurate. Piles of rubble filled the front hallway and the parlor. Much of the interior framework was gone.

You could look over the mounds of lumber and see where the kitchen used to be at the back of the house. I spontaneously cried out, "Anyone here?" Several ghostly embers answered with loud snaps and then quickly vanished. I called out again, "Anyone here?" A dazzling bolt of lightning arced the clouds, presaging a deafening clap of autumn thunder. A deluge of rain then began pouring through the open roof. The cold drops sizzled on the glowing timbers.

I spent the night in the carriage house with Master Taylor's beloved horses. I couldn't sleep. My mind oscillated between reminiscing and planning. My mind said, "Everything's gone;" my heart said, "Don't give up; keep searching."

The morning broke crystal clear. I walked back up to the charred shell. One look told me my mind was right. No one could have survived except perhaps the holy men in Nebuchadnezzar's punishing fire. I knew I would have to accept they were all gone now.

I slowly turned away, left J.P.'s lantern on the stoop, and walked up Jefferson Street toward my old office. I pulled out my key and tried turning the lock. The door was already open. I shouted, "Doc, you here?"

"Is that you, Thomas?"

"Yeah, Doc."

My partner entered the front office carrying an armload of supplies. "I hope this is the last of the fever medicine we have to see for a while." He put the packages down on his desk and gave me a big hug. "Good to see ya, Thomas. Well, I know you missed the telegram."

"Telegram? No. When?"

"Sent it this morning."

"I was already back in Memphis. Must be about the fire."

"Fire? What fire?"

"Master Taylor's house."

"My God! Everyone okay?"

"They're all gone, Doc. Master Taylor . . . Amanda . . . Hannah . . . Lil' Jim."

"My God!"

"Yes, it's awful. The roof collapsed. All's left is the brick shell. The firemen have already recovered Master Taylor and either Amanda or Hannah. They couldn't tell. Got them over at the undertakers. They'll begin looking for the others this morning. I just couldn't bear to stay and watch them digging though the rubble."

"Pull up a chair, Thomas. We need to talk."

I sat down behind my desk and asked, "Talk about what?"

"First of all about Hannah. Now that you've told me about the fire, things have gotten a little bit clearer. I don't want you to get your hopes up, but just listen. I'll tell you all I know. Hannah didn't die in the fire, Thomas."

"She's alive?"

"Yes. Over at the Mansion House Hospital."

"Working?"

"No. That's why I said don't get your hopes up. She's got the fever, Thomas. She's in pretty bad shape, but they don't think it's hopeless. At least not yet. Let's finish talking and then I'll walk up there with you right away."

"But everyone assumed she was in the fire."

"I know. And more than likely she was, but somehow she

managed to escape. Ya see, since I didn't know about the fire, I couldn't explain the talk about singed hair and burns on the arms. But now it begins to make some sense."

My head was spinning. Hannah survived the fire only to end up fighting the fever? I had so many questions bubbling up inside me, I no longer knew how to feel.

"How'd she end up at the Mansion House?" I asked.

"Some church folk saw her walking up Gayoso. She was naked and shouting she didn't deserve to be in hell. The people who found her knew the Mansion House was just up the street, so they took her there."

"They say anything about a boy being with her?"

"I'm sorry, Thomas, no. No mention of Lil' Jim. Hannah was apparently alone."

"How'd you find out she was there?"

"Anna. She came by the office early this morning suspecting someone would know how to get in touch with you. I promised to send a telegram and speak with Hannah's father."

"Why don't we start walking up toward the Mansion House? We can continue talking on the way."

"Let me grab my bag, and we'll get going."

As we approached the hospital, I recognized Anna standing out on the front lawn. She was smoking a cigarette. I waved. She stared in our direction and then began waving back excitedly. She rushed toward us, gave us both a hug, and cried, "I'm so glad you're here! I hope you can do something to help Miss Hannah. The doctors who've come by treating our patients haven't had much encouraging to say about her situation."

"Let's get inside, review the notes, and then evaluate her

condition," Doc Landrum responded.

Anna fetched the file, and Doc began reading and relaying information. "Looks like we're dealing with stage two pending our examination—confusion and slight bleeding from the nose and gums."

"Any signs of anuria?" I asked.

"Urine output appears to be diminished but steady," Doc replied.

"Haven't noticed any significant changes," Anna interjected and added, "With the high fever you'd expect to get some decrease. But we've been monitoring output carefully, and her urine hasn't stopped."

Doc continued surveying the notes. "Fever's come down and pulse is low normal. Has she been conscious, Anna?"

"In and out, Doc. But when she's awake, she doesn't recognize us or the hospital. She's been pretty much confused the whole time she's been here. I did notice, however, the agitation and aggressiveness toward us stopped when the fever broke. It spiked at 103. These all look like good signs, but the physicians who've seen her think this may be the quiet before the storm."

"Well, let's reserve judgment until we've examined Hannah for ourselves," Doc replied. "Where is she?"

"Down the hallway on the right," Anna replied. "I'll lead the way."

As we entered the room, I whispered, "Doc, I'd prefer you take the lead, and I'll record the notes." Hannah was resting quietly. She was propped up on several pillows and covered with fresh sheets. Doc moved to the left-hand side of the bed and I to the right. She was wearing my mother's locket. It took everything in me to resist leaning over and kissing her forehead. Doc handed me the chart and asked, "Ready to begin?"

I grabbed the pencil from my coat pocket and replied, "Ready."

"Pulse 80. Heartbeat regular. Temperature 99. Skin dry and warm to the touch. Anna, when she's been awake, did she mention pain in the head, back, or legs?"

"No, Doc. But it's hard to ask questions. She's so confused."

"Okay. Now Thomas, back to you. Face slightly flushed. Eyes sensitive to light. Tongue slightly swollen and coated. Stomach quiet. Refresh me, Thomas. What have the docs prescribed so far?"

"Let's see. . . . Ten grains of calomel, ten grains of quinine, Fleming's tincture. That's all I see here."

"Since I can't interview her, that's about all I can do for now. Let's step outside and devise a plan."

"Doc, what should I say to the other doctors who've been dropping by to help us out?"

"Explain that her personal physician will be taking over this particular case. With all the work they have to do, they shouldn't mind one bit. I'll drop by twice a day, before and after seeing my regular patients. Thomas, I suspect you don't mind staying here, keeping an eye on Hannah and helping out with the other patients?"

"Not a problem, Doc. Happy to help Anna out." Although I meant what I said, I was even more grateful for the opportunity to be near Hannah and to stay busy. I knew if I was helping I would not think so much about all I had lost.

"So what do we propose to do?" Doc Landrum said. "Thomas, take some notes. Remember, what I'm about to say is contingent on Hannah becoming coherent and her fever staying down. If her stomach's irritable, give her five grains of bismuth in a tablespoon of peppermint water every two hours until the symptoms resolve. As we know, urination's important. If she's having trouble, give her a teaspoonful of sweet spirits of nitre in two ounces of hot or cold tea. If she's thirsty, give her some crushed ice or cool water, which will also help with the urine output. Since the fever has subsided for now, it's okay to give her a little beef tea, chicken broth, or milk. And later on, if she's having trouble sleeping, give her bromide of potassium. I like to stay away from the opiates; they can cause serious complications. Let's see. . . . Anything else? No, that's about it.

"I'll have to be going now," Doc concluded. "I've got patients coming by the office this afternoon. I'll drop back by early this evening to see how things are going."

"Thanks so much, Doc," Anna said.

"It's the least I can do for my dear friend's daughter."

As promised, Doc returned after his office hours. Hannah was semiconscious and stable. But overnight it became clear the discussions of bismuth, nitre, or beef tea were premature if not academic. It was painful to acknowledge the symptoms, but I had been down this path a thousand times before. The fever spikes, and the patient shows remarkable signs of improvement. And then just as quickly, the fever returns, and the victim stands at death's door. Hannah had been in stage two remission and was now surely headed into stage three where less than half survive. As Hannah's fever climbed, her pulse slowed dramatically. We were now on the slippery slope. For the first time, I detected a yellowing of the skin, and her urine output had ceased—telltale signs her liver and kidneys were under siege. And within another hour the nosebleeds had returned.

With every additional symptom my love for Hannah dragged me farther away from the cool professionalism I had practiced daily with strangers. I kept repeating to myself, "Hold on; don't let your emotions show around the nurses; stay in control; Doc will be here later this morning." But by eight o'clock, resignation had replaced my dread. Two violent episodes of black vomit meant the end was near. The bastards were now ripping her stomach lining away.

Once the retching stopped, two of the volunteer nurses bathed Hannah and changed the bedding. When I returned, she was sleeping peacefully. I moved over to the side of the bed, sat down, and held her hand. Again, my head said "no" but my heart said "yes, she can hear you." So I whispered my deepest feelings. "Hannah, I'm sorry I couldn't do more. . . . Hannah, you keep Mama's locket. Know my heart's with you and with Lil' Jim. My heart's where my home is. God, I remember seeing you that first day setting the table for my first meal with the family. . . . Two days later standing beside you in the receiving line waiting to welcome Grand Duke Alexis . . . . And only days after he left, there you were riding beside me in the coach, a goddess in your flowing gown on your way to your first Mardi Gras. And then together again in the fever fires, following little Amber into the shuttered house. . . .But we found a rainbow, didn't we? We found Lil' Jim. The Memphis Reds. Irving rubbing the Christmas wrinkles from our brows . . . .Yes, we found a rainbow."

In life, Hannah was always accommodating. She didn't want to be a bother to anyone. And in death she was the same. Her breathing became labored and her pulse irregular. I was watching my best friend slip away. She struggled to sit up, extended her arms, and murmured, "Mama's coming, boy. I see ya there, Lil' Jim." She settled back onto the pillows, sighed heavily, and found the joy on the other side of sadness.

19

A KILLER FROST taunted us the morning of the joint funeral. The undertaker said it was the most mourners he'd seen in two years. Following my special request, Reverend Woodburn fashioned a forceful sermon out of last year's Christmas message that hope is an anchor of the soul. After the funeral reception at Doc Landrum's, Aaron and I walked back to the Peabody where he chose to stay after the fire. We settled into overstuffed chairs in the hotel parlor and ordered whiskies and cigars. I opened the difficult conversation. "With all that's happened, you gonna just come down here for a day or two, stay at the Peabody while you work, and then head back to Nashville?"

"Actually, Thomas, I'm thinking about doing the opposite."

"Spending most of your time in Memphis?"

"I've already spoken with Father's attorney. He's the executor on the will. He said Father had insurance on the house. I'm gonna rebuild it, Thomas, and move back home. Going to get started immediately."

"And keep your job with the governor?"

"Absolutely. He's been very kind and offered me a great deal of flexibility. He's seen enough of my work now to trust me. He said I could mail the reports directly to his secretary and come into Nashville only when necessary."

"Just between you and me, that's a lot of house for a bachelor. You plan on renting out rooms?"

"No, but I won't be the only one living there. I had a surprise prepared for Thanksgiving. Was gonna bring a lady out to meet the family."

"Sounds serious."

"It is. I was gonna tell y'all I had proposed, she'd accepted, and we were moving back to Memphis. The plan was to buy one of the vacant cottages. After two years of the jack, there'd be plenty of 'em on the market at a fair price. But now with everything that's happened I'll just rebuild and move them all into the old house."

"Them?"

Aaron smiled and replied, "She has three children. She's the widow of the late Senator Rodgers—one of the few freedmen who made it to the Senate. You may remember all the hubbub surrounding his death. Mysteriously disappeared off a steamer between Vicksburg and Natchez. Left Jane with three little ones and a boatload of money he'd made in catering. She's somewhat older, but the bloom isn't off the rose yet. Well, ya know what I mean. . . . Her children seem to like me. Smart and respectful. The attorney general introduced us at a campaign rally. She still has a keen interest in politics; and having spent a lot of time around the governor, I've acquired a taste myself."

"Does Jane know what she's getting into moving out here? Settling in a place where there've been three epidemics in the last six years."

"She's fearless, Thomas. You'll know it when you meet

her. You should have seen how she lit up when I suggested I'd like to run for a seat in Congress from our district here some day. It's a win-win. She's got the money, and I've got the drive to do it. She wants to recapture what she had before. I guess you could say in her book, ambition trumps fear."

"Well, I wish you and Jane the very best."

"So what about you, Thomas? Where you staying now?"

"With Doc and his wife. They've been gracious hosts."

"What are you going to do for the long haul? Rent a place here and continue your practice?"

"I believe you and I see Memphis differently. You see an opportunity; I see a tough row to hoe. Population's declining. The wealthy have run away, and many won't be coming back. Many of my patients already can't afford to pay; and for the foreseeable future, it's only gonna get worse. If Doc and I both stay here, neither of us can make a decent living. So why not give him the practice and let the younger fellow move on to new challenges?"

"Any idea where you'll go?"

"Toying with the idea of going back home where I grew up and opening a practice there."

"I forget; where's home?"

"Near Warfield . . . where I helped out with the jack this year. I rode all over the county, and it's booming. There's going to be a shortage of physicians, I can tell. So there's my opportunity."

"That's good news, Thomas. Then it looks like we're both running toward something, not away from it. Any idea when you'll be pulling up stakes?"

"Probably sometime between Thanksgiving and Christmas."

"If you'd like, you could come back to Winchester with me for Thanksgiving. The governor's invited Jane and me to stay out at his estate. I can check, but I'm sure he wouldn't mind an extra guest. You could meet Jane and the children....Listen now. I'm serious about the invitation. I'll be back and forth from Nashville to the Peabody until the Tuesday before Thanksgiving. Just let me know. It would do you good."

I didn't travel to Winchester for Thanksgiving. I shared a quiet day with Doc and his wife. It gave us a chance to reminisce and tie up loose ends about the business. I explained I would be leaving Memphis by the fifteenth, which would give me time to clean out the old files and draft explanatory notes about my most difficult cases. I knew I could make the fifteenth because the month between Thanksgiving and Christmas is usually a quiet time for us physicians. Most patients choose to focus on Christmas preparations rather than on seeking treatment for minor aches and pains.

But as is often the case, our plans were interrupted by the unexpected. Doc and I spent the last week in November and the first two weeks of December treating patients who had returned from the camps with influenza, which had deepened into pneumonia. So my administrative work had to take a backseat to the health emergencies. Despite the serious setback, I was determined to be out of Doc's hair by Christmas Day. I even borrowed a cot from the Howards so I could catch some sleep at the office between seeing patients and working on the files.

Christmas was almost on us. It was coming down to the wire. Despite still having a quarter of the work to review, I just had to take a nap. My eyes were blurring, and my concentration was shot. Within minutes of stretching out on the cot, I had fallen into a deep sleep and begun to dream. I was guiding Master Taylor, Hannah, Amanda, and Lil' Jim along a forest path. But every time I looked back, another of my hikers had disappeared into the darkening woods.

Finally, as I was walking all alone, I heard a distant thunder calling out my name, "Thomas. . . . Thomas." And within minutes the storm was on top of me booming out my name, "Thomas! Thomas! You there?" Somewhere between sleep and consciousness, I realized someone was banging on the door and shouting my name. I rolled off the cot and staggered toward the front of the office. I heard the voice shout again, "Thomas, you in there?"

As I struggled with the lock, I shouted back, "Aaron, is that you?"

"Yes! Quick, open up!"

When I swung the door back, I murmured drowsily, "Clever, clever dream but cruel joke."

Aaron protested excitedly, "No, Thomas. We're real. Flesh and blood real. See for yourself."

I extended my hand and touched Aaron's arm. I began shaking as I moved to his left and grasped Clara's hand. As I moved toward the sleeping child Aaron was holding in his arms, tears welled up in my eyes. "My God, Aaron. Where'd you find him? Clara, how'd you get here? This can't be real. I'm dreaming."

"Let's get in out of the cold, and we'll explain everything," Clara replied.

"Okay, okay. Follow me. Aaron, you can lay Lil' Jim on the cot over there and take a seat here next to Clara. I'll slip in behind the desk. Now tell me, how'd this miracle happen?"

Aaron looked over at Clara and said, "I know you're really tired, but I think it best you take the lead. All I know is what happened after you got here this morning."

Clara leaned forward and began, "Remember, Thomas, the day you left Hurricane Creek, you suggested I keep working at the orphanage after the fever ended. I took your advice. William relented. And ever since then, I've been working Tuesdays and Thursdays helping with the record keeping. Since a number of children have come in from outside the county, the state board has insisted we create files and track every one of them. Part of my job has been interviewing these children to create their files.

"About a week after you left, we got the last of the children our Memphis asylum couldn't handle. Among the group was a boy with bandages on both hands. Since the cloth was soiled, I took the boy to the nurse's station to apply ointment and clean wrappings. As I was rolling up his sleeves, I noticed an unusual birthmark on his right forearm . . . in the shape of a heart. Remembering your description of Master Taylor's 'godsend' as you called him, I gently grasped the boy's shoulders and asked, 'What's your name, boy?' He answered, 'Lil' Jim.' I continued, 'How'd you get the burns?' He replied, 'In a fire with my mama.'"

"Well how'd he end up at the Memphis asylum?" I asked.

"I got a chance to speak with the chaperones before they left Camden. They said one of our brethren found him wandering alone in the streets and took him to the orphanage."

"Must have escaped the fire with Hannah and then got separated from her somehow," Aaron suggested.

"What'd you do next, Clara?" I asked.

"I went to the administrator, told her I knew the boy's identity and where he lived in Memphis, and offered to get the boy back to his relatives. To be honest, at that point I didn't know the address. I'd misplaced the note you'd given me, but I thought I could find the street by looking through your reports for a forwarding address. So the administrator accepted; I looked up the files; and Lil' Jim and I caught the train.

"You can imagine how my heart sank when we pulled up in front of the house. There were a lot of workmen clearing debris but no sign of you. Lil' Jim and I climbed down from the carriage and just stood there, stunned, staring up at the ruins. Just as I was about to approach one of the supervisors, a gentleman, who turned out to be Aaron here, tapped me on the shoulder and asked if he could help. Before I could answer, Aaron caught a glimpse of Lil' Jim's face and exclaimed, 'Boy, is that you?'

"Well, after Aaron explained who he was and how we could get in touch with you, we climbed into his carriage and hurried over here. And that pretty much sums up how we unlikely three ended up standing outside your office shouting and banging on the door this morning."

I looked over at Aaron and said, "Who in the world would believe? . . . My God, what are the odds?"

We then sat there staring at each other for a few seconds, smiling and shaking our heads. Aaron looked over toward the cot and broke the silence. "Now that we understand what happened, I think we'd better consider the future while we have the time. I mean while the boy's sleeping."

"You have some thoughts, Aaron?" I asked.

"On the way over here I got to thinking how close we are to Christmas and the boy doesn't know about his mother, his grandfather, and his Aunt Amanda. . . ."

Clara interrupted, "Perhaps you don't say anything about them until after Christmas. He's been through so much already and then to pile all that on top. I think it's too much."

"I agree, Clara," I said. "But then that brings up the question of Christmas. How can we make sure it's a happy one for him—like last year, remember, Aaron?"

"Oh, I remember. It was the happiest I'd seen Father in ages. Reading Irving with Lil' Jim in his arms. That'll be hard to repeat. But I have a suggestion. Why don't I take Lil' Jim with me to Jane's house in Nashville? We'll have a tree, and we'll make sure he has plenty of presents. Besides, he'll have Jane's children to play with."

"Sounds ideal, Thomas," Clara said. "What do you think of Aaron's plan?"

Knowing the endgame, I paused and then replied distractedly, "It seems to make for a great Christmas."

"Well, that settles it. I'll take Lil' Jim back to the Peabody with me, and we'll leave for Nashville at noon."

"Since I'm going to have to file a report on Lil' Jim, what are your plans for him after the holidays?" Clara inquired.

"Since he's lost all his other close relatives, I assume it will fall to Jane and me to take him under wing. He'll stay in Nashville until the house is finished and then move out here with the rest of us."

"Splendid," Clara said and added, "The boy's had a lot of misfortune, but he's lucky to have someone like you come to the rescue. What do you think, Thomas?"

I thought, "Checkmate!" but replied smilingly, "Things seem to have a way of working out. Don't they?"

Perhaps sensing some reluctance on my part, Aaron made a suggestion. "Thomas, I know how much you care for Lil' Jim, and I want you to know right now you'll always have a place to stay when you visit Memphis."

"I appreciate the offer, Aaron. I look forward to meeting Jane and the children."

Aaron pulled out his watch and said, "We're gonna have to wake the boy up and get over to the house. I want to make a final check of things and give the workers a Christmas bonus before leaving for Nashville. You can ride along with us, Mrs. Emmett. We can take the same train back to Warfield and Nashville."

Clara looked toward me and then turned to Aaron. "Thanks for the offer. . . . but if Doc doesn't mind, I'd prefer taking a later train. I need some advice on medical issues we have at the asylum."

"No, no. I'll be happy to see you to the depot," I said. "And if you folks don't mind, I'll sneak over and wake Lil' Jim up." I moved over to the side of the cot and sat down next to my son, who was curled up under a quilt Hannah had sewn for me for the previous Christmas.

I shook him gently. "Boy. . . . Boy. . . . It's time to wake up."

He stretched his legs, rubbed his eyes, groaned, and turned away toward the wall.

"Boy. Time to wake up."

He rolled over, opened his eyes, and stared.

"It's me, Lil' Jim. It's Thomas."

He sat up and wrapped his arms tightly around the back of my neck.

"We got to get going, Lil' Jim," Aaron interjected.

"You're going to Nashville with Uncle Aaron," I said.

"Nashville?"

I paused and then answered, "That's where Saint Nick knows to find you and leave your presents this year. Next year he'll know to find you back here in Memphis. Now let's get your shoes back on. Uncle Aaron has to make a stop before you get the train."

Clara and I walked with Aaron and Lil' Jim out to the carriage. I extended my hand to Aaron and said, "Thanks for all you're doing for him. He's had it tough, and you know there's so much more to come."

I leaned over, picked Lil' Jim up, and whispered, "Happy Christmas. I love you, boy."

He whispered back, "Happy Christmas. I love you too, Thomas."

As I lifted him up onto the carriage bench, I promised, "I'll see you in the summer, boy. We're gonna see them Memphis Reds again."

"Mama too?"

"Yes, Lil' Jim. Yes, Mama too."

20

AFTER THE CARRIAGE disappeared around the corner, Clara and I turned and walked arm in arm back toward the office. Light snow had begun swirling about in the air.

"Thanks for staying, Clara," I said. "It's really been hell around here since I got back."

"It's nothing, Thomas. I wanted to stay."

"Well, I'm up for some hot coffee. How about you?"

"Sure. It'll take the chill off, and I remember you made the coffee just right at the orphanage."

Clara folded her arms and began rubbing her shoulders.

"You're cold. I'll stoke the fire and get the coffee brewing. But first, let's see if I can find something you can throw around your shoulders until it warms up in here."

I went into the storage room and retrieved one of Hannah's light jackets she'd left at the office during the '78 epidemic.

"Here, try this on. Hope it fits. . . . Well, not exactly. A little large, but it'll keep you warm until the room heats up."

After adding several small logs to the fire, I measured out the coffee and added the secret ingredients to the percolator basket—two extra tablespoons of fine grind and a pinch of salt to mellow the flavor. When I returned with the steaming cups, Clara smiled and said, "Smells delicious. It's just like before."

"It's so simple making coffee for you," I replied. "We take it the same way. Straight and strong. Nothing added."

"You remembered?"

"How could I forget, Clara? We were a team. Fighting the battles together."

"Yes, Thomas, a fine team." She paused, took several small sips of the hot liquid, and asked, "With the fire and everything, what will you do now?"

I ran my finger around the edge of my cup, buying time to craft a response. But before I could answer, Clara continued, "Reading between the lines, Thomas, sounds like you're leaving Memphis. Aaron hinted at it. Said 'when you visit Memphis.' I picked up on that." Clara peered at me over the lip of her cup, smiled slyly, and said, "So it's time to fess up. What are you doing?"

"I was gonna surprise you. Three waves of the jack and the fire forced me to think things through. Memphis is on the downswing for now. Not enough patients left who can afford to pay. So I'm leaving the practice to my partner and moving on."

"Where you headed?"

"Lot of folks streaming out of the cities into Magnolia County. And as you and I learned during the scourge, there aren't a lot of doctors around to handle the load. Besides, you know I grew up east of Warfield. All my close family's buried there, and I have cousins whom I've never met. So I guess something's telling me to start over by closing the loop.

"You remember old Doc Marshall who helped us out at the asylum? Well, not long after the fire, I wrote him a letter proposing to join his practice in Warfield. He accepted,

Clara! And he even found me a temporary place to stay until I can find a house of my own. So that's my surprise. I'll be right next door to Hurricane Creek." I looked at Clara and noticed tears in her eyes. "What's the matter? Why so sad? I thought you would be as excited—"

"I would have, Thomas, but . . ."

"But what, Clara?"

"I told William."

"Told him what?"

"Everything."

"Everything?"

"About us. About the afternoon you left."

"For God's sake, Clara, what moved you to—"

"We'd done so much good together, Thomas. Why undercut all that by keeping a secret, living a lie? Regardless of why I married William, I'd made a commitment, and I broke it. I had to tell him, come what may."

"What'd he say?"

"Nothing at first. He just turned and left the parsonage. It was terrifying sitting there waiting for him to return, not knowing what he would say or do. But when he came back, he calmly asked me to join him in the church. We sat down in one of the pews. . . . It was a clear day, slants of light streaming in through the stained glass, light piercing the darkness, the sanctuary my confessional. William looked straight ahead toward the altar and asked, 'Why, Clara?'

"If he or anyone else had asked me earlier, I'm sure I would have sat there shaking my head in confused silence. But the truth flowed out of me in the shadows. In some ways it was strangely mystical. I was explaining both to him and to me. While your courage pulled, his fear pushed me into your arms. The combination overwhelmed me."

"His fear?"

"Ironically, the constant fear of losing me."

"How'd he respond?"

"He didn't become angry or berate me as he had in the past. He just said we have to pray on it, pray to help *him* change."

"Him? Not you?"

"Yes. I couldn't believe what I was hearing. It was as if my infidelity had conquered his fear of betrayal."

"So what'd you do?"

"Just as he wished. We prayed on it. Prayed for several days. He then asked me to join him again in the sanctuary, where he swore to change his ways, if I would in turn promise to remain faithful for the rest of his days."

"What'd you say?"

"I told him I would, Thomas. I told him I would despite knowing I had fallen in love with you. But I knew he still loved me and would support me. So what was I going to do? Ask him for a divorce? On what grounds? Failing to provide financially? Charges of infidelity? A highly respected evangelist? Laughable. What was the alternative? Run away to Memphis with the hope of being close to you? And once I got here, where would I live? How would I support myself? Would you leave the Taylors and come live with me? What assurances did I have? You never spoke of love. So what was I to expect?"

"What will the reverend say when he learns I'm joining the practice in Warfield? That could be a problem."

"William's kept his word so far. I'll describe what really happened. I believe he'll accept my explanation that your move wasn't something we planned, that it had everything to do with you and not with us."

"So what'll we do when we meet on the street? Greet each other as casual friends? Forget the past?"

"How could we, Thomas? How could we ever forget the good we did? The lives we saved? And God forgive us, that Sunday afternoon we shared before you left? No, they're memories cradled in the soul. But Shakespeare had it right, Thomas, past is prologue."

She paused and smiled, nervously awaiting my response. I was determined to convey I understood and that everything was okay between us. I returned a warm smile and playfully extended her metaphor, "If past be prologue, how should we now begin this play?"

She leaned over, gave me a big hug, and joked, "You were the English lecturer. I'll leave that to you."

"Fair enough," I said.

But there really wasn't much need for dialogue. We had already said what had to be said. We spent the rest of the morning walking arm in arm through the city. First a circuit around Court Square to view the decorations; next a visit to the bustling shops to find a gift for William; and then a stroll up Main to Nicholson's for a catfish feast.

It was only a short walk from the restaurant to the depot where we waited on the platform for her train to board.

"Thank God they lifted the transfers and quarantines before Christmas," I said. "Three transfers to get to Warfield from here in the summer? Ridiculous. But I guess it was necessary."

"Lil' Jim and I didn't have any trouble last night. Slept the whole way until the sun woke us up."

"I wish you could have stayed until evening," I said. "But I know you've already had a long day, and the three o'clock will get you home just a little after dark. You know it comes so early this time of year."

Clara smiled distractedly but didn't respond. The conductor began walking up toward the front of the train shouting, "Humboldt, Warfield, Nashville, three o'clock, all aboard!" She turned to face me, slowly ran the palms of her hands up the front of my jacket, and whispered, "I guess it's really time for the play to begin."

"Just before the curtain goes up, I want you to know I love you and I'll miss you, Clara."

"I love you, Thomas. I'll never forget."

She stretched her arms up around my neck and leaned in to share a final kiss.

"What is it actors say before taking the stage?" she asked.

"Break a leg," I replied.

"That's it. So break a leg, Doc."

"Yes, break a leg, Clara. See you in Warfield."

Clara turned away and never looked back. I didn't see her sitting at any of the windows near me. She must have sat down on the other side of the car.

I finished the paperwork on Christmas Eve and rode out to Elmwood on Christmas Day. Little Grace greeted me at the gate. She had grown at least a foot taller since I'd seen her last. I asked her what she'd gotten from Saint Nick. She answered excitedly, "A new ledger, sir. 'Cause the old one's full." I then asked her to do a Christmas favor, to ring the tower bell four times a half hour from then. She said she would.

I moved through the main gate and passed the heroes' trench where thousands of caskets lay buried side by side and end to end—ministers, priests, nuns, and nurses among them—volunteers who'd come to help and landed here. I found the Taylor plot, hitched the mare, and walked over to the graves. I stood facing the markers and waited. And right on cue, the bell began tolling. After each of the four peals, I repeated the name etched on the headstone—Emma . . . Preston . . . Amanda . . . Hannah. I stared out into the yellow band of winter light packed between the horizon and the thick gray clouds. I offered up a silent prayer and then a goodbye, knowing my heart may never again be where my home is.